FOREVER
HIDDEN

Books by Tracie Peterson and Kimberley Woodhouse

All Things Hidden
Beyond the Silence

THE TREASURES OF NOME

Forever Hidden

THE HEART OF ALASKA

In the Shadow of Denali
Out of the Ashes
Under the Midnight Sun

Books by Tracie Peterson

BROOKSTONE BRIDES

When You Are Near
Wherever You Go
What Comes My Way

GOLDEN GATE SECRETS

In Places Hidden
In Dreams Forgotten
In Times Gone By

HEART OF THE FRONTIER

Treasured Grace
Beloved Hope
Cherished Mercy

SAPPHIRE BRIDES

A Treasure Concealed
A Beauty Refined
A Love Transformed

BRIDES OF SEATTLE

Steadfast Heart
Refining Fire
Love Everlasting

For a complete list of titles, visit www.traciepeterson.com.

The Treasures of Nome ⋗ 1

FOREVER HIDDEN

TRACIE PETERSON
AND KIMBERLEY WOODHOUSE

BETHANYHOUSE
a division of Baker Publishing Group
Minneapolis, Minnesota

© 2020 by Peterson Ink, Inc. and Kimberley Woodhouse

Published by Bethany House Publishers
11400 Hampshire Avenue South
Bloomington, Minnesota 55438
www.bethanyhouse.com

Bethany House Publishers is a division of
Baker Publishing Group, Grand Rapids, Michigan

Printed in the United States of America

ISBN 978-0-7642-3248-0 (paper)
ISBN 978-0-7642-3249-7 (cloth)

Library of Congress Control Number: 2019949995

Scripture quotations are from the King James Version of the Bible.

This is a work of fiction. Names, characters, incidents, and dialogues are products of the authors' imagination and are not to be construed as real. Any resemblance to any person, living or dead, is purely coincidental.

Cover design by Jennifer Parker
Cover photography by Mike Habermann Photography, LLC

Kimberley Woodhouse is represented by The Steve Laube Agency.

20 21 22 23 24 25 26   7 6 5 4 3 2 1

To Miss B (otherwise known as Miss B Havyn). Keep singing, beautiful girl. I miss seeing you every week for lessons, but it's a privilege to watch you blossom and grow from afar. (Thank goodness for the technology of today!) Oh, make sure you do the monkey exercise . . . at *least* once a day. For me.

And to Monica and Merle Powell, precious friends and an amazing couple. Thank you for allowing us to make fictional characters out of your girls. It has been so much fun. Although, we could never capture how amazing they really are! Keep on keepin' on—we cherish your friendship.

And to Chuck and Diane Bundrant. What an absolute privilege it is to know you and call you friends. Thank you for your generous spirits and love for people. You've touched thousands of lives.

To God be the glory!

Dear Reader

This series began with three beautiful young ladies whose cinnamon-colored hair and dark brown eyes stirred us to create stories to match their spirits. Whitney, Havyn, and Madysen Powell were my (Kim's) piano and voice students. In January of 2017, they came to one of our book events, so excited that not only did I *know* the amazing Tracie Peterson, but we wrote books together. Tracie was completely captivated by my girls and told me that someone *had* to write stories about them. The idea was born and we ran with it.

In researching our next locale for this series, I came across some historical pictures from Nome. A few in particular were of the Nome Dairy and Poultry Yard. Inspiration struck when I saw a picture of a man with a yoke over his shoulders, two pails of milk dangling, with walls of snow around him that rose in height above his head. On top of the snow, a chicken appeared in mid stride. It cracked me up. I had chickens when we lived in the country in Colorado. I loved those girls. And yes, they all had names. In fact, the mom of one of my piano students made a sign for my chicken house with all of their names. Check out my blog for pictures.

Apparently, I am not the "type" in most people's minds to have chickens. So "Kim's chicken adventure" amused my husband and my friends. Jeremy would often find me out there feeding them and carrying on conversations. (Don't judge. Yes, I talked to my chickens. Yes, they chattered back. One followed me around like a puppy, always at my heels.) I even had a wonderful lady bring me a chicken at a large women's event I spoke at—and much to Kayla's shock, I drove all the way from Nebraska back to Colorado with the chicken in the car.

Needless to say, all the chicken stories in this series will be based on real events from Kim's crazy time of having chickens. And one even from my dad. Well, my grandmother always told me the story. And made sure I saw the chicken grave. Every time we visited. Tracie also made me chicken pillows. I should post pictures of those too.

While Whitney, Havyn, and Madysen are named after the real girls, please remember they are fictional characters. But if you ever get the chance to hear the real-life Powell girls sing or play, you should take it. I promise you won't be disappointed.

As always, Tracie and I find it an absolute joy and privilege to bring you another story. Thank you for reading. For praying. For investing in us.

Enjoy the journey,

Kimberley and Tracie

Prologue

Cripple Creek, Colorado—1891

Y our husband is . . . well . . . he's *gone*." Chuck Bundrant bit the inside of his cheek after he gave the news to his daughter. "I'm sorry, Melissa." It was necessary to tell her the news, but the apology left a bitter taste in his mouth. The truth about Christopher Powell was much worse than Chuck would ever tell his girl, but at least it was over and done now. While he hated to see Melly hurt, what coursed through him was more than just relief. Gratitude and joy were the first words to come to mind.

His son-in-law had been a constant thorn in his side.

"Chris . . . is dead?" Melly blinked several times and half sat, half fell into the chair behind her. "But . . . what . . . ? What happened? Can I see him?"

"I'm sorry. No. He's already been buried. He was beyond recognition. I'd hate for you to see him like that."

She took a deep breath and put a hand to her mouth. After

several moments, she lowered her hand and looked him in the eye. "What will we do?"

"You don't need to worry about it. I'll take care of everything." Sighing, he touched her shoulder as he looked out the window to the snowy landscape around them. Down the hill, he could see men with wheelbarrows hauling rocks out of his mine. The clanking of picks and shovels echoed through the mining camp. "Why don't you and the girls move in with me? You spend most of your time here anyway, around the piano."

Her chin lifted and he got a glimpse of his strong and independent daughter. "I appreciate that, but I can't do that to you. When we're here, it's for the girls' lessons. And you're never here during that time. I don't think you realize what it would be like to have us around at all hours. The girls are rambunctious . . . playing their instruments or singing . . . *all* the time. You'd never have any peace. Besides, I can't expect you to take care of us . . ." Melissa used her hands as she spoke—a normal habit for her whenever an instrument wasn't in them. But her frantic movements now and the speed of her words showed her distress.

A fact that made him feel even more of a horrible father than when he couldn't control his son-in-law's actions. Was he doing the right thing? It wasn't like he could change the course of events now. "You're my daughter, and your three precocious redheads are my granddaughters. Who, I might add, bring joy to my life every day. I know quite well how energetic and . . . *loud* they are. They keep me young." His words seemed to go unheard. She just turned her face to look out the window.

"It's not supposed to be this way."

The words were hushed. Her hands still.

He started to make a retort about the no-good man she'd married, but when her shoulders slumped, it pricked his heart. By the look of her, shock had settled in. Why was Christopher's death so hard for her to believe? Didn't she know her husband for who he was? Or was he that good of an actor? Of course it wasn't supposed to be this way. Couples were supposed to grow old together and raise their children in loving homes. In a normal marriage situation, that would be true. But theirs?

Chuck had thought for sure the news would bring her a bit of relief. After all, she'd never again have to deal with a husband coming home drunk. Or worry that he would gamble away all their money. But watching Melissa now . . .

He'd thought wrong.

He'd been so focused on his own distaste for the lowlife that he'd let himself forget who his daughter was at the core of her being. She'd always had a heart for people, always believed there was good in them. When she eloped with the rogue all those years ago, she'd raved about what a good man Christopher Powell was deep down.

Chuck knew better the minute he met Christopher. He'd seen him for what he was: a gambler. A drunk. A man who made a habit of coming to his father-in-law for money to cover his debts. At family gatherings, Christopher always put on a show. Cleaned up real nice. Showered Melissa with attention. Knew how to talk the talk of society.

Of course, if Chuck was honest . . . he'd put on as much of a show himself. Pretending to like the man his daughter had married. All to keep the girls happy. The façade had become a way of life. But the girls were sharp as tacks . . . surely *they* had noticed their father's behavior or heard the rumors of Christopher's exploits around town?

No. They'd never given any indication of it. All they ever showed was adoration for their father.

Melissa stared out the window, still and quiet. And then she looked at Chuck. The depth of emotion in her eyes moved across the room like waves that rushed over him, threatening to swallow him up. Guilt filled his gut. Rather than the take-charge, everything-is-in-hand father he wanted to be, the moment—and even the future—seemed out of his control. She turned back to the window without saying a word.

One thing was clear.

His daughter needed his comfort.

He sat on the ottoman in front of her and listened to the rhythm of tools clanking against rock in the distance. The sound had always been soothing to him in the past. Now, it felt like a hammer to his chest. Pounding over and over that he'd failed. "My darling girl, I'm . . ." He swallowed. "I'm sorry for your loss."

The words pulled her attention from the window. A sheen of tears covered her eyes. "I don't know if I'll ever be able to get over this, Papa." The drops escaped and slipped down her cheeks.

Leaning forward, he took her hands and clasped them in his.

Lord, I need Your help. Your compassion. Give me the words . . .

"When I lost your mother, I thought I would die right along with her. But God had me here for an important reason. That reason was *you*. I had to be both parents to you and help you grieve the loss of your mother. You had so much talent oozing from your fingertips that the only thing I could figure was to give you more lessons. More instruments. With every teacher I could find. So every day, we traveled from one teacher to the next, filling our days with music. Music helped you heal . . . it helped me too. In more ways than you can imagine." Memories of those years brought a rush of feelings he couldn't distinguish because he'd tried to lock away the death of his beloved. "I can't take the pain and hurt of this loss away, but I can be here for you. We'll get through it. Just like we did before. Together."

She sniffed and pulled one of her hands away to wipe at her cheeks as she gave a slight nod.

Time to steer the conversation in a different direction. Take the reins of the situation back and encourage her that everything would be fine. Christopher was no longer part of the equation. Melissa would grieve. The girls would too. But they'd be back to normal soon enough. In the meantime, Chuck would have to be their strength, hold them together, comfort them, and take care of things. Something his son-in-law had never done.

"I still think it's for the best that you and the girls move in with me. I won't take no for an answer." He managed a smile.

The expression on her face was one of resignation. "But, Papa . . . once I married, you were relieved of your duty to take care of me. This isn't fair to you." Her voice drifted to a soft murmur as she looked away. "It wasn't supposed to be this way." The repeat of her statement, and the depth of pain in her voice, made his hands fist. He wanted to throttle Christopher, but that wasn't possible. How could the ne'er-do-well have thrown away his family like he had? All for what? Gambling? Other women?

He closed his eyes against the last thought. Melissa would never find that out. Not as long as he lived and breathed.

But he needed to help her understand the reality. "Melissa, I've been taking care of you behind the scenes for years whether or not it was my duty. So of course I'm going to continue to do that. There was nothing to *relieve* me of . . . I'll never cease being your father. The mine is doing very well and I'm by myself, tinkering around this large house."

She snapped her attention back to him, her brow furrowed. "What do you mean *taking care of me behind the scenes?*" Melissa grabbed the armrests as her eyes narrowed. "You don't mean . . . no . . . Christopher would never do that. . . ."

He let understanding come to fruition in her mind. He was so tired of all the lies and his daughter continuing to believe that Chris would somehow, one day, miraculously change.

She straightened. "I take it from your silence that yes, he did. I can't believe it. He *lied* to me. Over and over again."

Emotions played across her face as Chuck watched it all sink in. Disbelief turned to shock.

"I knew he had a gambling problem, but he tried to overcome it. At least he *said* he did. And it seemed he'd get better for a while and he'd be home more . . . and he told me that he paid the bills. We didn't have much, but, Papa, he treated me like a queen—even when he was drunk, he never got mean." Coming to her feet, she balled her fists at her sides and paced the room, jaw set and firm. The fire was back in her eyes.

So. She'd moved from shock to anger.

She shook her head as she paced. "Let me get this straight. . . . Christopher's been coming to you for money? For how long?"

At last, the truth was coming out. But he couldn't triumph in that fact the way he'd thought he would. It was causing his girl too much pain. "Since the week after you married."

A sharp gasp caused her to cough. "Things weren't great, but I would never have dreamed that . . ." She lifted her chin and pulled a handkerchief out of her sleeve to wipe at her nose and eyes. "I know how much you disapproved of him at the beginning, but I loved him. Knew that he had so much potential . . ." She sniffed. "What am I supposed to do now? I don't have any way to support myself and the girls." She turned away and looked out the window again. After several moments, her shoulders stiffened and she looked back at him. "It seems you were right all those years ago, and I should have listened." With slow steps, she headed back to her chair and sat.

He'd ached to hear those words, but they brought little joy. "It doesn't matter now. And it brings me no pleasure to be correct on this." If only he could take away the pain he saw in her face.

Dipping her chin, she drew a deep breath. "I suppose I should tell you that his creditors have been coming by the house for several weeks now." When she looked back up at him, her lips formed a thin line. "I haven't wanted to say anything because Chris said he'd take care of it. As much as I hate to inconvenience you, now I need to ask for your help with that too." Her eyes darted down to the hankie in her lap.

A deep pink color tinged her face and ears. It made Chuck wish he'd punched Christopher Powell in the face at some point over the past fifteen years for the obvious pain and embarrassment he'd caused Melissa. The one good thing the man had ever done was give them Whitney, Havyn, and Madysen. Chuck was glad the man was out of their lives. But he couldn't say that right now. "No need. I've already paid off his debts."

"But how did you . . . ?"

"It doesn't matter. I took care of it. He's buried. You can move on." He cringed as soon as the words left his mouth.

Even though he'd been thinking it, he never should've said it out loud.

"Move on? Isn't that a bit callous?" The look she gave him stabbed him in the heart. "Flaws and all, I still loved Chris. And how exactly am I supposed to *move on*? I just found out that my husband is dead!" Her voice rose in pitch. "I have three girls that need raising. And now it will be *without* their father—who they adored. The man that I loved." Hurt, anger, and fear all resided in her gaze. "And my girls . . ." She took another deep breath. "This loss will not be easy on them. On top of that, they need education, food, clothing. Good heavens, we live in a mining town. It was all right as long as Chris was attempting to be a miner, but now . . . I don't know. I don't think Cripple Creek is the right environment for the girls. How can we possibly stay here?"

Blast Christopher! What a predicament he'd left them all in. "Where are you going to go? Your husband never amounted to anything. You should have told him to get a job and work if you didn't want to live in a mining town, where all he did was drink and gamble away the hours rather than actually *do* the hard work of a miner. And before you say another word about raising the girls in a mining town, please remember that my livelihood has provided for you the entire course of your life, and I happen to have a very *successful* mine here. We've *always* been successful, from the Black Hills Gold Rush until now."

Her eyes grew wide. "I'm so sorry, Papa, I didn't mean . . ." Her voice cracked. "That sounded so ungrateful of me."

Oh, why did he say all that? This wasn't about him or his pride. It was about taking care of his daughter. Chuck sighed. "I'm sorry, Melly. I never should have said those things." Swiping a hand down his face, he clenched and unclenched his hands. "My frustration with your husband all these years was hard to keep shoved down."

Melissa's face had gone pale. She licked her lips. "I'm sorry too. I didn't mean to insult the hard work that you've always done, Papa. It's just . . . I never saw the ugly side of mining until Chris . . . that is, I never had a problem with you mining or living in a mining town until Chris started at it and failed. I don't know what I feel. Every negative remark I've ever heard about miners and mining towns has rushed to the surface—like it's my fault that I chose to raise my children in this. I probably should've stood up to him about staying here, but I have to admit that it was a comfort knowing that you were here." She held up a hand. "Not that I expected you to have to do what Chris asked of you, but having family around made me feel secure. I loved my husband . . . believed him when he said he was taking care of things. I simply can't believe he's gone." A sob shook her shoulders.

"Oh, Melly. This isn't the time to be speaking of such things with you just getting the news about Chris."

"I didn't realize everything Chris had done. . . . I guess he had too many vices." She shook her head and swiped at her eyes. "I can't believe I was so blind."

"Don't beat yourself up over this. Give yourself time to grieve." It would take a lot for her to heal, especially if she found out the whole truth. And she did have a point. In fact . . .

The more he thought about it, moving away had a great appeal. "I understand it's hard to stay here. But for right now, this is where we are. How about we make a deal?"

She narrowed her eyes. "What kind of a deal?"

"If you agree to stay here for a bit, I'll look into selling the mine and finding us another place to call home."

For a moment she looked like a little girl again, wanting her daddy's approval. "You'd do that for me?"

"I'd do anything for you and the girls. I hope you know that."

Her lips made a thin line. Either she was trying to control her emotions, or she was still perturbed with him. "That's a deal I can agree to. I appreciate all you've done for us over the years, but I would prefer not to raise the girls here. That doesn't mean that I want to take you away from your liveli-hood. We've done just fine in different mining areas over the years. I just don't want to stay *here*, where everyone will remember Chris for his failings. As the girls get older, I don't want them hearing things . . ."

Of course she didn't. He should have thought of that. Chuck nodded. "Perhaps we can head north. I hear there's some beautiful country yet to be discovered."

"Thanks, Papa." She stood and twisted the handkerchief in her hands. "I think I need to lie down for a while and figure out how to break this to the girls. Would you keep an eye on them for a bit until I'm ready?" Leaning down, she kissed him on the cheek.

"Of course."

Melly walked out of the room, the weight of the world appearing to rest on her shoulders. This whole conversation had been harder than he'd expected. But then, he hadn't thought it all through. He'd been thinking of himself. What a relief it would be to *him*. How this would affect *him*.

Getting to his feet, he wandered to the window in the kitchen area. When he'd come home to give his daughter the news, a neighbor's wife had been having tea with Melly and the girls. He'd asked the woman to take the girls outside.

As he gazed out the window, he smiled at the girls tramping around in the snow, their cheeks pink and faces full of smiles. Completely unaware of the news their mother would share with them later.

How would they take it?

Whitney, as the oldest, would try to hold her tears back . . . but then she would take the other two under her wing. Like she always did. Havyn adored her father, at least from what Chuck had observed, but she had a good head on her shoulders and would be strong for her mother and sisters. Madysen, though . . .

She was the one he worried about the most. At seven years old, she was also the most tenderhearted of the three.

The girls' laughter drifted to him. If only there were an easier way for his dear granddaughters. But there wasn't. What was done was done. With a tap to the windowsill, he made a decision.

Tomorrow, he'd put the word out that the mine was for sale. Melissa was correct—the sooner they left Cripple Creek, the better.

ONE

Guiding the bow over the strings, Havyn Powell played the final run in Tchaikovsky's Violin Concerto in D Major. Her fingers flew over the fingerboard as she raced to the end of the piece she'd worked on for the past three years. As the last notes resounded from her violin, Granddad stood to his feet in the parlor and clapped. Even though they were alone, she couldn't help but let a smile bubble up and spread across her face. She took a deep curtsy as Granddad continued to applaud.

She'd finally conquered the great piece!

"Magnificent, my dear. Absolutely magnificent!" He came to her side and put his hands on her shoulders. "I believe you've mastered it."

"Truly?" Praise from Granddad came on a daily basis. But this? This was different. He knew how important this piece was to her. She couldn't hold back her exuberance as her heart pounded in her chest. Bouncing on her toes, she clutched the violin to her chest. "Do you think Mother will be pleased?"

"*Absolutely*, and won't she be surprised?" He tucked his thumbs behind his suspenders and looked as proud as her prized rooster. "She'll never guess that you've prepared such a piece for her birthday. Now if only we had one of those big bands—"

"Orchestras."

"Yes, one of those." He pointed at her and winked. "To play the part that backs you up. Not that you need anyone to back you up. You sound splendid."

Havyn laid her bow and violin on the piano bench in their large parlor. The sun sparkled off the snow outside and filled the room with glorious light. "Don't you worry, Granddad, Whit has been looking at the orchestrations and she's made up a piano part to play along with it." Her older sister was such a genius on the piano. No matter what she played, it would be beautiful accompaniment.

"I'm sure it will be the likes of nothing we have heard before." His eyes twinkled.

"Thanks for listening to me practice. I knew this was my chance while Mama was in town with Madysen. And poor Whitney has heard it too many times already."

"Your mother will love it." He moved forward and kissed her on the cheek. "Where is Whitney?"

"Out with her dogs. She wanted to get another run in with the sled and the new pups. All this late snow has been good for the new litter to practice. They're quick learners."

He clapped his hands together. "With Whitney as their teacher, do they have any other choice?" Granddad wiggled his eyebrows.

"Very true. It's a good thing she's the eldest, because she's definitely the best at barking out orders."

They laughed together and Granddad put an arm around

her shoulder. "A couple weeks until your mother's party, and then we can all go back to our regular shenanigans."

Placing a hand on her hip, she gave him a look. "*You* are the only one who's allowed to get away with shenanigans. And it's highly unlikely you'll stop them for that amount of time. Am I supposed to believe you are going to be on your best behavior for the next *two* weeks?" She shook her head and went to put her violin back in its case.

"Of course not. It's a rite of passage that you too will one day enjoy . . . once you're old like me and have earned it." He tugged on her braid and then headed to the door. "I best get back out there. More calves should be making their appearance any day now."

Havyn smiled as her grandfather walked out the door. How she loved her family. With a glance around the room that had been their gathering place every night since 1892, images washed over her.

The exquisite grand piano that Granddad paid for in gold and had shipped up from Seattle so their mother could play for hours each day and teach all of them music. The massive windows that looked out upon the beautiful rolling hills surrounding their farm—how many fingerprints and smudges had she and her sisters made on those panes when they were younger? The dark, wood shelves filled to the brim with music and books.

Oh, how she loved this room! It was so warm and inviting, with the massive stone fireplace in the corner. They'd practiced their instruments, sung their hearts out, had their own concerts, and even held Sunday services here.

She'd also been told more than one secret in this room. Probably because she was a good listener and she also knew how to keep a confidence—

She wrapped her arms around her middle and looked back to the window.

Dad.

He used to tell her secrets.

Oh, how she missed him. Her little-girl memories of him were a treasure.

Why did they have to leave him buried on the mountain in Cripple Creek? It seemed so cold and unforgiving up there. As a child, that was the part she couldn't understand. Even now as an adult, it felt . . . wrong somehow.

Stepping closer to the large picture window that faced south, Havyn blinked at the brightness. The days were getting longer, but the snow lingered. Which happened often up in their little hamlet near the top of the world.

When they'd moved up to the Alaska Territory after Dad died, she'd been enchanted by the area from the very beginning. The new adventure had made it easier on her young heart, helping her heal. She'd always been a daddy's girl.

But the first few years had been rough on their mother. She'd grieved their father and refused to talk to the girls about him. Oh, she put her best foot forward for the girls' birthdays and for Christmas . . . but celebrating her own birthday hadn't been allowed. Because it had also been her wedding anniversary. As Havyn and her sisters got older and the grief became memories, they'd tried to surprise their mother with something special on her birthday. With no success. Somehow, Mama always figured it out. She'd smile and hug them all, but the sadness behind her eyes always showed up on that day.

This year would be different. It *had* to be. She and her sisters had planned and planned, and Granddad had helped. Hopefully they'd be able to pull off their plans. Especially since the party was to be a full week before Mama's actual birthday. Havyn clapped her hands as excitement filled her stomach. They'd bring such joy to Mama!

She'd taught them all music since they were old enough to pick up a bow or sit at the piano. The delight that music brought to their lives was immeasurable.

So their plan was perfect. A special night to honor their mother and thank her for the years she'd invested in them, teaching them what she loved most. They were going to perform pieces that they wrote themselves or had practiced without their mother's knowledge.

No, Havyn couldn't imagine a better present—any more than she could imagine her life *without* music. Without singing. Without performing. Havyn loved the violin, but singing was her favorite—not that she wanted to tell Mama that. Besides, so far her largest audience to her solo vocals had been her chickens.

The chickens! She turned from the window and her mind's wanderings and rushed to the door. In the mud room, she grabbed her apron. Maybe her girls wouldn't give her too hard a time. It was well past the time for feeding, and they tended to get a little ornery when she was late. Whit said it was because Havyn spoiled them, but she refused to believe it and rolled her eyes whenever her older sister said anything of the sort.

Just because they all had names, she treated them like pets, and she'd made them their own individual nesting boxes didn't mean she spoiled them.

Most people didn't understand her special relationship with them. They *talked* to her. Well, in their own little way. And they all had distinct personalities. A point on which her sisters had debated her at the dinner table on more than one occasion.

But Havyn's chickens were for egg laying and egg laying alone, a fact that produced many an argument with Grand-dad over the past year, after they added the poultry farm to their dairy farm. He'd made her promise that the next batch of chicks would be raised for eating. Of course, she would let someone else deal with that. After all, she did enjoy eating chicken.

Just not *her* chickens.

As she trudged through the path they'd shoveled to the farm area, the walls of snow on either side of her made her feel cozy and protected. It always made her a bit sad when spring breakup happened and all the snow melted away. But when the weather was brutally cold and it froze her lungs every time she inhaled, she did think of warmer days. Still, that was the great thing about Nome—there were wonderful seasons in addition to the long winter. The seasons were short. But beautiful.

On her trek to the chicken house, the soft lowing of the cows in the birthing shed floated over the cold air toward her. Several of them would probably become new mamas today.

As her feet crunched closer to the chicken yard, the chatter of her girls soon took over all sound around her.

"I know, I know, I'm coming. I'm sorry I'm late." Opening the gate, she stomped some of the snow off her boots and picked up the feed bucket. "Go ahead and get your feathers unruffled, because food is coming." Filling up the bucket, she listened to the uproar and then took the first round out to the gathering of hens. Angry Bird led the entourage. Her black feathers shone almost blue in the sun, with the red around her head giving the appearance of a flame. Angry Bird earned her name the day she hatched by pecking and squawking at everyone that came into her space. Havyn was the only one she'd allow to pick her up. Havyn laughed every time she saw the chicken puff out her breast feathers and try to make everyone else listen to her.

Then there was Buttercup, the mother hen to everyone else. She spent most of her time at the back, helping to herd the rest of the girls where they were supposed to go. She was also one of the loudest, which always made Havyn giggle. Even if Havyn couldn't see the golden beauty, she'd hear her. Bossing all the other girls around.

Within seconds, Havyn was surrounded by the one hundred fifty chickens that made up her flock. Counting heads, she made sure everyone was there. The roosters were in another yard right now, since they tended to cause arguments among the hens.

Havyn filled up the bucket again, then hummed as she spread feed in the short trough. Next came the watering hole, where she broke the ice so all the chickens could get fresh water. There'd been a lot more snow this past winter, and the temperatures continued to dip well below freezing. Even though Havyn loved the snow, she was ready to see the ground again.

About a dozen of the girls followed at her feet like little puppy dogs, chattering away. Havyn joined in. "Oh, really? That's fascinating. Everyone staying warm enough?" As she continued caring for them, the jabbering continued.

A loud crash made most of the hens jump and flap their wings.

What . . . ? Havyn looked toward the birthing shed.

Thud!

Oh no! "Granddad?" She yelled for him across the yard. No response.

She set the bucket down at the gate, rushed through, and

set the latch. Her heart sank even as it picked up its pace. She raced through the troughs of snow. Granddad *always* answered. That was one of their rules. A sort of game they played as children, but one meant to ensure safety. Whenever anyone called out on the farm, whoever was present answered.

Every time.

Except this one.

Opening the door to the barn they used for the birthing, she blinked to adjust her eyes to the dim interior. As she scanned the room, she spotted her grandfather lying on the floor, tools scattered around him. "Granddad?"

A lump swelled in her throat as she raced to his side and knelt beside him. What had happened? Havyn rolled him over onto his back and put her ear to his face, praying she would hear the soft whoosh of a breath.

A light flutter of air brushed over her cheek and she let out a long sigh. "Thank You, Lord." She sat up and gripped his shoulders. "Granddad. Granddad, wake up."

A moan escaped his lips and his eyelids fluttered.

"Please, Granddad. I need you to look at me." Her heart beat faster with every silent moment. What could have brought her strong grandfather down?

His eyes finally opened. "Havyn?" His voice sounded so unlike him. He sounded . . . weak.

"I'm here." She lowered her face closer to him again. "What happened? Can you move?"

He closed his eyes, sucked in a deep breath, and then opened his eyes again. "I'm all right. I simply fell down."

She narrowed her eyes. This seemed worse than that. "What made you fall?"

He looked around but lay pretty limp in her arms. "I must have tripped. Don't worry about it."

"I don't believe you for one minute." Placing her right arm under his neck, she lifted. "Let me help you sit up and then you can tell me the truth."

"I told you not to worry about it."

But he sounded so out of breath, she couldn't help worrying. What wasn't he telling her? "You can say that all you want, but it won't make it happen." Once she had him sitting up, she kept her arm around his back. Then she quirked an eyebrow at him. "Now, how about the truth?"

He took several deep breaths and sat there. Still as she'd ever seen him.

"Well?"

"Pushy, aren't you?" A disgruntled groan left his lips.

"You taught me well."

He huffed. "I know." Wiping at the hay that covered his trousers, he clenched his jaw.

What was going on? Granddad *never* minced words.

"Do you promise you'll keep it to yourself?"

"Of course, I will." That didn't sound good, so she braced herself.

His nod was weak, but the slight smile was good to see. "I've fallen a few times in the last few weeks. It's like my legs all of a sudden don't work anymore."

She tried to hide her dismay, but a tiny gasp escaped. "I'm calling the doctor . . . right away." She started to stand, but his arm shot out and stopped her.

"No need. Doc Gordon and I have already been discussing this. But Doc is leaving soon. And there's a couple new doctors. I don't know either of them . . . and you know how many untrustworthy people have come to Nome because of the gold. Liars and thieves trying to pull the wool over people's eyes. Doc said to give him a bit of time to find out who would be best to work through this with me. He said there's another one coming too that he'd like to evaluate."

"What are you saying?" Was his problem that severe? Life-threatening? That he needed a specialist of some sort? For Granddad to need Doc's advice about a new physician made her cringe. She could count the times her grandfather had seen the doctor in Nome on one hand. So it must be serious. She swallowed, determined to get to the bottom of it.

"I'm saying you need to give me time to settle on one of the new docs." Wiping hay from his shirt, he squared his shoulders.

"Settle on one before what? It's serious, isn't it?" She narrowed her eyes. Granddad should know she could read him like a book. She'd keep pushing if she had to. "What aren't you saying?"

He gave her a resigned look. "The doctor thinks I'm at risk for apoplexy."

All the air in her lungs left her in a whoosh. Apoplexy? Didn't people *die* from that?

"Don't look at me like that, Havyn." He pointed a finger in her face. "Now you promise me right now that you'll keep this secret from *everyone*. You understand me?"

Havyn crossed her arms over her chest. She'd never divulged a secret before, but how could she keep this from the family?

"Ha-vyn?" His tone brooked no argument.

She had a hard time not feeling like a little girl when he spoke to her like that. They'd been raised to obey and respect their elders. But what if this wasn't for the best? One look at his face made her blurt, "I promise. But you have to promise *me* that you'll get this taken care of."

"As soon as Melly's birthday is over. I promise."

She stood and reached down to help him up. "And you'll let me know if you have any more episodes?"

He groaned but looked steady enough. "Of course."

She nodded, and he walked away. Slow and with a limp. The weight of this new secret crushed her chest.

What would they do if something happened to him?

Two

John Roselli stretched as he climbed out of the dog sled basket. It had been a long and arduous trip to Nome. He'd thought reaching it would be an easy task, but soon enough he found out that ships didn't sail to Nome in the winter months. Locked by ice in Norton Sound, the town was impossible to reach by water until May. The only way to get there this time of year was by dog sled.

Even though it was late April, he hadn't wanted to wait on a ship. Besides, he'd been almost out of funds.

Now, as he stood on the edge of town, he shook his head. What had he gotten himself into?

The sled driver looked at him. "Are you taking a room at the hotel?"

"Not just yet, Sam. I need to see if I can find a job." John glanced first one way and then the other.

The man nodded and extended his hand. "You more than earned your keep by helping us get these supplies to Nome. I want you to have this." He handed John a leather pouch.

"I don't understand. We agreed I'd work for transport here."

"It's just a little money to get you through a couple of days. Nothing more. It's expensive around here, as you'll soon learn. Food, drink, beds. All of it comes at a premium price ever since they found gold here."

"Thanks." John pulled off his mittens so he could tuck the strings of the pouch into his belt. In truth, the few dollars and change already in his pocket weren't going to get him very far. "You've been more than fair with me. Want me to help you unload?" He glanced back at the other two sleds, each pulled by twelve dogs.

"No, I know you have business. Besides, the store owner will have men to help. You go on and find your people before sunset. It'll get mighty cold after the sun goes down."

Laughing, John rubbed his hands together. "You mean this isn't cold?" He pulled on his pack, grateful for the added warmth against his back.

Sam grinned and gave him a pat on the shoulder. "This is a balmy day. Must be at least twenty degrees. Warm, I'm telling ya."

John quirked an eyebrow at the man. All the same, he was grateful for his mittens and hurried to put them back on. He started toward the main part of town, surveying the area around him as he went.

Norton Sound was full of ice, and the beaches of Nome were lined with tents as far as the eye could see. He'd heard that not only did the creeks and rivers bear gold, but nuggets and flakes were also found in the beach sands. Hundreds of men had set up tents to prospect the sands. Because it wasn't legal to stake a claim on the shoreline, there was often fierce fighting. In fact, on the boat to Seward, someone had told John that if he thought he was coming to civilization, he was wrong.

Traveling all the way from Cripple Creek, Colorado, to

Alaska had been a wearying journey. But he'd promised Nonno, right before his grandfather died, that he would hand-deliver the package tucked inside his rucksack to Chuck Bundrant. All he had to do was find the man.

He turned from the sea and faced the busy town.

The salty air around him competed with the racket of the hordes of people to overwhelm his senses. Nome was not at all as he'd expected. In Seward and elsewhere, the mountains had been glorious, but up here, it was more of a flat landscape with rolling hills in the distance. After the long sled ride in, he knew the mountains weren't far. But they weren't right here. The mountains had been his companions most of his life. . . .

This would take some getting used to.

Of course, he wasn't planning on staying in Nome. Especially after all the stories he'd heard. Living in the middle of the wilds of Alaska would suit him better. He wasn't exactly fond of cities and all their noise.

And lawlessness.

Which was rumored to be rampant here.

He'd gone to Denver to catch the train to Seattle. How so many people could live crammed in so close together was beyond him. When he reached Seattle, he was further convinced that life in the city wasn't for him.

But Alaska . . . maybe. The territory boasted amazing beauty and grandeur. Nome, however, wasn't holding a lot of appeal. There were more people and buildings than he'd anticipated. Closer inspection, however, showed that many of the buildings were nothing more than tents with false fronts, and most of those were saloons and brothels. A typical mining town.

Why on earth did men work so hard and then waste what

little they'd made on drink? Of course, he'd spent every last dime getting here and people would probably call him just as foolish. Had Sam not given him money, he'd be in dire straits.

Probably best not to judge.

He was here to fulfill a promise. No matter if he liked the town or not. No matter what anyone thought. It wasn't like anyone knew him anyway.

Before he could set out to find his grandfather's old friend, he needed to find something to eat and a place to sleep. That meant finding a job to be able to pay for that. Good thing it was still early in the day.

John maneuvered his rucksack into a better position on his shoulders. Nome reminded him a little of Cripple Creek when the gold rush had been on. The same looks of anticipation and hope pasted on the faces of the men. Who were everywhere. The closer he made it to the center of town, the more claustrophobic he felt. Men clamored for information on staking claims, shoving anyone who got in their way. The mass of humanity, supplies bundled up on their backs, moved through the streets.

John heard the word *gold* every few seconds from a cacophony of voices until it almost made him sick to his stomach. But when he stopped and looked closer, he noticed many a man sitting on the sides of the street. Faces thin and gaunt. Eyes staring. Had they lost everything? Did they know where their next meal would come from?

It had been the same in every mining town John had ever seen. The depravity of man, the greed, the defeat.

Was there anything more sad?

Forcing himself to move forward, John pushed the negative thoughts aside. But he had to sidestep a man throwing a punch, tripped over a drunk lying in the street, and then stopped in time for two men to tumble out of a saloon, their fists intertwined in the other's collar.

John tried to tune out the horrid, tinny saloon music and picked up his pace. How long would he need to stay in this mess of a town? He didn't exactly have a home to return to—his family was all gone. How long would it take for him to earn enough to leave? Where would he go?

His parents had died when John was twelve, and Nonno took on the responsibility to raise him. Now he was gone too—

A tug on his coat sleeve made him look down. A young woman looked up at him and batted her eyelashes as she slipped her arm around his waist. "Buy me a drink? We've got the best beer to be had and hot toddies that will melt your frozen toes." A smile filled her hollow cheeks but didn't take away the haunted look in her eyes.

John shook his head. "No, thanks."

With a frown, she tugged again on his sleeve. "Come on, Mister. I haven't had a bite to eat all day." She unbuttoned his coat and slipped inside, close to him. "Besides, if you buy me a meal, we can sit inside by the fire. I'm so cold."

He pried her from his body and rebuttoned his coat. She'd been so swift and brazen! He put his arm out to keep her from advancing again, though pity made him shake his head. Tucking one hand under his arm, he tugged off the mitten and fished a dime out of his pocket. "Here, go buy yourself something to eat and get warm."

She couldn't have been more than sixteen and was skin and bones. She snatched the coin and hurried away.

John pulled his collar up and glanced around before moving on through the crowd. No doubt there would be others looking for money, especially if anyone saw him give the coin to the girl. Better pick up his pace.

The closer he came to the middle of town the noisier it grew. Sled dogs yipped and howled, men shouted, metal clanked, and people stood shoulder to shoulder. John fought his way through the throng.

As he scanned local businesses, the brothels and saloons outnumbered everything else by probably twenty to one. Weren't there any jobs available other than panning for gold?

Wait. There was a mercantile ahead. Perhaps he could try there.

Five minutes later, he was back on the street. They weren't hiring. Too many men looking for work.

Maybe he should stop and eat. After all, it would do him little good to collapse from hunger. He'd eaten some dried fish at dawn. Ah, but now he had Sam's leather pouch. He smiled. At least he had plenty of money for the next day or two. He reached inside his coat and felt for his belt.

The pouch was gone!

He unbuttoned the coat and searched the full length of his belt. He shook his head. Where could he have lost it?

The young lady who begged him to buy her a meal. He'd mistaken her bold actions for something else entirely. He couldn't believe it. She'd robbed him! There couldn't be any other explanation.

His stomach turned. No use spending what little money he had left on a meal. Especially if he needed a place to stay for the night. He needed a job and fast. He rebuttoned his coat and headed toward the next building that wasn't a saloon or brothel.

An hour later, he'd tried every decent establishment he could find. All to no avail. Finally, he spotted a two-story structure with a sign that read *Holy Cross Hospital*. Perhaps it was run by the Sisters of Providence he'd heard about. Maybe they needed some nonmedical personnel? It was worth a try.

His stomach rumbled as he made his way into the large building. He shook his head. An empty stomach was the price for his stupidity. He should have secured the money better. Out of the reach of pickpockets.

Oh well. No food until he secured a job.

Heavenly Father, it would sure be nice to have a bit of Your divine intervention right now. It's my own fault the money was stolen, but I'm powerful hungry and in need of Your help.

He walked toward the desk. The change in his pocket might buy him one meal at Nome's prices, but he doubted it. No doubt that young woman had learned to steal to survive. He'd felt that kind of despair and worry himself. Grandfather's sickness the last two years had depleted all of the fortune he'd amassed. Something John didn't tell his grandfather when Nonno asked him to go to Alaska and find his long-lost friend. He didn't want Nonno dying with concern for John on his mind.

An older gentleman walked down the hall toward John, his gaze fixed on the papers in his hand.

John cleared his throat.

The older man—clearly a doctor—lifted his head enough to peer over the top of his glasses. "How may I help you? Are you sick?"

Such compassion etched in the man's face. Clearly, he was a healer. "No, sir. I'm actually here looking for a job. Any chance you need an able-bodied man to assist with moving patients or cleaning?"

The man pushed his glasses up on his nose. "We can definitely use the help, but I'm afraid it's not in our budget." He stuck out his hand. "I'm Dr. Gordon. I take it you're looking for a job?"

"Yes, sir. Preferably something honorable."

"Ah, so you're not here to find your fortune in gold?"

"No, sir. Although I have to admit that my grandfather owned a gold mine and I grew up doing the hard work of a miner. I've seen my fair share of labor there and what the search for gold does to a man. Frankly, I would prefer to work another way."

Gordon nodded his head. "That's admirable, young man." He stroked a hand through his beard and squinted at him. His gaze was piercing. Like he was assessing John. "You know, I have a patient who is also a good friend. He's been talking about hiring another worker on at his farm, and I've been prodding him to do it. Do you think you're up for that kind of work?"

"What kind of farm is it?"

"Dairy and poultry."

His heart lifted. "My family had a dairy farm back in Italy. That would be perfect."

"Sounds like a good match. Why don't you head on out to his place now and tell him that Dr. Gordon sent you. I doubt you'll have any trouble." The man scribbled a note on a small paper. "Here are directions."

"Thank you, Dr. Gordon. I can't tell you how much I appreciate it." That God had seen fit to answer John's prayer with such swiftness made him want to shout, but he held it in.

The doctor laid one of his hands on John's shoulder. "You go work for Chuck and take some of the load off the man's plate, and I'll be the one thanking *you*."

"I'll head there right now." He let a smile split his face.

40

"Chuck Bundrant is the man you need to speak to. He owns the place."

John froze. He knew that his jaw had dropped, but it took a few seconds for him to regain his composure.

"You all right, son?"

"Yes, sir." John shook his head. "Did you say Chuck Bundrant?"

The doctor's eyebrows lowered and he tilted his head. "I did."

"Wouldn't you know . . . my grandfather was friends with Chuck Bundrant and sent me here to find him. That's why I'm in Nome."

"Isn't that amazing. God works in mysterious ways, doesn't He?" The doctor slapped him on the back. "I guess the sooner you find Chuck, the better. Tell him that I insist he hire help, all right?"

Quick footsteps drew their attention to a nurse running down the hall. "Dr. Gordon! Come quick!"

Dr. Gordon turned. "I guess I'm needed." He pointed back to John. "Make sure you tell Chuck that I sent you."

"Yes, sir. Thank you."

Heading back toward the door, John couldn't believe this was all a coincidence. Nonno had sent him to deliver a package to his friend. Now the good doctor had sent him to the same man for a job. Providence was shining down on him once again. He would ask Mr. Bundrant for a job, and then he'd find a good time to sit down with the man and deliver his grandfather's package. No. Maybe he should do it the other way around. That was why he'd come.

His stomach rumbled again. He didn't want any special favors. A man had to earn his way. He'd have to be honest with his grandfather's friend. Maybe Mr. Bundrant would agree to keep John on long enough to earn the amount he needed to sail back to Seattle when the waterways opened. Or maybe at least as far as Seward. The mountains there had been beautiful. Perhaps he could go into some sort of fishing industry? That sounded heavenly compared to the life he'd lived in a gold mine.

Outside the hospital, he stopped long enough to study the directions the doctor had written, then headed west. The Bundrant Farm was two or three miles from town. He considered trying to hitch a ride, but the walk would do him good. He'd keep warm enough if he kept to a quick pace.

A farm in Alaska. It likely didn't warm up much this far north. Pity the poor livestock—and the man who had to work out in the bitter cold of winter. But people needed milk and meat. Had to be almost impossible to get those things shipped here.

Besides, John could handle farm work well, could even favor the cold. Gracious, he'd lived way up on the mountain in Colorado.

The possibilities of working on a dairy farm again brought memories from childhood to the surface. Up until he was twelve, he'd worked on the Roselli dairy farm back in Italy. His heart clenched a bit at the scenes of rolling green hills, of the large barn, and of jumping into piles of hay. A hazy memory of his mother laughing as she sat on the milking stool holding up a pail of milk brought it all back.

"*Patatino*, come help me." Her term of endearment had always made him feel special, although why she called him her little potato was something he never quite understood. All he knew was how much he loved her, and how much she loved him.

How he missed her! And his papa. To have them both

taken from him by measles . . . it had been almost more than he could bear. If not for Nonno, John didn't know what he would have done.

They'd had a good life . . . as good as it could be without his parents. But then the time came when Nonno said they had to leave Italy and go to America. The troublesome changes in Italy, with the ruling politicians pressing their socialistic agenda and the devalued farms, left Nonno declaring, "If we're going to have so many changes, we might as well go to America and change everything."

And so they did. Fifteen years ago, they came to New York City and learned English. It didn't take long for them to buy into the promises of getting rich quick in the goldfields of the West, like so many other Americans. And that was what they had become—Americans. As the days in America became years, John's memories of Italy faded. Some days it felt like that life belonged to someone else.

Now, with Nonno gone, the memories of family made him feel more alone.

John pulled his mind back to the matter at hand. Crunching his way through the snow, he followed wagon tracks on a road that was filled with icy ruts. A fair amount of traffic must cross this area.

"Ho, there! Watch *out!*"

John turned and stepped aside as a dog team and sled approached. The driver guided the sled between existing tracks. The eight dogs ignored John, but the driver gave a brief salute, then turned his attention back to the dogs.

John thought to call out to the man and ask for a ride, but before he could, the team turned from the road and headed north across open land. Just as well. John needed time to think about what he would say to Mr. Bundrant. But as he practiced words over and over in his mind, his thoughts returned to the fact that he had no family left. No home to return to. No job or business. He . . . was all alone.

At twenty-seven years old, he should be settling down. His own grandfather had encouraged him to do that, but in a gold-mining town, there hadn't been a lot of decent, unmarried women. On August the first, he would turn twenty-eight.

God, what do You have for me? I wasn't expecting to have to start over—by myself—at this stage in life. I guess I don't understand . . . why?

Why . . . the question that plagued him the most. His parents' deaths. Moving to America. Nonno's death. His last request. And now? For John, left with nothing . . . and this trip with all its ups and downs. No job. No money. In an unknown place that seemed on the edge of the world.

Best not to focus on the negatives and all his questions. Once he accomplished his task and earned enough money to start fresh, John knew what he wanted. To move forward with his life. Find a good church and a decent job. Maybe the good Lord would still bless him with a family.

He gave a sigh and squared his shoulders. The pack was getting heavy, just like the burden of wondering what the future might hold.

Stop. No good could come of trying to figure out the details of what he wanted. Best to focus on what God had for him. One day at a time.

The raw feeling in his stomach made him feel like his body was gnawing on itself as it let out another loud rumble. Picking up his pace, he decided he'd have to settle on one *meal* at a time—and pray Mr. Bundrant had a job for him.

Otherwise, he'd run out of options.

THREE

Everything was falling into place. The more gold diggers that stayed in Nome, the more supplies they'd need, and the more indebted to him they would become. Eventually, they'd have to give him their claims.

The thought made Judas Reynolds chuckle. But a wise man didn't put all his eggs in one basket. No. He'd planned for more than those foolish simpletons. For the most part, he had control of all the business owners. All except Norris—the man who owned the Roadhouse—who wanted to keep gambling and alcohol out of his establishment, and that all-too-quiet Bundrant. But they'd come around. In time. Everyone would owe him.

He tapped his fingers on his desk. Now why would a man who'd had a successful mine in Nome, and plenty of gold, just up and start a dairy? He'd investigated Bundrant. The man had been very successful with other mining operations over the last couple decades. There wasn't any way the farm was more prosperous than the mine, plus it was grueling work. But as soon as the crowds had flocked to find gold, he'd watched Bundrant turn his land into a dairy and poultry farm.

It didn't make sense.

But he intended to find out why. And with that, he'd learn the man's weaknesses.

It wouldn't take too long to be the benefactor of the entire town.

Then he could make even more money.

All he had to do was give it time.

The metronome ticked, and Havyn tapped her foot in the same rhythm.

"Let's start again." Whitney gave a nod to her and Madysen. "One, two, ready, play."

Havyn kept her eye on the music as she moved the bow in rhythm. The sixteenth notes in this piece made it tricky for her to stay in tempo—especially since the piece was relatively new to Madysen and she had a hard time keeping up on the cello. If it were the two of them playing a duet, it would be one thing, but Whitney tended to try to pull them along like a steam engine, her head bobbing with the beat as her fingers flew across the ivories. Havyn wanted to ask her to slow it down a bit, but Madysen hadn't asked for help, so perhaps they would make it.

Whit was very much the leader. It was her job to lead them and mother-hen them almost as much as Mama. From the time Havyn could remember, her elder sister had been dragging her along by the hand or making sure she understood what to do. But Whit was also a fierce protector and loyal friend. Havyn couldn't have asked for a better older sister. Even if they got annoyed with one another, it never lasted.

The piece continued into a *ritardando* that led to the *largo* movement. Taking a deep breath, she lifted her bow for the rests in her music and closed her eyes as Madysen took over the lead part.

Their youngest sibling could make the cello sing. It gave Havyn chill bumps to listen to the haunting melody. It was almost time for her to come back in, so she opened her eyes and looked at her sisters. Whitney's curly red hair was tied back in a braid with a ribbon. She never fussed much with it because she liked things simple and out of the way—her focus was on helping run the farm and on practicing their music, *not* on her appearance. Even so, Havyn didn't think their elder sister knew how truly beautiful she was.

Madysen sat with her head slightly ducked as she played. Her frame was much more petite than either Whitney or Havyn, but her red hair was just as curly as Whit's. She chose to wear it down most of the time, pulling it back with combs like their mother used.

Madysen glanced up as if she knew Havyn had been watching and smiled.

Havyn blinked. It was her turn to play again. As she moved her eyes back to the music in front of her, a memory of Madysen's birth took over her mind. Early, and oh, so tiny, the youngest Powell had captured all their hearts. Havyn had been three when her younger sister was born, but she had vivid memories of fighting with Whitney over who would get to hold the baby. And how the whole family had prayed daily for Madysen for many weeks.

The tempo picked back up in the last movement, and Havyn forced her mind back to the present. She loved her sisters, but she didn't want to be on the receiving end of their ire if she flubbed her part because she was distracted.

A fight would only give Granddad another reason to tease them for their fiery tempers. Poor man. Living with four redheads had to be a challenge. But the truth was, Havyn didn't want to incense either of her sisters. They'd done too much of that when they were younger and stretching their boundaries.

As the piece headed into the *vivace* section of the finale, their complete unity in the timing and harmonies gave her a little thrill. What was it about music that brought them together so beautifully?

The final notes rang out. Havyn watched for Whitney's pedal to release before she lifted her bow.

In perfect unison, they stopped. Madysen set down her bow and clapped her hands. "Whew! I wasn't sure I could keep up with you two there for a bit, but we made it." The smile that filled her face made her almost glow.

"I'm so proud of both of you!" Whitney turned on the bench to face them. Her smile warmed Havyn to the core. "This will be a wonderful addition to our repertoire for the Roadhouse, don't you think?"

"Oh, I do!" Havyn set her violin down and straightened the pages on her music stand. "It's definitely a challenging piece, which will keep the audience on their toes, and it's emotional enough to draw them in and pull at their heartstrings."

"Exactly." Whit turned back to the piano and glanced at her music. "I think perhaps we should practice a bit more around measure 128 through to the end of the movement before Mama gets back from town. Then we could play this for her after dinner."

"Agreed." Havyn glanced at the clock. "As long as we don't take too long—I've got to check on the chickens and then get to preparations for dinner."

Madysen leaned back in her chair. "Don't forget Mama wanted to go through some new harmonies she wrote for us on that song for church, as well as the other music she wanted to work on once she got home."

"Let's get back to it, then, shall we?" Whitney set the metronome for the tempo of the first movement again.

Havyn lifted her violin under her chin and nodded.

They started the piece together again, and Madysen didn't seem to struggle in keeping up at all.

Havyn let the music wash over her, filling all the cracks and crevices of her soul. There was nothing more perfect in the world to her. A true gift from God.

Applause from behind them made them all stop and turn. Mama beamed a smile at them. "What outstanding improvement you all have made! It's simply beautiful." She strode toward them across the great room they used for the family's gatherings and stopped abruptly by the window. "Why don't . . . you . . . start . . . back at the . . . beginning?"

Whitney came off the bench in an instant. "Mama, what's wrong?"

Their mother held up a hand. "Just . . . having trouble . . . catching my . . . breath." She sat in a wing chair. "I'll . . . be fine. Go ahead." The smile she aimed at them was weak.

Havyn looked to Whit for her cue. Should they continue? Or was something wrong?

Whitney glanced at her and then to Madysen. Even though Havyn wasn't looking at their mother, she listened to each breath, pretty certain that her sisters were doing the same.

She rearranged her sheets of music.

Madysen applied rosin to her bow.

After a few moments, Whitney nodded.

Their mother's breathing seemed slow and steady now. Maybe she had run in from the wagon when she'd heard them playing? Could that be why she'd been out of breath?

"Let's—" Mama cleared her throat—"hear it." The words from their mother brooked no argument.

They went back to the beginning and started again.

An hour later, Havyn took a clean apron from the hook in the hallway. Her skirt was a sight. When she'd gone out to check on the chickens, she'd found them having a squabble over the scraps she'd taken out after lunch. So she had to separate a few of the troublemakers until they calmed down. Which had made a mess out of her skirt and blouse. Not to mention the depth of the snow in the new pen where she'd placed some of her ornery girls. She'd had to dig out part of the corner by the fence. Oh, for the day the snow would melt. It was almost May, for goodness' sake!

With no time to change, she'd cleaned up the best she could, washed her hands and face, pulled her hair back into a tidy bun, and headed to the kitchen.

Lifting the apron over her head, she put it in place and then tied it around her waist. She wanted to make her sweet cornbread to go along with the chowder tonight, but there wasn't enough time for it to bake, so she'd have to make do with biscuits.

Between all their music practice, chores on the farm, and trading off fixing the meals, they kept quite busy. It didn't bother Havyn. She loved it. But she also hated to get behind.

"At least I'm more flexible than Whit . . ." She shook her head. Her older sister couldn't handle things not going according to her plans. When she got it in her mind to do something, everyone else better step out of the way.

Then there was Madysen. She was so compassionate and merciful. All that mattered to her was that everyone was happy—

Tones from the cello came from the living room, as if Havyn had commanded her little sister to play with thoughts of her. It made her giggle as she chopped vegetables for the chowder and placed them in a large cast-iron skillet with butter to sauté. She really shouldn't be thinking of Madysen as little. Sure, she was tiny, but they were all adults. Madysen was already twenty years of age!

Where had the time gone?

Whitney appeared in the doorway, tying her apron around her waist. "Mama wanted to work on some cello specifics with Maddy, so I came to help you." She grabbed a fish and slapped it on the counter. "I see Granddad's been fishing through the ice again. I thought he normally did that on Saturdays."

"He said he had a hankering to go fishing early this morning. Said the aurora was quite beautiful."

Her older sister took a knife to the fish. "I'm worried about him. I don't think he's sleeping well—especially if he's getting up that early to go fishing." Whit's brow was furrowed, her lips pursed.

While Havyn agreed, she couldn't let on that anything was amiss. "Maybe we could ask him about it at dinner. I think he's working way too hard."

"Which is why he should let me take over more responsibilities. He knows I'm capable of running things, and the dogs don't take near the work that all the cows do. I hate to keep reminding him, but he's not getting any younger."

The aroma from the buttery onions, carrots, and potatoes filled the room with a divine fragrance that made Havyn's mouth water. "I'll bring it up at dinner if you think that will help."

"Would you?" Whitney finished cleaning the fish and wiped her hands on a towel.

"Of course. We're all concerned about him. Mama mentioned it the other day, but then said that we all might think we're stubborn because of our red hair when in all actuality it came from Granddad." Havyn cleaned her work space so she could start the biscuit dough. "Don't be surprised if it takes him a bit to warm up to the idea of having help. He's been running this farm, and his mines before that, for a long time without much help from us."

"You're right. But that still doesn't negate the fact that he's aging. Slowing down. Maybe he needs the reminder that we're fully capable of helping out. Even running things." Her older sister cleaned up the fish guts and scales.

Havyn poured boiling water over the fish bones so she could make a stock for the base of their chowder. Even though Whitney was right, Havyn worried that Granddad wasn't ready to hand things over to them just yet.

But if he didn't do something about it soon . . .

It might be too late.

Four

The road stretched before him. After all the chaos of the morning, John had finally left the town of Nome behind. Good. There wasn't much out here but snow on the ground, and from the look of the clouds, a threat of more to come. He picked up his pace.

While the town held its own perils, was it dangerous to be far from civilization in this territory? He didn't have a weapon, other than a small knife. He scanned around him for wild animals. The wind picked up, and he pulled his coat close. A hundred thoughts ran through his mind as he trekked up the snowy road. He'd come a long way from anything he knew. What was he doing here?

Fulfilling a promise. But now that he'd come this far . . . it almost seemed ridiculous. He didn't remember much about Chuck Bundrant. The last time he'd seen the older man, he'd been fourteen. A vague recollection of Nonno's stories, and of a kindly face, came to mind. But little else.

He could almost hear his grandfather's voice on the wind . . . *"Do this one thing for me, John."*

He looked toward where the doctor assured him he'd find

a dairy farm. There was no sign of one. Or really anything, for that matter. At least, not yet. Should he press on? What if the farm was farther out than the doctor thought? What if the weather turned ugly?

Shaking his head, John continued on the road for the farm. Silly to have such fears. No doubt they were brought on by his hunger and thirst. God had already provided for him to find his grandfather's friend. John needed to press on in faith.

As he crested a slight rise in the road, the dairy finally came into view. His stomach rumbled loud enough that a cow behind the fence on his left turned to stare. John laughed out loud. One thing was for certain: Hunger was a good motivator.

Down the lane in front of him, a team of horses pulling a wagon converted to a sleigh kicked up snow. John had to jump to the side—into waist-deep snow—so the conveyance could make it in the well-traveled tracks. It slowed, and a man nodded to him. "Sorry to push you off the road there, but I'm so loaded down, we'd never get her unstuck out of the deep stuff." The man looked him up and down. "Though I 'spect you'd be strong enough to push me out. You new in town?"

"Yes, sir."

"I hear a slight accent. Don't think I've heard it before. You from abroad?"

"Italy, originally. Colorado recently."

The man chuckled. "Ah, so you've come to hunt your fortune in gold?"

"No, I can honestly say I haven't." John gave the man a smile. "I've seen enough of that in my lifetime."

The man relaxed back in the seat. "Good to hear. We've got plenty of 'em filling up our town." He nodded toward the pack on John's shoulders. "So what brings you so far north?"

"I'm looking for a friend of my grandfather's." John spied

the large metal cans in the back of the wagon. They must be from the dairy. He looked back to the driver. "Do you know where I can find Chuck Bundrant?"

"Sure, he's in the birthing shed. That's the first building on your left past the house."

"Thank you, sir."

"Name's Herb Norris. I own the Roadhouse on the outskirts of town. We offer good food and musical entertainment in the evenings. Clean. No gambling. No saloon." The man lifted his eyebrows and nodded at John. "Let me know if you need a place to stay."

"Thank you, I will. I'm John Roselli. It was a pleasure to meet you. I greatly appreciate your help."

"You're welcome." He lifted the reins, and the horses started pulling again.

John stepped out of the snow and back onto the ice-rutted road. Dusting the cold, wet snow from his trousers, he headed up the hill.

The sprawling house was much larger than anything he'd seen in Alaska so far. The rock apron around the base was a nice touch. Someone had taken great care to build a beautiful home.

As he hiked the rest of the way up the slight incline to where the homestead was situated, more buildings came into view. Chickens chattered and cows bellowed.

Now these were the kinds of sounds he could live with!

The door to the first building on the left was propped open with a milk pail. John walked in and allowed his eyes to adjust from the brightness of the snow to the interior of the barn.

Opening his mouth to call out for Mr. Bundrant, he stopped. He'd walked in on a man praying.

". . . forgiveness. If the girls ever found out what I did, it would crush them . . ." The next words were muffled. ". . . to understand *why* I did what I did if they come to know the truth." A shuffling noise sounded and muted the rest.

Who was praying, and what had he done? John had done plenty of things he wasn't proud of, but the man made his wrong sound so . . . ominous. Frozen in place, John glanced around. What should he do? The shed was silent for several moments, so the man must be finished praying.

John shifted, weighing his options. Should he step outside and make more noise as he entered again? If Mr. Bundrant had been the one praying, John definitely didn't want him to know that he'd invaded his privacy and overheard his prayer. But it was all so quiet now . . . if he moved, the man might hear him.

His quandary was solved when one of the cows started up a ruckus. From the sound of her, she was getting ready to calve. It gave John the perfect opportunity to walk outside and start again. This time he stopped in the doorway and knocked on the doorframe. "Mr. Bundrant?"

"Be right there."

The same voice he'd heard praying. The right thing to do would be to tell the man that he'd overheard his prayer. Maybe introductions first, then he could decide what to do.

A man shuffled through the straw toward him. "I'm Chuck Bundrant. How can I help you?" He didn't *look* like a man harboring some dark secret.

John extended his hand. "It's nice to see you again, Mr. Bundrant. My name is John Roselli—"

"You're Giuseppe's grandson, aren't you?" A huge smile filled the man's face as he took John's proffered hand and shook it.

"Yes."

Mr. Bundrant pulled him into the barn. "How is the old chap doing? He used to tell me so many stories about you and your folks. I haven't heard from him in almost a year."

John swallowed the sudden lump in his throat. "He passed away four months ago."

Bundrant's face fell. "Oh, I'm sorry to hear that. He was a very good friend. I'm surprised you remember me. It was a long time ago when we met." He walked over to the stall, where the cow made her displeasure known.

Maybe he'd misheard the man's prayer. The man in front of him had been Nonno's friend. There was no reason to judge him for his private words. "Yes, sir, well . . . I don't remember much, but my grandfather often talked of you and how much your friendship meant to him."

Mr. Bundrant shook his head. "It's hard to believe he's gone."

John dipped his chin as his stomach rubbed itself raw, and he looked at his boots for a moment. "Nonno asked me to bring you a package, so that's why I've come . . . but I'm also in need of a job, sir. It took everything I had to get here. I was inquiring in town when I ran into Dr. Gordon. He suggested I come see you and told me to tell you that he sent me . . . just in case you have any questions."

"So you ran into the good doc, huh? He's been hounding me for months to slow down and hire a foreman, but I haven't gotten around to it." He grabbed a bale of hay. "Not exactly like there's a lot of good men to choose from." Setting it down next to the moaning cow, he rubbed his chin. "What's this about a package?"

John took off his rucksack. "It must be awfully important because Nonno made me promise to bring it to you. Right before he died."

"Giuseppe was a good man. We helped each other a lot over the years, but I don't remember him having anything of value for me." Mr. Bundrant looked down at the cow and then back to him. "Ah . . . now I remember . . ." He shook his head and chuckled. "The old coot."

"Well, let me give it to you." John untied the flap to his bag.

The cow's abdomen undulated as she gave a cry. "Don't think we'll have time for that right now. I'm going to need your assistance." Chuck took up a looped rope and slipped it over her head. He tied the other end to the stall. "How are you with cows? Ever helped with a birth?"

"My family used to have a dairy farm back in Italy. But I was a kid last time I did that." John took off his coat and mittens, then rolled up his sleeves. "Tell me what to do, and I'll do it."

"How about you help keep mama calm, and I'll explain what I'm doing as I do it?" The older man pushed his sleeves up his arms. "Ya know, I always thought I'd be able to run this place myself, but the good ol' doc is right. I need help. I've got plenty of hands milking, and my girls do a good job helping out, but I need a foreman. A man who knows the ins and outs and intricacies of the whole business. You up for learning all that . . . handling that much responsibility?"

All thoughts of leaving Nome as soon as he could vanished. Even the few minutes he'd spent with Chuck Bundrant made him feel at home and reminded him of Nonno. Might as well learn the job, do it well, and see what God had in store for him down the road. "It's been a good long while since I did this sort of work, but I'll do everything I can to learn and do what you need. It'd be an honor to work for a friend of my grandfather's."

The older man's face broke into a smile. "It's all right, son. You don't have to convince me. I've already decided to hire you."

"Thank you, sir." His limbs relaxed as he stroked the cow's head. At least he'd have an honest job.

"And why don't we stop this *sir* business, all right? Your grandpa and me were mighty close. *Chuck* will do just fine. You might not remember me all that well, but I definitely remember you. Tall and lanky, a little awkward. You've filled out a good deal over the years, but I still see the family resemblance. How old are ya now?"

"Twenty-seven."

"Wow, it's been longer than I realized. Time sure does fly these days." Chuck's focus shifted to the cow again. "This little one's having trouble being born."

John's stomach took that moment to rumble loudly. He put a hand to it. "My apologies. I just got into town and haven't eaten anything since dawn."

Chuck gave a wry laugh. "Nothing to apologize for. As soon as you help me deliver this calf, we'll head up to the house and get you fed."

John stroked the cow's black head. "I'm not familiar with this breed."

"Canadienne." Chuck rubbed some sort of oil over his right arm. "Hearty breed, developed in Canada. Some folks call them Black Jersey. Most of mine are black, but they can be brown or even reddish. Now hold her tight. She's been at this for far too long. I'm going to check the position of this little one." He lifted the cow's tail and maneuvered his arm into the birthing canal. "Ah, just as I thought. One leg's forward and one's bent back." As he withdrew his arm he held fast to the forward leg. "Get me one of those ropes."

He motioned with his head to the stall gate, where several lengths of calf rope awaited.

John left the miserable mama and grabbed the first rope he could reach. He came back to Chuck.

"Tie it on the calf's leg right above the hoof and then tie off the other end to the stall fence."

John did as Chuck instructed and stepped back.

"Now go hold mama's head again while I push this baby back inside and see if I can't get that other leg in the right position."

The poor cow protested louder than ever, but Chuck had things well under control. After a few strenuous moments, he smiled. "There we go." He pulled his arm out, bringing the calf's leg forward as he did. He released the rope from the stall as the mother cow pushed the baby partway out. The front legs and face were delivered, and Chuck reached over and pulled the sack from the calf's face as the cow pushed her baby out to plop down onto the straw below. The miracle of birth. Was there anything more beautiful? Memories of witnessing it as a child came back and made him feel whole and complete again.

This was what he was meant to do.

"Untie her and step aside."

John did as Chuck instructed, then followed the older man from the stall.

The cow attended to her baby, seeming not to want anything more to do with the men.

"There. Now that's a sight to see." Chuck reached for a rag hanging on the rail of the stall, wiped at his hands and arms, and shot his smile toward John. "I'm glad to have you here."

"Thank you, sir—I mean, Chuck."

"Let me take you up to the house. We'll get washed up, eat, and meet everyone, and then I'll show you the ropes around here. It's a mighty big job, but I'm inclined to believe you can handle it."

"I look forward to it."

Chuck turned and eyed John as they walked out of the birthing shed. "Seems like the good Lord above sent you at the perfect time. How are you at handling redheads?"

FIVE

As she glanced at the bubbling pots on the stove, Havyn wiped her hands on her apron and then went into the dining room to check on the table. The background music of cello and piano filled the air around her. With a glance to the empty table, she planted her hands on her hips. "Madysen? You haven't set the table!" She raised her voice so it would resonate across the dining room and reach her younger sister in the parlor.

The cello screeched to a halt. "I'm sorry! I'm coming!" Footsteps accompanied her words. It only took a second for Madysen to come blazing into the dining room in her stocking feet, her hair flying behind her in a thick curtain of cinnamon. "I completely forgot . . . again. I'm sorry."

Havyn laughed and went to the sideboard. "Here, let me help you."

"No, this is my job. You have enough chores to do without having to do mine." She waved a hand at Havyn. "You go finish whatever you were doing. I'll get this all set in a jiffy."

Havyn covered a giggle. Madysen was the most stubborn of them all, but she was also the sweetest. Which was quite the juxtaposition. But then, they were *all* stubborn. And *hopefully* a bit sweet.

Whitney, the oldest at twenty-five, was the most passionate and no-nonsense. Always making sure they were all on track. She could remember a list seventy-five items long and not forget a thing. Whereas, twenty-year-old Madysen could forget what day it was if you let her. In fact, a mere two years ago, they'd all had to remind Madysen about her individual duties. Daily. It had become tiresome for them all until Mama finally had a stern meeting with her and laid out how the youngest sibling's forgetfulness was affecting everyone else. As Madysen was also the most merciful of them all, her heart about broke in two when she realized the time, effort, and exasperation she was causing everyone else. Since that day, she'd done a pretty decent job at keeping up—with the exception of a few mishaps.

Like today.

But oh, to cherish each day as Maddy did. That would be such a blessing. Tiny and full of life, Maddy focused on each day as it came and seemed to enjoy every moment. A luxury most youngest siblings had, perhaps? If Whit and Havyn hadn't spoiled their little sister when she was younger, maybe things would have been different. But Havyn wouldn't change Madysen for anything. They needed her to be just who she was.

A creak of the back door let Havyn know that Granddad would soon join them for dinner. Ladling the fish chowder into the large soup tureen, she hummed the new song they were going to sing tonight at the Roadhouse. It was one that Whitney and Mama had written for the three of them, complete with tight harmonies and glorious minor chords that sent chills up and down her spine. Their audience might not be refined and high society, but she and her family would still perform their very best.

Madysen came in and took the tureen out to the dining room, and Havyn dished up the creamed corn into another serving bowl.

The tips they received each weekend at the Roadhouse grew as time went on. Didn't that prove that not all men in their little gold-seeking town were at the brothels and saloons each night, like the paper reported? In fact, the crowds at the Roadhouse were increasing. So maybe there was hope for a God-fearing man to come along one day. Problem was, they'd need *three* God-fearing men, one for each sister. And that might be asking for a bit much. Even from God.

She placed the biscuits in a basket and wiped her hands on her apron. Maddy came in again, but her eyes were wide.

Havyn angled a look at her. "What's that face for?"

Madysen stepped closer and took the basket of biscuits. "There's a man with Granddad. I saw him as they were mucking their boots in the mud room."

Havyn smiled at her sister's hushed voice. "Granddad has lots of men who come to get milk, plus there's all the milkers. What's got you so surprised about this one?"

"He's . . . new. Someone I've never seen before. And he's not a native."

"Okay." Havyn tried not to giggle at her sister's expression. "That doesn't exactly raise the alarm."

Madysen hugged the basket to her chest. "You don't understand. Just wait until you see him."

"All right." Havyn pushed her way through the swinging door to the dining room, smiling at her sister's dramatics. Setting the bowl of creamed corn next to the chowder, she checked the table. "Madysen, you better grab another place setting, just in case."

The bass of their grandfather's tone, mixed with the baritone of another man, drew closer. The baritone had a bit of an accent. What was it? Ah! Havyn snapped her fingers. Italian. Their mother had taught them to sing many songs in Italian. A few in French and German as well.

Whitney entered the dining room with their mother, a slight frown on her face. "Why is Madysen setting another place?"

"Because we have a guest." Granddad spoke from the doorway, his face all smiles. "Girls, I'd like you to meet John Roselli. He's our new foreman."

Havyn, her sisters, and her mother fell silent. The man with Granddad was much younger than she'd expected.

And much better looking.

Blinking several times, she realized her mouth was open and shut it with a snap.

Whitney stared too.

Madysen coughed into her hand.

Wait . . . *what?* Did Granddad say a new foreman? Since when?

Mama gathered her wits first. "John, it's a pleasure to meet you."

"Likewise, ma'am." The tall, dark-haired gentleman nodded and bowed slightly at the waist.

"John, meet my daughter, Melissa Powell, and my three granddaughters. Whitney, Havyn, and Madysen." Granddad beamed at them, pride shining all over his face.

"It's an honor." John bowed to them as well.

Havyn caught her breath. Mr. Roselli's skin was a lovely olive shade, which made his dark brown eyes appear mysterious. A strong jawline and Roman nose reminded her of their Latin studies and the tales she'd read about Rome. His dark hair was almost black, a lot like the native people up here in Alaska.

Whitney elbowed her. Had she missed something?

Another elbow to her side.

"It's nice to meet you," she spit out. Had they been waiting on her? With any luck, the elbows would stop. It wasn't her fault. They'd never had a guest like this before.

Mama stepped around the table to her place. "Won't you join us for dinner, John?"

"Thank you, ma'am. That is quite generous."

Granddad went to the head of the table and pointed for his guest to sit at the other end. Which placed the handsome Mr. Roselli on Havyn's right.

She laid her hands in her lap and bowed her head. Where had this man come from? And why did Granddad hire him?

As Granddad thanked God for all of His provision, a horrible thought made her inhale quickly. Her skirt! Gracious. Underneath her apron, she was an absolute mess. Oh, why hadn't she changed?

She put a hand to her hair. Oh, was it a mess too? Well, nothing she could do about it now. After Granddad's *amen*, she gathered everyone's bowls and passed them to him so he could serve the chowder.

"Now, John. I don't know if you've had a good fish chowder yet, but you're about to have the best. Havyn is an excellent cook, and she makes this magnificent creamed corn to go with it." After he'd served everyone the chowder, he began to pass around the steaming bowl of creamed corn. "My favorite way to eat it is to put a nice big spoonful of it right in the middle of the chowder."

"Sounds wonderful to me." Mr. Roselli took two biscuits from the breadbasket and buttered them. Setting them down on his bread plate, he accepted the bowl of corn and did exactly as his host had done.

Havyn took the bowl as he passed it to her, and she did the same. What was it about this man that seemed so . . . intriguing and different?

Mama cleared her throat. "So . . ." She dipped her spoon into her bowl. "Papa, did we have any new calves make an entrance?"

Granddad laughed. "Did we ever. Five, just today."

"Wonderful." Mama tasted her chowder and turned to Havyn. "Delicious, as always."

"Thank you, Mama." She looked across the table at her siblings. Madysen looked cheery as usual, but Whit's expression didn't bode well. The air around the table sizzled with an odd awkwardness.

Oh, hopefully Whitney would keep her thoughts to herself.

The eldest Powell sister picked up a biscuit and tilted her head. "When did you decide to bring on a foreman?"

So much for keeping her thoughts to herself.

Whitney loved this farm. And had offered numerous times to run it for their grandfather. His hiring a foreman without even talking to them? Whit's feathers were clearly ruffled. Like one of Havyn's hens.

Granddad took a sip of his water and set the glass back down on the table. "That's a really good question, Whitney. You know things have gotten a lot more demanding around here, and even with all the hands that help with the milking, I still find myself busier than I'd like. I admit I'm getting a bit older, so it's only wise for me to bring on some help." His tone was light but firm enough to brook no argument.

Mama reached over and patted his forearm. "That's a very wise decision, Papa. I've been telling you that you work too much, and so has Dr. Gordon."

Havyn wholeheartedly agreed. "I think it's a great idea." She looked to their guest. "We're glad to have you here." She turned back to Granddad. "And maybe now you'll have more time for fishing so you don't have to go in the middle of the night."

He laughed again. "Exactly my thoughts, Havyn. Which, of course, means more chowder."

She looked across the table at her eldest sister. Oh boy . . . *something* was simmering in that head of hers, but thankfully, she let the subject drop.

For now.

Their guest polished off his first bowl of chowder.

Granddad waved his hand. "Send your bowl up this way, and I'll fill it again."

"Thank you, Chuck." He did as ordered, then wiped his mouth with his napkin and looked around the table. If he felt any of the tension around the table, he didn't let on. "Let me see if I remember . . . Whitney, Havyn, and Madysen? Did I get them right?"

"Yes, you did." Mama smiled at their new foreman.

Granddad passed the full bowl back.

"I don't believe I've ever heard such lovely names before. Do they have special meanings?"

Mother laid her napkin down and turned toward John. "My husband—God rest his soul—had a best friend when he was a child with the surname of Whitney. He was determined that whether we had a girl or a boy, we needed to name our first child Whitney."

No matter how many times Mama told this story, Havyn loved it. Memories of her dad were so precious.

"Then he decided we should be as creative and unique with our second child. When Havyn came, we were in the middle of a crazy lightning and thunderstorm. Which turned to snow. In August mind you. Cripple Creek is way up the mountain."

"John here came from Cripple Creek. His grandpa and I were good friends."

"I knew I recognized the Roselli name!" Mama beamed a smile at their guest. "You're Giuseppe's grandson, aren't you?"

Their guest's face lit up. "Yes, ma'am. And I remember well the snow we often had on the mountain in the summer months. Please continue with your story. I'm fascinated."

"Well, this snowstorm was unlike anything we'd ever seen. Thankfully, we made it back to our little cabin, which he called a safe haven. So he named her Havyn, using the Old English spelling of a *y* instead of an *e*."

John glanced at Havyn and smiled.

"Then we had our last little surprise." Mama looked at Madysen. "At the time of our third baby girl's birth, my husband had a good friend with the last name of Madison. So once again he changed the spelling and called her *Madysen*."

Havyn took a sip of her water. Mama left out the fact that Dad's *friend* was actually the bartender who served Dad drinks every day. All day. And all night. Havyn found that out when she heard Mama crying one night and went to console her. When Mama discovered who Dad's best friend was, she'd felt horrible for naming their newborn after him.

Yet another secret tucked away in Havyn's heart.

Granddad stood up and put his napkin on the table. "Well, girls, I think it's time I got John settled for the night so that tomorrow I can show him the ropes."

John stood as well and nodded at them. "It was nice to meet you all." He turned to Havyn. "Thank you for a wonderful meal."

"You're welcome."

Silence engulfed the table as the men walked out the door. Once the door shut, Mama raised her eyebrows at all of them.

But Whitney didn't hold her tongue. "I can't *believe* that Granddad would hire a foreman without talking to us!" She crossed her arms over her chest.

Mama's brow furrowed, and her tone sharpened. "And exactly what would you have him do? He's getting older, Whitney, and I've been worried about him for some time. This farm is growing, and the demands for milk and eggs are higher than ever."

"Well, at least it didn't have to be a stranger. You know how long it will take my dogs to get used to someone new? And if he's going to be here all the time, that's going to get them riled up every day. It will completely mess with their training."

Havyn sighed. "You and your dogs. They're smart enough—I think they'll do fine. Besides, he's not a stranger. He's obviously a friend of the family. You don't like him because you wanted the job yourself."

Whitney came out of her chair, her curly hair escaping the braid she'd thrown over her shoulder. "Don't even *start* about my dogs, or I'll sic them on your chickens."

Madysen stared at her from across the table, her jaw dropped. *No* one messed with Havyn's chickens. "I'm going to ignore that comment because I know you don't mean it," she said. "You're just mad that Granddad didn't consult you."

"*Girls!*" Mama stopped the argument before their tempers really took off without them. "Now, it is not our place to question your grandfather. This is *his* farm, and we will respect his decisions."

"But—"

Now it was Mama who stood. "There will be no *buts*, Whitney Elizabeth Powell."

Uh-oh. Mama used Whit's whole name . . .

Her tone was firm. "We *will* support whatever Granddad does." Her expression softened a tad. "Besides, I think it will be wonderful to have a foreman. Might help things run smoother." She lifted her chin and gave them all a stern look. "Now, it's time to clean up the kitchen and get to the rest of the chores. Then we need to go to the Roadhouse to perform. So I do not want to hear one more word of argument out of any of you. Please act like the ladies you are."

"Yes, Mama." Havyn started to clear the dishes.

"Fine." Whitney straightened her shoulders. "But if this new foreman doesn't work out and it all blows up in our faces, you can't say I didn't warn you." She strode out of the room, and in seconds they heard the beginning of Liszt's Hungarian Rhapsody no. 2 echoing through the house.

With a bit more ferocity than normal.

Havyn followed Mama into the kitchen.

Madysen carried a stack of plates in and looked to their mother. "What's gotten into her? And you all say that *I'm* the melodramatic one. She acts as if Granddad hiring a foreman is going to start a war."

"Don't worry about your sister." Mama patted Madysen's shoulder. "She doesn't like change, and this wasn't what she envisioned happening here."

"Well, I for one think it's a wonderful idea. Granddad

has been working too hard." And it didn't hurt that the new foreman was fascinating. Havyn liked him already.

"Yes, he has."

She restrained a frown. Mama's voice had that worried tone. The kind that meant there was more to the story. Did Mama know about Granddad?

Havyn started a pan of soapy water. Well, John was here now. That would take a lot of strain off Granddad. He would be all right . . .

Wouldn't he?

Six

Pride filled Melissa as she watched her girls grace the stage at the Roadhouse. The three were arm in arm, singing the new song she'd written for them. A capella. In perfect harmony. A haunting ballad about the loss of their father, the song had come to Melissa late at night, when she allowed the tears to flow. Thoughts of Chris had come often of late.

She missed him.

In all the years since Chris's death, no other man had interested her. Maybe because she'd been too engrossed in raising and teaching the girls. Maybe because living with Papa had been easy. Comfortable. Or maybe she didn't want to open up her heart only to be hurt again.

Every day she prayed for her girls and what their heavenly Father held for their futures. More than anything, she longed to see them stay together as a family. If she had her druthers, it would be right here. On the family farm.

A standing ovation erupted around her, and Melissa joined the men in applauding as she smiled up at her daughters. The next song was a lively one, so she moved to the edge of the crowd to allow for the boisterous knee-slapping that almost always took place. Last thing she needed was to get caught in the middle again and have one of the men ask her to dance.

Herb Norris came to her side. "They're getting more popular every time they get up on that stage. That last song was a tearjerker for sure."

"Thank you for asking them to perform. They love it."

"I'd love to have them more often, if you're willing." He pointed to the stage. "The men would come every night if they knew your girls were here."

"The farm keeps us pretty busy, but we'll think about it. Maybe for some special occasions or holidays?" The sound of forks clanking against dinnerware filled the room. Funny how the men seemed to do most of their eating when the girls weren't playing or singing.

He tilted his head. "That would be wonderful. Just know that the invitation is open." He walked away as Whitney started the next piece on the piano.

Melissa scanned the room. Herb was right—the crowds had grown for her daughters' performances. How wonderful that they were able to use their talents.

A man at the table in front of her struck a match and then lit a fat cigar he'd put in his mouth. Herb didn't allow for alcohol or spitting, but for some reason, he let the men smoke. Probably because Herb liked to smoke a pipe himself.

When the sweet-spicy scent from the cigar wafted her way, she waved a hand in front of her face and moved toward the back—

Oh no! It was happening again! Her lungs tightened. Tears rushed to her eyes. She couldn't take a full breath.

Racing for the back door, she put a hand to her chest. It felt like someone was pressing down on it. She tried to suck air in, but it only seeped through on a wheeze.

Outside, she leaned against the building and bent over at the waist, trying to force air in through her nose. Closing her eyes, she worked to calm herself. Tried to take slow breaths. But when she couldn't seem to get enough air to satisfy her starving lungs, panic built.

No. She couldn't let it overtake her. She had to calm down.

A tiny breath in. Slow breath out.

Another small breath in. Even slower breath out.

This was much worse than what she'd experienced before. She kept at it for several excruciating minutes, but her breaths still came shallow and pinched.

Oh, she mustn't get sick! The summer months in Nome were the busiest. Papa needed her. So did the girls.

Standing upright, she looked to the sky. *Please, Lord, help me. . . .*

But no answers came.

She wrapped her arms around herself. There was no choice. She'd have to go see the doctor soon. Before her family suspected anything was wrong.

———

John sat on the edge of his bed and tugged his boots off. Four days at the farm now, and every muscle and bone in his body seemed to ache. How had Chuck managed this on his own for all these years? While the older man shuffled and paused every now and then, John was still amazed at everything his boss accomplished. Every. Single. Day.

Maybe John had gone soft. Taking care of Nonno and then all the traveling were the only reasons he could come up with as an excuse for being so out of condition. How long would it take for him to get into the swing of things?

The room that Chuck had given him above the milking shed—a humble name for such an enormous barn—was warm and cozy, with its own fireplace in the corner. Not that he'd had time to even unpack. He worked with Chuck, ate with the family, worked some more, and came to bed.

As he went to pull a clean shirt out of his rucksack, he spotted the package on the floor next to the end of his bed. They'd been so busy these first few days, what with Chuck insisting that John learn every inch of the farm and every detail of the daily workings, that John hadn't been able to give it to him. In fact, he'd forgotten about it.

Shaking his head, John ran a hand through his hair. First thing in the morning, he would give it to Chuck. Before chores. Before breakfast.

Nonno's wish would be fulfilled.

A knock at the door startled him.

"John, it's Chuck."

He went to the door and opened it. "Did I forget to do something?" John's heart pounded for a moment. No matter the family friendship, he couldn't bear the thought of letting his new employer down.

Chuck held up a hand and entered. "Not a thing. I just wanted to talk to you."

John let out his breath as he closed the door. "Good. I need to talk to you too. I'm so sorry, but after that first day, I forgot to give you the package from Nonno." He walked to the end of his bed and retrieved the paper-wrapped box. "Here it is."

"Thank you, John. And thanks for coming all this way to deliver it." The older man chuckled. "If I know Giuseppe,

I know why he did it." He pulled the one chair in the room closer with his boot. "May I?"

"Of course."

Chuck sat in the chair with a sigh and set the package on the floor.

"Is there a problem?"

"With you?" Chuck shook his head. "No. Not at all. But we will get to all of it in a moment. First, I wanted to ask you about your plans."

"My plans?"

"Yes. I realized I hadn't asked how long you plan on staying. The ships will be able to reach us in a matter of weeks, so I can't help but wonder if you plan to stay."

"Oh." John looked down for a moment. "I'll be honest with you, Chuck. At first, I thought it would be short term. I've spent the last fifteen years in gold-mining towns with my grandfather and figured I'd like to try something different."

Chuck looked at the floor for a moment and then back up, his face serious. "I see. Well, do you like it here?"

"Very much. Even though it's merely been a few days, this is the best job I've ever had."

"Would you consider staying?" Chuck's probing gaze was steady.

John looked at him for several moments. "I honestly hadn't thought about it until you offered me the foreman position. I came here to deliver Nonno's package and was going to start fresh somewhere after this. I just hadn't figured out where."

"I'm guessing it wasn't just a simple request for you to bring me the package. Your grandfather wanted to get you up here for a reason."

That sounded like Nonno, still . . . "I don't understand. If that's true, why didn't he tell me?"

"Ah, well, your grandfather always had a plan. He liked to dream too. I'm sure he didn't want to put you in dire financial straits, but trust me when I say that he wanted the best for you. I have to admit it impressed me that you went to Doc Gordon looking for a job. Shows you're a man of character. A man looking ahead."

"Thank you, Chuck, but I'm still confused. Do *you* know why my grandfather sent me here?"

"I have an inkling, but let me ask you this . . . will you consider staying?"

The man's voice almost pleaded. There must be more to this than John first thought. "I know I have a lot to learn, and it would be an honor to work for you, Chuck." He sat on the edge of his bed and placed his elbows on his knees. "But I feel there's something more to your request."

Chuck quirked an eyebrow and chuckled. "I knew you were perceptive." He paused for several seconds. "Son, I've been watching you. You're hardworking and you love the Lord. Those are my top two priorities. It also helps that you're quite capable at what you do. Your grandfather was a good friend to me, and I know you come from hardy stock." Chuck looked down at his boots again. "The truth is . . . I'm sick. Something is wrong with me. I need someone I can trust to take over the farm and to provide for the girls."

A deep ache hit John in the chest. Would he lose this man so soon after losing Nonno? He'd just found Chuck. This couldn't be happening. "What's wrong, sir?"

"I don't know for certain. I need to see Doc Gordon again before he leaves."

Of course. It all made sense. "That's why he sent me here."

"Yes, to help lighten my load. He's been scolding me for months that I needed to slow down. Fact was, I was too stubborn to listen. Until recently."

John leaned forward. "What can I do to help? You don't look sick, so there must be plenty of time for you to heal . . . right?"

"Are you saying you're willing to stay?"

"Of course. I've come to love working on a farm again. And Nonno would want me to help his friend."

Chuck held up his hand. "This isn't a charity case, John. Don't misunderstand me. I'm here to offer you a business deal. One that also includes my family."

John raised his eyebrows. "You already hired me . . ."

His boss took a long breath and held out both of his hands. "Let me be blunt. Years ago, your grandfather and I had a lengthy discussion about our families. It was shortly after the girls lost their father. Giuseppe and I had been quite close. We were both gravely concerned about you youngsters living in a mining town. What would happen to you, or to my girls, should we pass on. We made a pact to keep in touch, and should anything happen to one, the other would assure the safety and provision for the other's loved ones."

"Sounds like Nonno." John went over and stoked the fire. "But why did he never mention it? I mean, he talked about you all the time and told me how he loved you as a brother, but nothing of this."

"I didn't tell my girls either. Not until a couple years ago, when a letter from your grandfather came. I mentioned to Melissa that should anything happen to me, she needed to get in touch with Giuseppe."

John sat back on the bed. What would it be like to have a bond—a friendship—like that?

"The truth is, son . . ." Chuck leaned forward. "And this might sound a little crazy—but I'm hoping that you will marry one of my granddaughters and run the farm. It will be yours—and the family's—if I die. But you must promise to provide for them all until they are married and out on their own. Of course, Melissa has never remarried, so I would ask for you to provide for her as well. Perhaps you could even keep them all together on the farm and let them help you run it. I'm not worried about how you do it, because I trust your judgment. I know we've just gotten to know each other, but I believe God put our two families together a long time ago and that you are worthy of my trust. So the bottom line is—I'm asking you to take care of my family."

Was he really hearing what he thought he was? "Sir . . . Chuck, surely things aren't that grave—"

"They are. At least to me. I want to offer you this . . ." He pulled a large gold nugget out of his jacket pocket and held it out to John.

It was the largest nugget of gold John had ever seen. "That's *huge*, sir."

"Yes. It is, but I'm asking you to accept a huge responsibility. Something I don't take lightly. Please consider it a dowry of sorts."

John stood and placed his hands on his hips. "I admire you a great deal. Especially after all the stories Nonno told me over the years. But this is a bit overwhelming. I'm here to help you. You've already hired me. So why the need for an additional arrangement?"

Chuck grimaced as he shook his head. "There are men in this town who would kill to have this place. If something happened to me, they wouldn't hesitate to jump in and steal everything from my girls. Their futures are at stake." The weariness in the older man's eyes pleaded with him.

John swiped a hand down his chin. Chuck was right to be worried . . . especially in a town like Nome that had exploded with men all seeking their fortunes. Men who would do anything to gain wealth fast. Men who would take advantage of women. "And you want me to marry one of your granddaughters? But this doesn't have to happen right away . . . does it?" Not that marriage and settling down wasn't a pleasant thought.

"What? You don't think they're lovely?" The older man lifted one side of his mouth in a grin.

"Of course they're lovely, but your granddaughters don't know me. Or I, them. And I don't know if you've noticed, but Whitney doesn't seem to care for me one bit. What if none of them do?"

Chuck laughed. "Don't you worry about her. She's the oldest, and to be honest, I think she's peeved at me for hiring on a foreman—*any* foreman. She wanted the job. Look, I know this is a bit unorthodox, but I need you to promise me that you will marry one of them. It doesn't have to be anytime soon. Just within the next year or so. I need to make sure that they are taken care of and that my farm will be in good hands."

The thought of the proposition in front of John overwhelmed him. He paced the room, his mind spinning in a hundred different directions. "What if none of them *want* to marry me? I mean that's a pretty important piece of the agreement."

"I've been doing a lot of talking to God about this. I'm content to let Him arrange it. The girls all have their good points and bad, but they're all loyal, faithful, and loving."

John nodded. "I'm sure they are, but love . . . well . . . that's something special. Something that needs to grow from a mutual affection. You can't force it."

"You're right, of course." Chuck's shoulders slumped, but his gaze was more fervent than ever. "You can't force love, but I believe God has made it clear to me that this will happen. I've already had a contract prepared, in fact."

"I understand you wanting to take care of your family, sir. It just all seems a bit . . . strange."

"I know. And I'm sorry. But I don't think I have a lot of time." He pulled some folded papers out of his jacket. "If you'll notice, it's pretty simple. There's two copies to sign. One for you and one for me. Just in case."

John studied the man a moment and then took the papers. Chuck was serious. What had he gotten himself into? Was this why Nonno had sent him here? No. His grandfather couldn't have known this would happen. But he *would* want John to help his friend.

Lord, I need some wisdom. And fast. Is this Your will?

John unfolded the sheets and read them. "So I don't have to choose now which granddaughter? I can get to know them?"

"Of course."

He nodded and continued reading. "Would you let me think about it and pray about it?"

"I hope that you do. But I'd like an answer soon." Chuck clasped his hands together and then slapped them against his thighs. "Am I asking too much of you, John? I mean, you will have quite a farm that will be in your name once I'm gone."

"No, sir." John swallowed. "It's a bit overwhelming. I mean, this is all very generous of you, and I'm grateful that you would entrust me with such an enormous task. And your family . . . it's an honor that you consider me—"

"Let me stop you right there, son." Chuck stood and picked up the box. "I'm hoping I'll be here for quite a while yet, but I'm feeling an urgency. It would give me a great peace of mind if you would agree to this now. I know it's a lot to ask, but your grandpa was the only man I ever trusted with my whole heart. And he had the same worries about you as I had about my girls. Won't you please consider doing this for an old friend of your grandfather's?"

John stared at him for several moments. Took a few deep breaths. "Of course, I will. Let me sleep on it and pray about it. But I want to add that I hope you are around for many years to come. I wouldn't ever want you to think I signed this because of what I would gain."

"I know that. That's why you're the man for the job." Chuck put a hand on his shoulder.

John's throat clogged a bit and he swallowed against it. To have someone believe in him . . . "It's been wonderful being at your side the past few days. You know I don't have any other family—but you've welcomed me with open arms, and I *feel* like family. And that makes me miss my grandfather a bit less."

"I'm glad I can help alleviate a bit of your grief. He was a good man. No, I take that back. Giuseppe was a *great* man. It was an honor to call him friend." He turned to the door. "I better let you get some rest. Thanks for hearing me out."

After the older man walked out of the room, John stood staring at the door.

When he'd come to his room a little bit ago, sleep had been his main priority. Now . . .

His mind swam.

The farm was a huge responsibility. But then, so was taking care of all four of the Powell women. Chuck hadn't minced words, which was nice, but the thought of promising to marry one of his granddaughters made John a little nervous. They were all beautiful. Talented. But he didn't know them.

The good Lord was going to have to guide him on this one. He placed the contract—a contract that, if he signed, obligated him to forever alter his life—on his bed next to the gold nugget and dropped to his knees.

SEVEN

Havyn pulled on her sealskin pants and grabbed her rubber boots to put by the door. The beginning of May had brought warmer temperatures—finally!—but now they had to muck about in snowy, slushy mud for a while.

It usually didn't bother her, but for some reason, having to trade her skirts for the pants wasn't appealing. Probably because they weren't all that flattering. And because of a certain new foreman.

She admitted it. He hadn't been here that long, but she liked him. And what was wrong with that? It was the first time a decent man close to her age had been around. It didn't hurt that he was handsome, had a smile that made her stomach flip, and had her grandfather's approval. In the past twenty-four hours, she'd heard Granddad sing John's praises at least ten times. Either he wanted them to take notice or . . . what? Granddad had never raved about anyone like he had John.

Madysen had told Havyn that she thought John was nice. Then she'd gone right back to talking about the latest magazine she'd read about Boston and how she wanted to go there. So, obviously, there wasn't much interest in John from her younger sibling. Whitney, on the other hand, had plenty of interest. But not the good kind. She'd done nothing but shoot daggers with her gaze at John since Granddad announced he'd hired the man. And whenever Mama brought John up, Whitney was the first to express her concerns.

Over and over.

But Whitney's worries were for naught. John had so easily assimilated into the family that even the dogs were comfortable with his comings and goings. Havyn knew that was due in part to all the time John spent letting them sniff him as he petted them when he and Granddad walked and talked about the farm. Not that either man had leisure time—the two worked long hours to make sure John understood every little inch of the farm. But the fact that John took the time for the animals showed her a lot about his character.

If only Whitney would acknowledge that.

John was so . . . intriguing. She hated that her grandfather suffered from his affliction, but her worry for him eased with John around. Before he'd come, the thought that they might lose Granddad if no one was around to help him was almost more than she could bear.

Oh, she missed her father at times like this. Ten years old was a hard age to lose anyone, but it had been especially hard to lose her dad. What would her life have been like had he lived? Would he have stopped drinking? Would he have made a farm for them like Granddad had?

Highly doubtful. She couldn't imagine her father enduring the isolation of Alaska and the physical labor of farm work. Just keeping up with their stock was hard. There was a lot to do in making sure those animals survived the bitterly cold temperatures and heavy snows. Of course, some years the snows weren't that bad, but all the same, the stock had to be fed and watered whether it was fifty degrees above or fifty below. Dad had never been all that fond of the cold.

Ready or not, it was time to grab some breakfast and face the mess her chickens had surely made in the mud. How wonderful it would be when all the snow melted and she could tend to them without getting covered in muck.

As she neared the kitchen, a commotion sounded. What was going on?

Madysen's voice screeched and squealed.

Havyn couldn't decipher the words, but when she entered the room, she saw Madysen running around and spinning while her mother and Whit watched, amusement etched on their faces.

Madysen spotted her, raced over, took hold of Havyn's arm, and gave her a twirl.

"What's this madness?" Havyn grinned and looked at the others. "Did we find gold in our part of the river?"

"No, silly. The first ship is in the Sound! The *Corwin* is back!" Madysen sang the words.

Ah . . . excitement understood. With exception to the mail and freight that came on occasion during the winter months, Nome was completely cut off from the United States. So the first ship of the year was always cause for a huge celebration. There would be new supplies and people. The town would throw a party and everyone was invited. Of course, for the Powell girls it could mean a much larger crowd at the Roadhouse. And a lot more tips.

"Mr. Norris will expect you to come early tonight." Mama wiped up the counter. "So you'd best eat your breakfast and get chores done."

Havyn glanced back toward the parlor. "Where's Grand-dad? And John?"

"They're the ones who told us about the ship. They took the milk to town and brought back word." Their mother untied her apron. "I hope they've brought all the music we ordered."

Whitney's eyes lit up. "I hope it doesn't take them too long to unload. I'm itching for a new challenge." Stuffing the last piece of her toast in her mouth, she waved at them all. "I'll be out with the dogs."

Mama shook her head and laughed. "I never could keep enough music on hand for you girls."

Havyn walked over and kissed her mother on the cheek. "You've taught us well." She grabbed a piece of buttered toast from the counter and then went to the stove, scooped a mound of scrambled eggs, and plopped it in the middle of the toast. Folding the concoction together, she shrugged her shoulders. "I'll take my breakfast with me. My girls await."

Doctor Geoffrey Kingston unpacked his second trunk, taking special care to put his medical books in alphabetical order. Just as all his peers did. Not that he'd ever paid much attention to what was *in* the books, but this was a fresh start for him. It would be good. Nome was a bustling town and no one knew him here.

He could do it.

Memories rushed into his mind of who he had been before. He shook his head to dispel them. No. He would move on and do the right thing for once. No sense rehashing the past.

A knock sounded at the door.

With a hefty stack of tomes in his arms, he couldn't open the door. "Come in," he shouted over his shoulder.

The door scraped as it opened. "Good morning, Geoffrey."

"Ah, and good morning to you, Dr. Gordon." He set the stack of books down and dusted off his hands. "I'm afraid I don't have any refreshments to provide you, as I have yet to go to the mercantile for supplies, but I can offer you a seat." Pointing his hand toward the settee, he smiled at the man who had hired him.

"Not to worry. I'm not going to stay. Figured it might be a good moment to schedule a time for us to discuss my patient load, which you'll be taking over. I'll be here for a couple of weeks to help you out, but it's best that you understand all the cases first."

"Of course. How about Monday morning at seven? You mentioned all the hours of daylight we'd have, so I presume it will be plenty light."

"A man after my own heart." The older man smiled. "I do appreciate an early riser and yes, you're absolutely right. As you've no doubt noticed, the dawn's first light starts as early as three thirty now. But I can come as early as sunrise— around five thirty—if that suits you."

Geoffrey swallowed. He'd never been up before seven! He'd heard Dr. Gordon liked to get started early, but earlier than seven? Ridiculous! Of course, he couldn't say that. Besides, he *was* turning over a new leaf. . . .

Dr. Gordon laughed. "I'm joking. Seven will be perfect. Meet me at my office. I'm sure you'll have no trouble finding it. Then you can follow me for a few days and I'll introduce you to your patients. After that, you'll take over."

"Thank you. This is a wonderful opportunity." He reached out to shake the man's hand.

"I'm thankful you've come. The other two doctors have their hands full. It's perfect timing." Dr. Gordon headed to the door and smiled. "Don't worry, I can let myself out. It looks like you have a good deal of unpacking to do yet. Welcome to Nome."

"Yes, sir. Thank you." The man's trust in him felt good. He'd heard good things about Dr. Gordon. Not just good things. Amazing things. The doctor was adored by everyone. Maybe this was Geoffrey's chance to become a respected citizen of a community. Healing people, helping people, serving people. He could make a difference and forget his former life.

By the time the bookcase was filled to overflowing with every medical book he had been able to get his hands on, he stepped back to check his organizational skills. It appeared everything was in order. It would simply take him time to learn which resources he would use the most. Perhaps he could ask Dr. Gordon on Monday. Might as well learn everything he could from the good doctor before he left.

Taking a rag from the table, he went to dust the shelves and books one final time, but his nose began to twitch and a fit of sneezes overcame him. Stupid dust. Oh, how he hated the way it stuffed him up.

"God bless you."

Geoffrey spun on his heel. A man stood there. "I'm sorry, I must not have heard you knock." How strange that the man would let himself in.

"My apologies." The man before him was attired in a fine suit and had his hair slicked back in the latest fashion. His stance was one of complete confidence—almost arrogance. "I came to introduce myself." He bowed ever so properly. "Judas Reynolds, at your service. I own Reynolds's Shipping and Freight." The man stuck out his hand.

"Dr. Geoffrey Kingston. It's a pleasure to meet you." He took the outstretched hand and shook it. But something made the hair on his neck prickle.

Mr. Reynolds sat on the settee, crossed his legs, and lifted his right arm to the back of the couch. Looking like he owned the world. "I service all the doctors in the area—well, I *am* the only shipping company—and so if you have need of anything, simply let me know and I will get it ordered for you."

"That's good to know. I will probably need to make an order pretty soon, once I inventory everything that Dr. Gordon still has in stock."

"I figured as much. I must say, it's good to have some fresh blood in this town. Our doctors have been such sticks in the mud. Old fashioned, you know what I mean." He waved his hand and nodded as if Geoffrey would agree with everything he said. "I've been waiting for a man such as yourself to get here."

"Oh?" A ripple of pride coursed through him. It would be nice to be looked upon as respectable and full of wisdom. But weren't the other doctors relatively new as well? Maybe they were old? Or was the man referring to Dr. Gordon?

"Yes." Mr. Reynolds leaned forward and put his elbows on his knees. "In fact, I have a business proposition for you."

Business proposition? The rich types were all alike. Always wanting to be first in line or top of the list. "I'm a doctor, Mr. Reynolds. I will treat all of my patients with the utmost duty and respect. There will be no special treatment."

A rough chuckle left the man's lips. "I'm not looking for special treatment as a patient. I'm looking for a business partner. Doing exactly what you were doing at your last location. In Wichita, was it?"

Geoffrey felt the blood drain from his face. His knees went

weak, and he sat down in a chair across from his guest. How had he been found out? He forced his tone to remain calm. "I'm afraid I don't know what you're talking about, Mr. Reynolds."

The man *tsked* and shook his head. "Oh, I think you know very well. And I think you would make a fabulous business partner. I'm sure I can get my hands on all the fake medicine you want. Just like in your last city. Then we can charge a good sum to make a profit. Over time, if your patients get sicker, we can give them the real stuff, but at a higher price. As a last resort, you understand."

This man knew everything. But how? Geoffrey had changed his name. Gone back to school to get his medical certificate in his new name. How could this be?

"I can see that you are bewildered." Mr. Reynolds stood. "Let me be very clear, Herbert Winthrop. I know who you are. I'm not asking for much. Just the opportunity for a lucrative business." He looked down at his nails and flicked a piece of lint to the floor. "Are we in agreement?"

All Geoffrey's hopes and dreams crumbled around him. No matter what he did, he couldn't escape his past. And he'd thought he'd come to the very ends of the earth. Was there no way out?

No. Not without money or prospects.

He had neither.

Geoffrey swallowed the defeat in his throat. "If I agree to this, you'll keep my past a secret?"

"So you can start a new life and be known as the good doctor? Of course." Judas Reynolds extended his hand again. "You have my word."

"And you'll order the real medicine so that I have it on hand for a crisis?"

"Absolutely. I'm the last one to want to see an epidemic. I'm not heartless. But you and I both know that most people don't need medicine anyway. Their ailments are all in their minds."

He had no choice. Geoffrey gave a brief nod. "You have a deal."

John put on his best shirt and pants. Looking in the mirror, he hoped it would suffice. He hadn't been to a party in a while. Especially not one where his boss was hoping to surprise his daughter, and where the three granddaughters were all young and beautiful.

As he walked over to the main house, he hesitated. He didn't have a gift for Mrs. Powell. Would it be improper for him to show up without anything? Well, it was too late for him to do anything about it now. He would simply have to apologize.

Chuck's daughter was a kind woman. But how could she ever have fallen for a ne'er-do-well like her late husband? Chuck had told him all about the high hopes he'd had for his son-in-law and how it ended in tragedy. Melissa Powell and her daughters deserved better. Still, the younger Powell women had seemed to adore their father. Though why, John hadn't quite figured out. Not that it was any of his business.

Stepping up to the front porch felt strange. He always entered through the back door, but his instructions had been clear.

The door swung open and Chuck greeted him with a smile. "So far so good. She has no idea."

"Has everyone arrived?"

"Yes. They're all hiding in the parlor. Melissa went to dress for dinner, because I told her we were going to the Roadhouse for a special concert that Herb asked the girls to give."

"Sounds like you've thought of everything."

"I sure hope so. We've never been able to pull something like this off." Chuck shook his head. "Now get in here so we're ready when she comes down."

John did as he was told and found a group of men huddled in the corner. *Awkward* was the best word to describe them all. Typical men, not fond of parties. Unless they were given in their honor.

No. Not even then.

Madysen ran into the room, her green skirts swishing as she whisper-shouted to everyone. "Quiet. She's coming!"

Havyn and Whitney entered the room, looking beautiful. Their dresses looked like they were made of the same green fabric as their younger sister's. The fabric shimmered in the light.

Whitney took her seat on the piano bench. Havyn picked up a violin and bow.

Melissa entered, pulling on a pair of gloves. "Are we about ready to—"

"*Surprise!*"

Shouts emanated from all over the room as people jumped out of their hiding places.

Melissa put a hand to her chest, shock on her face. "Oh my gracious. What is this?"

"Happy birthday!"

"Blessings to you on your birthday!"

The salutations echoed from every corner.

Mrs. Powell's hands went to her cheeks. "But it's not my birthday!"

"We know!" Chuck went to her side. "That's why we

planned it for today. There was no other way to surprise you."

She blinked several times. "I can't believe it."

Chuck took his daughter's hand and led her to a seat at the front. He gave his granddaughters a nod.

Havyn lifted the violin to rest under her chin, a serious look on her face. Whitney began playing something lovely on the piano. Gentle and sweet, it began to build, like something exciting was about to happen.

Madysen stood up and addressed the crowd when Whitney paused after the opening notes of her accompaniment. "And now, Mother, for another surprise." She clapped her hands together and bounced on her toes. "Havyn has prepared Tchaikovsky's Violin Concerto in D Major, opus thirty-five."

Mrs. Powell's eyes went wide as her mouth made a tiny *o*. And then . . .

The most glorious sounds came out of Havyn's violin.

After a few seconds, the entire crowd was enraptured. *Oohs* and *aahs* were heard around the room.

As the song progressed, Havyn's fingers flew over the strings as she moved the bow, creating the most beautiful music. John couldn't take his eyes off her. With her eyes closed, her expression drew him in to the music.

When the violin paused, John caught the sound of the piano. Oh! Whitney was also playing. As she accompanied her sister, her whole form seemed to be engaged with the grand piano.

Time stood still. John didn't even want to take a breath for fear he might interrupt the beauty of the music. The clock chimed and a quick glance at it told him an entire half an hour had passed. His focus returned to the redheaded beauty and her violin.

Madysen slipped into a chair beside him. "This is my favorite part." Her voice was hushed. "She's amazing, isn't she?"

"Yes. She is." John watched as Havyn played notes so fast he couldn't even comprehend the hours it must have taken to practice such a piece. The music built and built, with Whitney leaning over the piano and almost appearing to attack the keys. Havyn's hands flew faster and the notes grew higher. When the piece was finished in a robust finale, she took a deep breath, and let the bow fall to her side.

The crowd surged to their feet and applauded. Cheers of *encore* were shouted. Havyn curtsied and then motioned toward her sister, who stood from the piano bench and curtsied as well.

Before the clapping stopped, Madysen joined her sisters at the front and Whitney nodded.

"'Rock of Ages cleft for me . . .'" Whitney sang the first line clear as a bell and held out the last note of the phrase.

"'Let me hide myself in Thee.'" Havyn joined her sister in harmony, and they held out the last note again.

Chills ran up John's spine.

"'Let the water and the blood . . .'" Madysen had joined them now. The blend was so beautiful, John couldn't figure out which voice was which.

"'From thy wounded side which flowed. Be of sin the double cure . . . Save from wrath and make me pure . . .'"

As the girls continued with the verses of the beloved hymn, John found himself taking a deep, satisfying breath. How he'd missed music. His father had taught him back in Italy, but when he and Nonno came to the States, the music ended. And it had left a large hole.

A hole that was now filled to overflowing by three sisters

and their amazing talents. He looked from one to the other. They were beautiful.

But for some reason, his attention kept going back to the one in the middle.

Havyn.

Their gazes connected and he swallowed.

Chuck elbowed him. "I saw that."

"What?" John's collar felt like it was getting tighter.

"Oh, this is going to be fun."

EIGHT

Chuck leaned back in his chair. He couldn't remember ever feeling so . . .

Exhausted.

Six more calves had been born in the middle of the night after the party. He had purposefully staggered the cows' breeding so they'd always have calves to sell and trade, as well as plenty of milk. The system worked well, but took its toll.

The constant worry about when his body would fail him again plagued his mind. John was a huge help and was learning fast, but last night . . .

Chuck shook his head. Whatever made him go out to the barn by himself? He hadn't wanted to wake his new foreman, but it just hadn't been smart. While helping one of the cows, his legs went out from under him again. His head twinged, and it took several moments for him to gain enough clarity to even think about standing up.

It was all too clear that he needed to see Dr. Gordon soon. Before the man left for his long trip. Time to stop worrying about how bad the prognosis would be and find out what was going on.

He'd meant to see Doc this morning, but the day had passed in a flurry of work. As he made his way just now to his study, he worked to breathe deep. To keep his heart from racing.

He leaned down to unlock the bottom drawer of his desk, where he kept a stash of gold nuggets and the ledgers. Let other men trust banks with their money. No robbers or crooked bankers would see, let alone have access to, *his* money. He had gold hidden in different places on the property.

He pulled out the ledgers to go over the numbers, but he couldn't focus. It would be good for him to hand this off to John soon.

Melissa and the girls didn't know how much money he had. When he was gone, they could rest knowing that he had provided for their futures. While his girls hadn't known a lot of want since their father died, they still worked hard to keep the farm prosperous. They weren't spoiled or demanding. Chuck and Melissa had both wanted it that way. By teaching them to do for themselves, they would never lack for provision. And because they'd learned to trust in God, they would never want for hope. With those two things . . .

His girls would be able to face life without him.

Thinking of them brought the sting of tears. He wasn't ready to leave them. Not yet. They brought him so much joy. And they needed a strong male figure in their lives. Someone to protect them. Someone to walk them down the aisle when they got married. Someone to be great-grandpa when the time came.

Please, Lord, let me be around for that time.

Doc Gordon had been telling him what to do, things to

help him improve for a while now, but Chuck had ignored it all. It was probably time to act on it. Especially if he wanted to be around for the future.

Bowing his head, he placed his forehead in his hands. *Father, I know I don't deserve all You've given me. I've failed You in so many ways, but I need Your grace and Your help. I don't want to leave my girls with a mess. But have I done the right thing? Is the contract with John right in Your eyes? He is such a good man. Thank You for bringing him here. . . . I hope I didn't scare him off by pushing so soon.* He let out a sigh. *I've been so stubborn in ignoring Doc's advice. Forgive me, Father. Help me to do what's right now. Don't let my foolishness hurt my family. Please.*

A tap sounded on the door.

"Come in." Chuck lifted his head.

John appeared in the doorway. "Two more calves."

Chuck smiled. "Just now?"

John nodded, walked over, and sat in a chair. "We definitely are going to have our hands full." The smile on his face showed how much he enjoyed the work here.

"That we are. Well, I should say . . . you are. I think it's time for you to take over a lot of the responsibility. I was just thanking God for bringing you here."

The smile slid off John's face. "Are you all right? Has something happened?"

How much should he tell him? Probably everything. But he was too weary tonight. "No. But I'm feeling the need to cut back soon. I've been ignoring Doc's orders to slow down for too long. You've got a handle on most everything now."

"I hope so. But I'm sure there's still a lot to learn." John placed a folded paper on Chuck's desk. "And I've made my decision."

"Oh?"

"I signed the contract. The more I prayed about it, the more I knew in my heart that God brought me here." John pressed his lips together. "But I have a request."

"Go ahead." Chuck leaned back in his chair. Thank heaven John would be there. Just in case.

"I don't want the ladies to know about it. I understand your need for this contract for the ease of your mind, but I think we should keep it between us. And once the good Lord allows me to marry, then I'll ask you to draw up a new contract. But it will be more of a will and last testament. I don't ever want them to think that I did any of this for your farm or your money."

"That's very honorable of you, John. And thank you for acquiescing to an old man's request. I'll keep it locked up here in my desk."

"Thank you." The younger man stood. "Well, I'm pretty beat. I should probably head to bed. Good night." He turned toward the door.

"John?"

"Yes, sir?" He looked over his shoulder.

Chuck put his hand on the ledgers. "There's a lot more that I need to tell you. The books here. Things that Melissa doesn't know about the money and how I pay the workers. But I'm exhausted. Why don't we meet in here tomorrow night after dinner?"

"I'll be here." John put his hand on the doorknob. "Oh, and one more thing?"

Chuck raised his eyebrows.

"I'll be the one to help the cows birth in the middle of the night from now on. Agreed?"

How did he find out? Oh well, it was for the best. Chuck couldn't help but chuckle. "Agreed."

———

The feed bucket swinging at her side, Havyn hummed a little tune to her chickens. What a glorious day. The sun was shining, the snow had melted down to a thin layer that glistened like diamonds, and she'd played the concerto for Mama without a single mistake.

Not only that, the family had pulled off their mother's surprise party! She'd talked of nothing else since the party and had thanked them all at least one hundred times.

Last night, Havyn and her sisters had discussed it at length. Now that they'd actually surprised their mother and helped her to have a happy birthday, they weren't sure what to do next year. But they all agreed that they better come up with something soon so they could plan.

What a joy it had been to see her mother's face beam with shock and then pride as Havyn began the violin concerto. Overall, the evening had been perfect. Absolutely perfect.

Working her way around the chicken yard, Havyn hummed a romantic tune and let her thoughts wander. More than once at the party, she'd noticed their new foreman watching her. While she didn't know John very well yet, her heart did a little flip every time she saw him. She looked down at the chickens and shrugged. "Maybe it's the accent."

Ethel clucked and chattered her response.

"I'm glad to see that you agree. Best to keep these things in perspective, you know."

Several of the other chickens voiced their opinions. Well, at least what Havyn imagined was their opinions. Why didn't more people have chickens as pets? They were good companions and they actually gave something back to the relationship. Eggs.

Besides, their personalities could cheer up even the gloomiest of moods. Especially once you got to know them.

All except Angry Bird, of course. It was best if everyone stayed out of her way. But Havyn loved on the hen anyway. No matter how prickly she became.

A wagon rolled up the lane.

Dr. Gordon raised his hat in the air and waved, but Havyn didn't recognize the man with him.

She set the bucket down and went to the fence to greet them. "Good afternoon, Doc. How are you today?"

"Quite well, Miss Powell, and you?"

"Lovely. The sun is shining and I'm out with the chickens. What could be better?"

"Your singing at the Roadhouse, that's what." Dr. Gordon laughed.

His comment made her smile. "You're biased. But thank you anyway. The chickens are my audience today."

"Not a bit of bias, Havyn Powell—even though I've known you since you were quite young. Let me introduce you to Dr. Geoffrey Kingston. He's going to take my place while I travel to see my mother in Walla Walla. I'll be gone at least a year, so he'll be a permanent part of Nome now."

She nodded at the wiry man. "It's a pleasure to meet you, Dr. Kingston. I hope you are enjoying our little town."

"The pleasure is all mine." He tipped his hat to her. "And I find Nome to be quite the town. I had no idea it was so large when I answered Dr. Gordon's advertisement for a partner."

"It hasn't always been like this, but finding gold changed everything."

Dr. Gordon cleared his throat. "Well, we are off to see your grandfather. Is he around?"

"Yes, sir. He's up in the pen right beyond the barn checking over the calves." Every morning and night she prayed that Granddad would take it slower so that he wouldn't have any more spells. Perhaps Doc Gordon could talk some sense into him.

The men nodded at her as the wagon rumbled up the lane.

After she fed the chickens, she brought several buckets of fresh water out to them. If the water wasn't freezing over, the chickens were spilling it, or they drank it all too fast. But with a flock as large as hers, it couldn't be helped.

"Havyn?" Granddad stood at the gate to the chicken yard.

She headed over to him. "What are you doing here? I just sent Doc up to the calf pen a few minutes ago to find you."

"Nice to see you too." Wiping his neck with a handkerchief, he looked down at the ground.

Something wasn't right. "Granddad?"

"Honestly, I'm not feeling all that well. Can you ask John to handle things?"

The longer she looked at him, the paler he appeared. Tossing the buckets aside, she rushed to the gate. "I think we need to get you to the house right now. I can go get Doc after you're settled, and then I'll let John know. Everything will be fine."

Several seconds passed before he responded. "Yeah, that's probably a good idea."

She latched the gate and then got her shoulder up under him and pulled his left hand around her neck. "Hang on, Granddad. I'll get you there. Let's take it slow, all right?"

"Sure." The word sounded slurred.

Wrapping her right arm around his waist, she stuck her

hip out toward him and pulled his weight against her. But the more steps they took, the more he began to slide.

"I don't think I'm gonna mamitanffff—" The rest of his air whooshed out of him and he collapsed to the ground, taking Havyn with him.

NINE

Landing with a thud, Havyn screamed. "Help! Somebody *help!*"

She'd tried to cushion Granddad's fall, but they had still hit pretty hard. Rolling him over onto his back, she checked for wounds. The right corner of his mouth was drooping. A trail of drool down his chin. No! Not apoplexy.

"Doc Gordon! Come quick!" Using her voice for all she was worth, she yelled toward the birthing shed. She grabbed Granddad's hand and pulled it to her cheek. "Stay with me, Granddad. You're not allowed to go anywhere." She turned her face the other direction again. "*Help!*"

The seconds ticked by. Tears stung her eyes.

Doors slammed and footsteps came from several directions.

Mama reached them first and knelt on the ground. "What's happened? Papa?"

"I don't know. I was walking him back to the house because he said he wasn't feeling well. Then all of a sudden he collapsed."

The doctors were at their side next. Doc Gordon put his head to Granddad's chest. "He's still breathing and has a heartbeat. Let's get him inside." The new wiry doctor helped Doc pick him up, and together they carried him to the house. Havyn followed on their heels, her mother and sisters behind her.

Once they got Granddad in his room, Doc turned to her. "I need you to keep everyone out for a little bit while I examine him. Keep them calm. Maybe go to the parlor and play some music. I'll come talk to you in a few minutes."

She nodded and gathered her family like they were her chicks and led them to the parlor.

Madysen went straight to her cello and began playing a hymn. Whitney joined from the piano.

Mama looked at Havyn with tears streaming down her cheeks. "Would you sit with me while I pray?"

Havyn took her mother's hand and knelt on the floor with her. Several silent moments passed as the music washed over them. It all seemed so surreal. What had happened? And how did it happen so fast?

Mama began to pray aloud, but Havyn couldn't even register the words. In her mind's eye, all she could see was Granddad fall. Over and over again.

The time passed in agonizing moments.

"Ladies?" Doc Gordon's voice made them all stand to their feet. He walked over to them. "I'm afraid your father has had a bout of apoplexy."

Mama gasped and put her hand over her mouth.

"He's actually doing all right at the moment. From what I can see, all the signs seem to be good that he will wake soon. But it does appear that his right side is paralyzed."

"Paralyzed?" Madysen squeaked.

Doc held up his hand. "Now, don't go rushing into any assumptions. During a fit of apoplexy, many people experience one side or the other going paralyzed. His facial muscles on the right are drooping—a signifier of the problem. But it's too early to tell for sure. If he wakes, he may not have use of the right side of his face, or his right arm, or his right leg. That could last. But it might go away."

The wiry doctor spoke up. "If I might interject, I've seen several cases where the patients progressed and regained the movement in the paralyzed side. But that was after a lot of exercises and help."

"Yes." Dr. Gordon clasped his hands behind his back. "For right now, you need to keep him comfortable. Pray for him. And then once he awakens, make sure he gets nourishment. But be careful. Sometimes it is hard for patients to swallow, or to keep food and drink in their mouths. You'll have to help him."

"We'll do whatever we need to do." Mama lifted her shoulders. "It's a good thing he's left-handed."

The situation was dire. Havyn felt it in her bones. Saw it on Doc's face. Was this her fault? What if she had shared Granddad's secret with Doc Gordon, or even with Mama?

John ran into the room. "I'm so sorry, I was down in the pasture trying to round up some stubborn cows when I heard the scream. What's happened?"

Mama pinched her lips together. "I'm so glad you're here. It's my father. He's collapsed."

"Is he all right?" He moved forward. "What can I do?"

She lifted her chin. "It sounds serious. Apoplexy." She smoothed her skirt and clasped her hands in front of her. "I need you to keep everything running, John. That's a lot to handle, but I'm sure you can do it. The girls and I will have to take turns caring for Papa until he's up and about again."

"I can do that."

Whitney scowled and moved forward. "I don't think—"

"Whitney." Mama sliced one of her hands through the air. Her commanding tone reminded Havyn of when they were little and drew close to danger. "Now is not the time to give your opinion or to argue. Your grandfather hired John to be the foreman. He's in charge. I won't hear another word about it."

"Yes, Mama." She clamped her lips together and stepped back.

Doc lifted his finger. "He's not going to be able to do much for a long while. You need to be prepared for that."

Havyn put her arm around Mama's shoulders. This wasn't going to be easy on any of them.

"May I see him?" Mama moved forward.

"Yes, it would be a good idea for all of you to see him and talk to him. Might help him to wake up." Doc Gordon shook his head. "I hate to leave at such a time, but Dr. Kingston here has agreed to come out twice a week and check on him. Someone will need to sit with Chuck at all times. Just in case he wakes or tries to get out of bed. It could be disastrous if he's by himself and takes another fall. The mind doesn't always have a lot of clarity after a bout, so we can't have him disoriented and alone."

"We understand." Mama nodded. "But you think that he's going to be all right? That there's a chance he can make a full recovery?"

"It's a chance, but yes." Doc looked so solemn, like the last hour had aged him several years.

"A chance is good enough for me." Mama moved past

him and stopped. "Thank you for taking such good care of us all these years."

"You're welcome." Doc Gordon watched her walk away. Whitney and Madysen followed.

Havyn hung back for a moment. "Doc Gordon, might I have a word?"

"Of course."

John cleared his throat. "I need to get back to the cows and let the workers know. Will you fill me in at dinner?"

"Yes. Thank you." Havyn waited for him to leave and then turned back to their doctor. "I have been keeping Granddad's secret for a while."

"Yes, I know, he told me." He patted her shoulder. "I'm sorry you've had to carry that."

"He told you that I knew?" None of it made sense anymore.

"Yes. I tried to convince him to let everyone know. I pushed and prodded and overstepped everywhere I could, but you know Chuck . . . he's extremely stubborn." Doc shook his head.

The emotions inside her were a jumble. "I didn't know what to do. He made me promise. But if I had said something . . . could I have stopped this? Is it all my fault?"

Doc laid a hand on her shoulder. "I warned him that you would feel this way if something happened. It's *not* your fault. Your grandfather wanted to get things in place in case something like this happened. I'd been advising him for the past two years to slow down and take care of himself, but sometimes it takes a health crisis for us to pay attention."

"But it feels so wrong. Like I did something wrong. Should I tell my mother and my sisters?" Her stomach churned.

He shook his head. "No. If he wakes up, which I hope and pray he does, you can talk to him about telling the rest of your family later. This was his secret. His decision not to let you all know."

Swallowing against the lump forming in her throat, she gave a slight nod. "And if he doesn't wake back up? Do I still keep it to myself? I don't know if I can do that."

"Sometimes secrets need to stay hidden. Forever. For the good of everyone."

———

In search of Whitney, John took off his leather gloves and slapped them against his thigh. More than a week had passed since Chuck's fall, and it had been pretty much a blur. Chuck had finally woken up a couple days ago, but all the Powell women had been so busy with chores and sitting with their patient that there hadn't been much time to tell them what was going on with the farm. And he needed to discuss several things with . . . at least one of them.

They all ate meals—much simpler fare than they were used to—in shifts. It took two of the women to keep on top of their granddad's every need. One to run for whatever was desired and one to stay with the patient. They were determined never to leave him alone. Mrs. Powell usually fed him, but she had enlisted each of her daughters to help. And she'd asked John to help with Chuck's personal needs.

John was busy keeping up with the farm, but happy to help whenever he could. But every time he wanted to bring up the business side of things, the timing had seemed off.

Since Whitney was the eldest, maybe she would be the best one to speak to. Maybe it could even help her get over whatever it was she had against him. As he approached the large fenced-in kennel area, he couldn't help but appreciate the work that had gone into it. He scanned the area. There she was . . . feeding her dogs. Perfect timing.

The sled dogs were amazing, but they took a lot of work and attention.

"Good afternoon." He put on his best smile. Out of everyone here, Whitney made it clear that she wasn't fond of him.

She hardly responded as she moved from dog to dog, delivering mixtures of fish and blubber. There were more than forty dogs, and Whitney told him once that they needed thousands of calories every day if they were to be at their peak. He'd volunteered a few days ago to help her take care of them, thinking it might afford him the perfect opportunity to get to know her better, but she'd refused. She was every bit as stubborn as Chuck had warned. So stubborn that she was barely getting any sleep. As attested to by the circles under her eyes.

She'd been congenial enough this morning at breakfast, when everyone else was around the table, but had hardly said more than a sentence to him when they were alone. Either she was completely exhausted or she still didn't think he should be there.

He was pretty certain it was the latter. "I'm making a list of things to purchase in town. I thought maybe you might need something for the dogs."

She continued her feeding task. "No, I'm fine. I've already arranged with Amka to bring me seal and fish."

"Well, what about the dogs that are about to whelp? Your mother said something about your grandfather needing to make a whelping box? That the other had been destroyed?"

"I've already seen to it." Her words were curt and left little doubt to her annoyance.

He'd gotten about all the information out of Whitney that he was going to get, and he simply hoped and prayed that she would let him know if she needed anything for the kennel of dogs . . . or herself. One thing was clear: She wasn't at all interested in him as a potential mate. If anything, she was interested in him leaving them all alone. "Please, let me know if you do need something."

No response.

Well, that was that. He turned and went to the chicken yard. When Chuck had first asked him to marry one of his granddaughters, John thought perhaps the eldest would be the best idea. That thought vanished almost immediately. But while he didn't want to waste his time trying to get her to like him, he at least wanted to earn her trust and respect.

As his steps brought him closer to the large chicken yard, he couldn't help but smile. Havyn was the one who'd captured his interest. Not that he could do anything about it right now, but he looked forward to every moment they could spend together.

She did such an incredible job with the poultry side of their farm, but Chuck had warned John that Havyn's chickens were for eggs *only*. Her attachment and fierce loyalty to the animals was unlike anything he'd ever seen. Eventually, it would be his job to bring on chickens for butchering. Half the town had already showed up begging to buy fryers, and he'd had to turn them away. There would be a lot of money in selling chickens for meat, but he didn't even want to think about the conversations he would need to have with Havyn about that.

As he approached the chicken house, he heard her voice. She was singing . . . "Santa Lucia." And in Italian. She stopped abruptly.

"I am *not* singing off-key. You are the one who is off."

He frowned and glanced around. Who was she talking to?

"I accept your apology, AB."

He heard nothing but chickens clucking. Then he smiled. Of course. Everyone teased Havyn about talking to her chickens. But she wasn't talking *at* them. She was having full-blown conversations with them. Albeit one-sided. With words anyway.

"Good afternoon, Havyn." He shoved his hands into his pockets and enjoyed watching her. The sun caught her red hair and turned it into a ball of fire. She hadn't braided it or pinned it up, and the way it rippled actually made his breath catch. He'd never seen it down before.

She looked up at him and smiled. "Good afternoon, John." Then she went right back to talking to the chickens. "Oh, is that a fact? Well, we will need to speak with Angry Bird about that, won't we?" She walked over to a dark-feathered chicken. One who pranced around like she was in charge of the show. Havyn pointed a finger at the hen. "Now, Angry Bird, we've talked about being nice to one another. It's about time you took my advice to heart."

The chicken ruffled its feathers out, lifted its beak, and began to give quite a squawking to Miss Havyn.

John covered his mouth to keep his mirth hidden and kept watching.

"I don't care what you think about the other chickens, you need to be nice." And then, to his complete surprise, Havyn bent down and scooped the agitated chicken up. The hen pecked at her hands a couple times until Havyn stroked the chicken's back. Then, all of a sudden, the chicken settled and looked like she was the queen sitting on her throne. "That's much better. Let's just remember our little chat next time you decide to peck at one of your friends." Havyn carried the large bird over to him and kept stroking her back.

The hen gave him the evil eye.

"Did you need to discuss something?" Havyn offered him a sweet smile.

He cleared his throat. "Um . . . yes. In my attempt to keep up with all the foreman responsibilities, plus everything your grandfather did, I realized I hadn't checked on the chickens." He held up his hands, just in case she got offended like her elder sister. "You do a splendid job with them, so I'm not questioning any of that, I simply thought perhaps I had neglected your needs. Er . . . any needs you— the chickens—may have." Letting out a sigh, he put his hands down. "My apologies. As you can tell, I'm still learning all the workings of a farm as large as this one. All of my bumbling around was simply to ask, do you need feed or anything else for them? I'm making a trip to town later today, in case you do."

Setting the hen she'd called Angry Bird down, Havyn worked her way through the gate, making sure none of her little pets followed her. "That's very nice of you, John. But I can't think of anything at the moment." She wiped some feathers off her apron and then reached up to her hair. "Oh, what a mess." Running her fingers through her hair, she *tsked*. "Fred got himself up on the fence and decided to pull the pin out of my hair." She deftly twisted her hair up and tucked it in and around itself. Somehow it stayed.

John blinked, trying to push his fascination aside. On the top of her right hand, a faded scar made a zigzag trail across her skin. John pointed to it. "What happened to your hand?"

She lifted up her hands and turned them over and back. "Oh that." She let out a slight giggle. "Do you really want to know?"

"I do." They stood by the fence and watched the chickens.

"When I was a little girl, we had a few chickens in Colorado. Mama made sure that we all knew how to handle them with care, but Dad was the one who knew how much I *loved* those chickens."

Leaning on the fence, he turned toward her. "Doesn't seem like much has changed."

She shook her head. "Goodness, I hope I've changed. I was such a young thing. But as you've probably heard, people with red hair are prone to losing their temper."

"I have heard that, yes." He kept his tone light and teasing. "But I can't say that I've ever witnessed it."

She gave him a mischievous grin. "Be thankful you haven't. Poor Granddad. He's had to live with *four* redheads. Gracious, the man has the patience of a saint." She gripped the top rail of the fence.

"So how'd you get the scar from loving chickens?"

"Oh, I was determined to *hug* one of the chickens one day. And not just a little hug, mind you, we're talking a big, squeezing hug."

"Oh boy, I can guess what happened next."

"I'd named her Sue." Havyn started giggling. "And if you're guessing that the chicken didn't want to be hugged, you'd be correct. But what you probably didn't know was that Sue decided to let me know exactly how she felt about being squished by a six-year-old and pecked my hand over and over again, while I stubbornly held on. Thus the scar."

Eyebrows raised, he waited a moment to ask his next question. "Why didn't you let go?"

"Because some things are worth holding on to." She grinned, and John felt his heart skip a beat.

"What happened to Sue?"

A faint blush filled her cheeks as she looked back to him. "It's embarrassing and horrifying to say the least. But my little temper flared when I saw all the blood, and I decided she wasn't worth holding on to after all. I was so mad that I threw her to the ground, and she started running around me like a regular cyclone. I tried to kick her with everything my little leg could fling at her. But I missed, and the momentum from that kick made me fall backward." She bit her lip and grimaced. "I landed on top of Sue and killed her."

The picture she'd given him was vivid. For a little girl of six, it must have been quite traumatic. "What happened after that?"

"Oh, I was in big trouble for killing one of the chickens, but even more trouble for losing my temper like that. To prove a point, Granddad made us put Sue in a box and we carried her out to the garden, where we had a funeral for her."

"For a chicken?"

"Oh my, yes. We marked the grave and everything. Because they wanted to make sure that I would never forget the day I killed a living creature because of my temper."

"Did the lesson work?"

"It certainly did. Not only was I reminded on a daily basis about the death of that chicken, but whenever anyone came to visit, the story of the chicken—complete with a visit to the grave—was shared." She smiled. "You know, I can honestly say that I've never lost my temper quite like that ever since. But Whitney and Madysen . . . let's just say they didn't get the early lesson that I did. It's not that I don't lose my temper, mind you. I can get as angry as the rest of them. I just don't act on it like I did back then. Hopefully."

"Remind me not to get on your bad side." He enjoyed standing by the fence with her, getting to know her. Watching her profile.

"You're a smart man, John Roselli."

"I'm glad you think so. What did Madysen and Whitney do after that whole episode? Were they scared of you?"

"Scared of me? No. That's silly. We're all too close for that. But I will admit that as I got older, they did tease me several times by calling me CK."

"CK?" He studied her, but she didn't answer. Just grinned at him and waited. When understanding dawned, he nodded. "Ah. Chicken Killer."

He laughed along with her.

"And one time, we had a bully in Sunday School. He was bigger than everyone else and stronger than everyone else. But he wasn't the brightest."

Her stories enchanted him. "What happened?"

"Whitney got tired of it. One day—in the churchyard—she marched right up to him, hands on her hips, and told him an overly dramatized version of that story. Yes, I killed a chicken, but apparently my thirst for killing was awakened by that first incident and I went on to kill other things. She implied that there was even a rumor that I had killed another bully in another churchyard years before, although no one ever found the body."

Havyn was now laughing so hard that tears streamed down her cheeks. "Oh my goodness, I'd completely forgotten about that until now. For the longest time, I didn't know why all the boys were scared of me. Until Granddad came home one day and said he'd heard a story. Whitney confessed that she had told the lie, but refused to apologize for it because she was sticking up for everyone else."

"I bet it was never a dull moment around your house growing up."

"Not one. Ever. And not just growing up. Gracious, there's never one now. Between the three of us, we keep Mama hopping."

"And what about your father?" He turned toward her and studied her.

Her face fell slightly. "He wasn't around a whole lot. But I do remember he told great stories. Probably where Whitney got her talent." She turned to watch the chickens, wisps of hair blowing around her face, begging John's touch. "I remember he taught us how to fish and to hunt. Those were really good memories." Her voice had softened.

"You must miss him." No matter what the man had done, he was still her father. John needed to respect that.

"I do."

"Do you and your sisters talk about him often?"

She shook her head. "No. If Madysen or I bring him up, Whitney is quick to remind us how bad things were. I don't think Madysen even has many memories of him. And mine are often clouded by choosing to remember just the good times. With Whitney being the oldest, she saw a lot more and understood a lot more than we did."

"What about your mother?"

"She never speaks of him. But her birthday is the same day as their anniversary. That's why birthdays have been so hard on her all these years. I think she's over grieving him, but I get the sense it still haunts her at times. She loved him so, and even when people spoke ill of him, she would stand up for him."

From the sadness in her eyes, this conversation was painful for her. John looked across the yard. There were still patches of snow, some larger than others. While it was nearly summer in Colorado, they were still finishing winter in Alaska. John glanced back at Havyn and saw her wipe at her eye. He needed to get her thinking about something happier. "I hear that you have all these chickens named?"

"Sure do."

"All of them?"

She nodded and gave him a smile. "Yep."

"And you remember them all?"

"Of course I do!"

He pointed to the one in front of them. "All right, who is this one?"

"That's Lucy."

"And that one over there that looks dirty?"

"Speckles."

That one made him laugh. "Well then, how about that group over there, can you recognize all of them?"

"You are ridiculous. Of course I can. That's Sally, JoJo, Ginger, Mae, Ethel, Petals, Lulu, and Becky."

She was remarkable. "I'm amazed."

Those wide eyes fixed on him. "Why? The people or things I love are very important to me. Certainly important enough to remember their names. That's why I won't tolerate Granddad killing them for the people in town . . . or for our table."

That was the perfect opportunity for John to bring up raising some chickens for food. "I wonder if you might reconsider that. Obviously, none of *these* chickens. But what if we added another flock? It would make a lot of money for the family farm, and with your grandfather ill, it might encourage his recovery if you spoke to him about raising some other chickens for meat."

Havyn frowned. "I don't know if I could. Especially when it came time to kill them."

"Well, I'd never expect you to kill them or clean them. We have hired hands for that, or I could do it myself. Of course, it won't be easy for me if they all have names." He gave her a smile. "Maybe the eating chickens could have numbers instead."

"Maybe." Her voice was hesitant.

"Just think about it. You don't have to make a decision now, but it might cheer your grandfather if you told him you were working on it."

She nodded. "I *am* fond of fried chicken. I don't mind the idea of eating them. I mind the idea of eating ones I know— ones I've befriended and told my troubles to."

"Well, you could always tell your troubles to me."

Good gravy! Did he say that out loud? Well, now that he had, he'd better face Havyn's surprise. "I mean . . . well . . . I do care about you . . . and your family. You've all become important to me, and I promised your grandfather I'd take good care of you."

Her look softened and her brown eyes seemed to study him in a way that he'd never been studied before. What *was* it about her that made him feel like he was standing on a cliff's edge, about to jump?

She tugged on his arm, breaking the spell. "Why don't you come meet the rest of the chickens. Perhaps I'll discuss your ideas about raising a separate group for meat. I'm sure Angry Bird would approve."

Good. A change of subject.

He followed her through the chicken yard for the next half hour, trudging through the snow and talking to chickens. Yes, he actually talked to them too. He wasn't sure what had come over him. Either he'd lost his mind . . .

Or his heart.

TEN

Whitney pounded the piano keys. First Granddad brought on a foreman without talking to her about it. Then he had to go and get himself laid up. Which meant she had to deal with the foreman even more.

It didn't matter that he was a nice guy. Nor that he seemed capable enough. What mattered was that she didn't want an outsider here. It made her feel . . . out of control. And she hated that feeling.

Even though the man had taken an interest in her dogs, who seemed to like him already—which should have made her like him as well, since her dogs were the best judge of character—she still wanted to punch something every time Mama mentioned the foreman.

It shouldn't be that way, but there it was.

When John had talked to her earlier, she'd fought with herself. One side told her to give him a chance. The other side said to ignore him. And if she did, maybe just maybe he'd eventually go away.

The more she thought about it, the louder she played.

What was *wrong* with her? Was it wrong to be so fiercely loyal? To not want to get hurt by anyone? Ever again?

Shoving the intruding thoughts aside, she focused on the piano piece. She knew it so well, she could almost hear the symphony orchestra in her mind playing the accompanying parts. It spurred her on as the music built.

If only it were time to go out to the Roadhouse. Those nights had been her saving grace. Playing until her fingers felt like they were going to fall off. Singing with her sisters until Mr. Norris said they needed to close. The problem was, they only played on Fridays and Saturdays. Today was Monday.

Music had always taken her away from things. And provided a way to vent her emotions. But with everything that had happened lately, there were too many emotions to deal with and not enough time.

Pounding out the ending of Rachmaninoff's Piano Concerto no. 2, she sucked in a deep breath and let the music pour out of her. When the piece was finished, Whitney let her hands fall to her lap.

Her perfectly ordered world had fallen to pieces. And she wasn't sure what to do about that.

But that wasn't what pushed her over the edge. It was overhearing John asking Havyn about their father.

Whenever anyone brought up their father, her defenses went into place like archers on a castle wall. The man had been her father, yes. She couldn't deny it. But she didn't want to remember him, much less talk about him or hear others talk about him.

The memories of her father haunted her sometimes at night. His drunkenness, which had been constant—at least that's all she remembered. Especially the last few years of his life. The way he talked about other women to his friends when he didn't know Whitney was listening. Then, of course, he gambled away everything they had. Over and over and over again.

Her sisters might not remember what it was like to scrounge for enough money to buy milk and eggs from their neighbor after their father gambled away their cow and chickens, but *she* did.

Mama hid her feelings well. All Whitney ever saw growing up was a loving and caring wife and mother. But deep down, did Mama despise the man she'd married? Was that why she refused men now?

Whitney stared down at her hands. How could Havyn and Madysen not remember any of the ugly things about their father? Did they just choose to focus on how fun he had been? How he'd acted out funny stories from his boyhood. Or that he taught them how to fish.

It was all a bunch of hogwash to Whitney. She knew better.

Her father had been no good, just as Granddad said. Christopher Powell had been incapable of keeping his promises and incapable of being true to their mother. Mother forgave his drunken behavior, but not Whitney.

Not ever.

Forgiveness wasn't for her—especially for people who didn't deserve it. Mama said it wasn't her responsibility to decide who deserved forgiveness and who didn't, but that was silly. Why, when she knew the person wasn't sincere in their request for forgiveness, couldn't she withhold it? After all, forgiving released them from responsibility, freeing them to repeat their sin all over again. All it did was set her up to be hurt . . . again and again . . . and again.

No man would hurt her. Ever again.

That's why she loved her dogs. They were loyal, no matter

what. They never turned on her. Never did anything other than love her unconditionally.

She took care of them. They took care of her.

But now, with Granddad laid up . . . what would happen to them? To her dogs? To her family? Was there enough money to keep the farm going?

She closed her eyes. Her heart could only take so much. She might not express her emotions like her younger sisters, but that didn't mean she didn't hurt or didn't feel.

Tears came unbidden.

She loved her family, and protecting them was the most important thing she could think of. Granddad had asked John to see to the farm, but that should have been *her* job. She was next in line. She was fully capable of doing any job on the place. Besides, there were the hired hands who knew her and followed her instructions. With their help she could have been foreman.

She gritted her teeth. *Why* had Granddad given John a job that should have been hers? And why did he get sick? That just threatened her peaceful world. Her fists clenched. If he died . . .

No! She couldn't think that way. Granddad *had* to live and he *had* to get rid of John Roselli so that she could prove she could run things. Take care of her family. After all, Powells should take care of Powells. They didn't need a stranger.

They didn't need anybody.

If anything happened to Granddad, *she* would take care of them all. No matter what it took.

———

"Sometimes secrets need to stay hidden. Forever. For the good of everyone."

Havyn sat up in bed with a jolt. Dr. Gordon's words kept repeating in her mind. She'd argued with him at first, but when he explained how much it would hurt her sisters and her mother to know that Granddad had kept that secret from all of them—then that *she* had kept that secret too . . .

He'd been correct. It didn't seem right.

Oh, she'd kept a lot of secrets over the years. Too many to count. But there was only one other than Granddad's secret that burdened her.

One she kept buried deep.

One that would hurt everyone she loved.

And the good doctor's words had brought it all crashing in to her mind.

Well, she wasn't going to be able to go back to sleep anytime soon. Maybe some tea would help. It was three in the morning. Perhaps she could sit by the embers in the fireplace for a while and watch the sun come up.

In the kitchen, she picked up the teakettle right before its telltale whistle and set her tea leaves to steep. As she peered at the window, the darkness beyond made her reflection appear. Then, in her mind . . .

Another face replaced hers.

With a quick turn, she headed for the parlor. Her favorite room in the house. It housed all their instruments, so many memories stored in the wood-ensconced walls, and some of the prettiest views of Nome. She took a deep breath and closed her eyes, trying to dispel the image she'd seen.

But no matter what she did to get her mind off the topic, it always went straight back.

Dad.

Tucking her feet beneath her on the settee, she held the cup of tea up under her nose so she could inhale the steam.

Closing her eyes against the memory and the pain that it caused, she tried to force it back to the depths of her mind.

But without her permission, it came to life anyway.

She was back in Cripple Creek. Barefoot, standing beside her father, who was lying in the straw. It all seemed so real, she could smell the manure and feel the straw under her feet.

The man she'd adored all her young life was holding a bottle to his chest and telling her that he needed more. Could she please get him some more?

No. She'd shaken her head. Little girls didn't buy alcohol. And they shouldn't.

He'd tossed and turned and wailed like a baby.

Then he'd opened his eyes and looked at her. Straight in the eye. And said, "Don't ever tell your mama."

"Don't tell her what?" That he'd been drunk? He always came home drunk nowadays.

"There's another baby on the way, and pretty soon everyone will know what I did. . . ."

"A baby? Mama's not pregnant. What are you talking about?"

He sat up for a brief moment and grabbed her shoulders. "No! Not your mama. Esther's the one carrying my baby. Esther's pregnant."

After he'd passed out again and fell against the straw, Havyn had let the words roll around in her mind. Did that mean what she thought it meant? Her dad would *never* do such a thing . . . would he?

"Oh, stop it!" Havyn pushed the memories away. She took a long sip of tea.

A week after that night in the barn, Granddad told Mama that Dad was dead. And she'd told Havyn and her sisters.

Her heart broke, but it also felt relieved. Mama would never have to deal with the pain that Dad's indiscretion would inflict on her. On them all. And from that day forward, she resolved never to speak of that night or of what Dad had confessed.

Whitney accused her time and again of remembering only the happy memories of their father. Every time Havyn defended the man she'd loved and adored. But had she done it to cover up the horrible secret that she held? No. She refused to believe it. Because even though their father hadn't been perfect, he was their dad. She had loved him and forgiven him.

But now, all these years later, she had to deal with the fact that somewhere out there, they probably had a sibling.

The sound of soft footfalls drifted over to her.

"Couldn't sleep, Maddy?"

"How'd you know it was me?"

Her younger sister's voice was soothing to Havyn's heart.

"It's a sister thing."

"Yeah, I woke up when you got up, but when you didn't go back to your room, I decided you might want some company." Madysen was so tiny, but her heart was huge. If anyone was hurting, Madysen was there, ready to fight for their cause or to bandage their wounds.

Havyn smiled at her. "I'm sorry I woke you."

"It's all right. I've done it enough to you over the years." She brought her knees up to her chest and wrapped a blanket around herself. Hair flying every which way, Madysen looked like a little fairy. If only she had tiny wings.

"You're so adorable, Maddy."

Her little sister's eyebrows rose. "You must be seeing things in the middle of the night."

"No, I mean it. You're beautiful, even in the middle of the night when your hair needs a good brushing. I think it's not just your outer beauty, but the fact that you shine from the inside."

"Hold on a minute. Isn't this a bit intense for a middle-of-the-night discussion when I'm still half asleep?" Her younger sister rubbed at her eyes.

"Probably." Havyn took another sip of tea. "But I don't tell you enough how beautiful you are. Or how much I appreciate you."

Madysen's eyes widened. "Wow. You should wake up in the middle of the night more often." She let out a giggle and then laid a hand on Havyn's knee. "Seriously, sis, what's going on?"

The great thing about having chats in the dark in the middle of the night was that she could take all the time she wanted. And for the most part, her expressions would be hidden. But now was not the time or the place to tell her little sister a horrible truth about their father. Even though Madysen might be the most merciful of them all, some things were best unsaid.

"Well? Come on, I'm not a baby anymore. I'm twenty years old. You can tell me what's bothering you."

Letting out a long sigh, Havyn stirred her tea. "I'm worried about Granddad. He's worked so hard and poured everything into this farm. It means everything to him, and I'm worried that he won't be willing to truly rest and recover. If he doesn't, if he tries to go back out there, he may not live the next time."

Her little sister gasped. "That's awfully harsh, Havyn. It's only one attack."

Havyn swallowed her guilt. Should she share the secret?

She declined and buried those thoughts. "I'm sorry, Maddy, but it's the truth. Granddad means the world to us, but we need to make sure that he doesn't overdo it as he's recovering." After another sip of tea, she went on. "Then there's Whitney."

"What about her? She seems pretty strong and stoic to me."

It didn't surprise her to hear Madysen say that. Whitney was the strongest person she knew. "That's just it. She's refusing to let anyone in. After watching Dad drink and gamble and what that did to hurt Mama, she's shut her heart off toward romance. And forgiveness too. She's got these giant walls around her heart, thinking it's going to protect her, but I'm afraid it's going to hurt her more."

"But she's fine with us." Madysen shrugged her shoulders. "What's your concern?"

"Don't you want her to be happy? To have a family? Good grief, she's twenty-five years old—"

"And that's simply ancient, isn't it?"

Havyn jumped a little when Whitney's voice came from the doorway, but at least it sounded amused and not angry. They didn't need a tempers-flared argument to wake up the house.

Arms crossed over her chest, Whitney walked toward her sisters.

Havyn swallowed. The last thing she'd wanted to do was hurt her sister. "Whit, I'm sorr—"

"Don't apologize." Whitney gave them a soft smile. Her curly hair was a thing to behold when it was down. She sat next to Madysen, pulled her close, and looked at Havyn. "Look, I know you're worried about me. But don't be. I may be a little against romance at this stage of my life, but I *am* happy."

"I'm glad. We care about you so much." Thank heaven Whit took her words that way.

"I know you do. We're sisters. We're going to take care of each other, right?"

"Right." Madysen chimed in.

"Good. Now why don't we talk about how we can work together to help Granddad and Mama." Take-charge, big-sister Whitney was back, and gone was any chance of cracking the barrier around her heart. "Maybe together we can figure out a way to get rid of John."

"Get *rid* of him?" What a terrible thought! But then again . . . why did she feel so protective of a man she hardly knew?

Whitney gave a firm nod. "Yes. He's not family, and I resent that he's running our farm. It's not his place to do it. I think he bamboozled Granddad. Maybe tricked him."

"Granddad is hardly one to be tricked." And John was hardly the kind of man to trick him. He was kind and friendly and . . .

"Normally, he wouldn't be," Whitney said, interrupting her thoughts. "But he's obviously not been feeling well. It has only been a matter of weeks since he hired John on. The apoplexy could have been coming on for that long, and it might have caused him confusion."

Havyn looked away for fear her older sister might see how close she'd come to guessing the truth about Granddad. Thankfully Madysen spoke up.

"I like John. He's fast to learn and fun to be with. And he's quite handsome. I'm surprised you aren't swooning over him instead of trying to get rid of him. You *are* the oldest, and decent men are hard to find up here."

Whitney grimaced. "So we're back to that, are we? I'm not interested in marriage to *anyone*—but especially not

John Roselli. Yes, he's kind and handsome and any number of other things, but doesn't it bother you that a complete stranger walked in here and took over the farm? Doesn't it concern you that Granddad seems quite willing to let John make important decisions? If I didn't know better, I'd think John owned the place." She shook her head. "We need to get rid of him, before *he* thinks he does too."

ELEVEN

Melissa swallowed hard. She couldn't have heard right. "What did you say?"

"You have asthma, Mrs. Powell." Dr. Kingston's lips made a thin line. "It's an incurable lung disease. An inflammation and bronchospasm."

This new doctor must not know what he was talking about. If only Doc Gordon were still around.

"Did you hear me?"

She straightened her shoulders and clamped her hands together in her lap. "Yes, I'm sorry. Are you quite sure?"

"Yes, Mrs. Powell. Quite. I can't imagine Dr. Gordon not speaking to you about this before. How long has this been going on?" The new doctor looked at her as if he pitied her.

"That doesn't matter." She cleared her throat. "What does this mean?"

"You'll continue to struggle with your breathing." He flipped through a medical book on his desk in front of him. "I can't do a lot for you, but I can research and try to order some medication that might help. I have some asthma cigarettes that you can take with you today. And I've heard of epinephrine—but it's very new. I'll have to look into it and see if we can get it up here."

Her chest tightened. Asthma. Her breathing events had increased lately, what with the stress of Papa being laid up. She'd finally asked John to shave her father today and sit with him for a little bit so she could run to town and see the doctor. But this was not what she expected. She'd wanted answers. But not this. "There's nothing you can do to fix this?"

"No. I'm afraid not." He stood, walked over to a cabinet, and unlocked it. "But I do have these. When your breathing gets difficult, smoke one of these and it should help."

He handed her a small package.

The box was white with a brown stripe. *Kinsman's Asthmatic Cigarettes.* Smoking wasn't a pleasant thought, but if it would help, she'd try it. Maybe she could keep her condition from the girls. Just until Papa was better. They didn't need to worry about anything else.

"Thank you, Doctor." Lifting her chin, she put on her best smile. "I need to get back to my father." She stood and moved to the door.

But he stopped her with a hand to her shoulder. "I must advise you, Mrs. Powell, that if you don't take enough time to rest, you run the risk of making your condition worse. I know you are worried about your father, but you also need to worry for your own health. Tell your daughters. Let them assist you more. And that new foreman your father hired? You should tell him too."

No chance she would tell anyone. Not now. This man didn't know her . . . didn't understand how things worked up here. There wasn't room for the weak and the sick. Living in Alaska was difficult enough when a person was healthy. And with Papa sick . . . well, she could deal with some breathing problems for a little while. "Dr. Kingston, I'll ask you to kindly keep this to yourself. My family has enough on them right now. I'm fine. In fact, when it first started, I did quite well just calming myself and taking slow breaths. I'm sure if I work at it enough, I'll be able to keep it under control."

"But, Mrs. Powell—"

"Please"—she held up a hand—"I've stated my wishes. I'll see you when you come out to see Papa. Thank you for your time." With that, she turned on her heel and left his office.

Melissa untied her horse from the hitching post in front of Dr. Kingston's office, mounted, and turned the animal toward home. Asthma. Incurable. Well, she'd just have to make the best of it. It wasn't that bad. Now that she knew what she was dealing with, she would find a way to control this disease. Too many people were relying on her for her to be sick.

She would be fine.

She had to be.

June came before John realized it, bringing with it even longer hours of daylight. Yesterday evening, he lost track of the day and ended up out in the field with the calves until past eight. If Havyn hadn't come looking for him, the sky was so light he probably would've stayed until midnight. But he loved it here.

Not only Alaska. He loved what he did and he loved seeing the success of the farm. It finally felt like he was the foreman and making progress.

Thank heaven for the time he'd had under Chuck's tute-lage. But there was still a lot he needed to learn. Especially the things that Chuck took care of himself. All that knowl-edge in his head that he hadn't been able to share before he collapsed.

There was an ongoing list of questions that John had to ask daily.

Thankfully, all the workers Chuck hired to do the milking understood a good portion of the routine around the farm. The Powell women had been helpful too. Well, all except Whitney. One of these days, he was going to need to sit down with her and figure out what bothered her about him. If he'd done anything wrong, he needed to fix it.

John cleaned up after the evening milking, then looked around the barn to ensure that all would be ready for the early-morning shift. The scent of fresh hay spread on the floor filled his senses.

"John? Are you in here?" Mrs. Powell's voice floated through the milking barn.

"I'm back here. I'll be right out." He made his way toward the front of the barn and took off his dirty work gloves. "How may I help you, Mrs. Powell?"

She turned a shoulder toward the door. "I was wondering if you would sit with my father for a bit again? The girls are practicing for their performance tonight at the Roadhouse, and I hate to pull one of them away."

"Of course. I don't mind a bit. It was good to see him so alert today. In your opinion, how's he doing?"

"He's acting more like his old self, but I know he's frus-trated that he can't form words well. The doctor suggested letting him use paper and pencil. It's a good thing he's left-handed, otherwise things would be much more difficult. Anyway, he's asking for you, and I thought maybe you'd like the chance to speak with him for a little bit. And selfishly, it would give me a few moments to myself."

"I'd love to." John followed her out the door and then latched the large barn doors.

She walked with him toward the house. "Dr. Kingston thinks he will make a full recovery. That is if we can get him to continue with the exercises. He's not a fan of them."

"Do you need my help?"

She pulled her shawl tighter. "No, but thank you. You're doing so much already, and we really appreciate it." Turning toward him a bit, she tilted her head. "Have you been out to Norris's Roadhouse yet to hear the girls?"

"Not yet. I find myself working until late in the evenings. I'm amazed how well your father managed a farm as large as this. His shoes are hard to fill."

"I imagine so. But nevertheless, everyone needs a night off now and again. And tonight is Friday. Why don't you go with them?" She made a little grimace and her cheeks turned pink. "I shouldn't be so bossy."

"You're not bossy. That's very generous of you, ma'am."

"Oh, I insist that you go, then."

"Thank you. I think I will."

"Good." She gave him a smile.

Once inside the house, he followed her down the hall to Mr. Bundrant's room.

"Hi, Papa!" Her voice was cheery and bright. "I brought John to see you for a moment."

John walked over to the side of the bed. It was hard to see a man who'd been so strong and capable bedridden like this, but there were signs that he was improving. His mouth might droop and his right side not function, but there was fire in his eyes. John could see every day that Chuck was doing more for himself.

"I'll leave you two alone for a quick visit if that's all right." She kissed her father on the cheek. "I'll fetch some dinner for Papa and then be back so you can get to the Roadhouse."

John nodded and then looked down at his boss. "Evening, Chuck. How are you doing? Mrs. Powell told me you were given the okay to write down what you wanted to say."

Chuck reached for the paper and pencil on his left side and nodded. After several moments of scribbling, he held it up. *Could be better, but thankful to be alive.*

"That's good. We're glad you're still with us too. Your daughter said that Dr. Kingston hopes you'll have a full recovery?"

The pencil scratched across the page again as he struggled to balance the notebook.

Yes, but Doc told me to watch it—I don't like those words.

John laughed. "I imagine so." He sat in the chair beside the bed. "Just so you know, I told your daughter that I have mighty big shoes to fill. It's taken me this long to learn the ropes, so I'm grateful I can ask you questions."

The pencil moved again. *I'm the one who's grateful. I owe you. Are you getting to know my granddaughters?*

John took in a deep breath and let it out slowly. "Yes, sir. In fact, that's one of the things I'd hoped to discuss with you when you were feeling better."

Chuck was already writing a response. *Let's discuss it now.*

"All right." John sat a little straighter, put his palms on his thighs, and glanced over his shoulder at the closed door. "I'm going to be honest. I'm a bit uncomfortable with the contract now that I'm beginning to care for one of them. Having a contract like that . . . doesn't seem right."

Once again, his boss was writing just as he finished. *Why?*

"Well, frankly, sir, I want to pursue her naturally. And I don't want you ever thinking that I didn't genuinely love the one that I chose."

Several seconds passed as Chuck studied his face. Then his attention went to the paper as he wrote. *I trust you, John. That's why I chose you. But the contract is in place for exactly why I'm here. Think about what would happen to them if I died. Which one?*

"Sir, first, let me say that I would take care of things anyway as your foreman. But if you truly want to give this farm to me and one of your granddaughters, let me continue to work for you and alongside you. Over the years, it will be greatly important for me to learn from you."

Chuck tapped the first question on the paper.

John leaned back in the chair. "That's why I signed it in the first place. So I understand your purpose, I do . . . but it won't be easy to explain."

Chuck wrote again. *Why would you need to explain?*

"I think it's only fair that I tell my wife the truth one day."

Chuck made a face and then tapped the paper again. This time to the second question.

John read it again. "Which one? Which one what?"

The pencil moved at a faster speed.

Granddaughter.

"Oh, my apologies. Well, you see . . . that is . . ." He swallowed. "I've taken quite an interest in Havyn."

Off went the pencil again. *Perfect. I had a feeling. Does she know?*

The words brought a smile to his face. "I'm glad you think it's a good match. And no, she doesn't know. At least, not yet. I'm hoping to get to know her a little better. If we can ever find the time. I'm going to go to the Roadhouse tonight."

Good idea. As you ride there and back, it will give you ample opportunity to talk and get to know one another better.

John wanted to shake his head and laugh. "Are you playing matchmaker now?"

Maybe.

"While we're talking about the contract, there's the piece about the gold that I would like to discuss."

Chuck raised his left eyebrow.

"I don't feel right taking it."

Why?

"I don't believe I've earned it, sir. And I don't want it just for marrying one of your granddaughters. If you want to give it to us as a gift later—much later down the road—that's fine. But it doesn't seem right for me to have what belongs to you."

I gave it to you.

"It was very generous of you, but I still don't feel I should keep it."

Chuck nodded after a moment. *I can respect that.*

"Thank you." John stood. He leaned over and gripped the man's hand. "I'm praying for you. Lots of people are. I'll be back tomorrow to check on you."

Another nod.

John went down the hall and found Mrs. Powell in the kitchen. An interesting—almost herbal—smell was in the air. "It's good to see him able to communicate. His mind seems to be sharp."

She nodded as she filled a tray. "He was out of it for a while, but seems to be getting back to his normal self. Now if we could just keep him from trying to jump out of that bed, we'll be doing well."

The thought made him smile. If anyone would try to do that, it would be Chuck Bundrant. "Do you need me to help you with anything before I leave?"

"No, but I appreciate it. I've already told the girls you're going tonight. Whitney is getting the wagon ready so you can all ride together."

"That will be wonderful."

"Just make sure you bundle up. It's chilly out there. Could come up a fog."

"Yes, ma'am."

He headed to his room. Time to change clothes and get freshened up before they needed to leave. With any luck, he'd be able to sit near Havyn, and they'd get to speak. Was it wrong to pray that he sat next to her rather than Whitney? He'd really rather not have the cold shoulder the entire drive to town.

When he went back to the house, the girls came out the door, instruments in tow. He helped load them and went to the driver's seat.

Whitney eyed the reins. "Are you driving us?"

"It would be my pleasure."

She shrugged.

God must have been in on the plan with Mr. Bundrant, because Havyn ended up in the front seat with him, while Madysen and Whitney sat in the back seat.

The four of them chitchatted about the weather, the farm, all the new calves, the chickens, and even Whitney's sled dogs all the way to the Roadhouse. An engaging and pleasant conversation. Easygoing. And the more time he spent with Miss Havyn Powell, the more he longed to know her better.

At their destination, the girls scurried out and thanked him for the drive. He parked the wagon behind the large building, where plenty of other conveyances stood waiting for their owners.

By the time he walked back up to the building, loud applause nearly burst through the walls and windows. Were the Powell ladies about to play?

As he opened the door, a rush of warmth hit his face. The glow from lanterns and lights filled the room until it almost felt sunny. The huge room was packed with tables and chairs, all of which were filled with eager guests. The food smelled hearty, even though John couldn't immediately identify what it was. It apparently was quite good, because the men were eating as if their lives depended on it.

Up on the stage, a flash of green caught his attention. He turned. Whitney, Havyn, and Madysen all appeared from behind the curtain. The green dresses they'd worn for their mother's birthday celebration—how many weeks ago had that been now?—brought out the gorgeous color of their dark red hair. Their hair color wasn't orangey, like some of the fellas had that he'd met in Cripple Creek. No, the Powell ladies all had a deep, dark shade of red that he couldn't describe. Havyn's had gentle waves to it. The way she'd pulled it into some sort of loose knot at the back of her head was elegant and lovely.

What a beautiful group of women.

The standing ovation continued even as the Powell ladies insisted the men sit down.

Whitney took her place at the piano, and Havyn picked up her violin. Madysen sat with her cello in front of her. Whitney played a note on the piano, and the other two tuned their strings.

The crowd hushed until he could almost hear the men breathing. And then the girls started a lively tune. How on earth did they start at the exact same moment?

Whitney's fingers raced up and down the keyboard, while Havyn's bow flew over the violin. Madysen's head bobbed fast as her fingers played up and down the neck of her larger instrument. Was that how she kept time? Pretty soon the audience started clapping along—but not too loud. These were seasoned customers. They knew how to be entertained and how to enjoy clapping along while still hearing the music.

John found a seat at a table, and before long, his foot was tapping out the rhythm. A young man came and asked if he'd like some dinner, and since his stomach growled at the very same moment, he gave the menu a try. Ordering a stack of sourdough flapjacks, or *hots* as they called them, with a generous side of bacon, John gave the boy a smile. It seemed normal that people around here ate breakfast food in the evenings. Plenty of the men were eating large stacks of the cakes, which made John's mouth water.

The lively song ended and applause erupted. A large tin can began making its way around the room. John caught sight of it at one point and noticed that it read *TIPS*. Ah, so this was a good way for the girls to make some extra income as well. Very smart. Especially in a town like this. Lots of men would be starved for entertainment, and yet, here the men had a chance at entertainment that was honoring to God. It was the only alternative to the brothels and saloons. But the Roadhouse proved that such a place could exist, and it was packed. It must turn a good profit.

The next song began with Whitney playing the piano. And then Havyn started to sing. Her voice—clear, bright, and angelic—soared to the rafters. Whatever the song was,

John had never heard it. But it was beautiful. And it wasn't in English. Nor Italian. He listened more closely . . . ah, French. When he was a child, he'd learned a bit of the language. After all, Italy was neighbors with France. Even so, he couldn't place many of the words from the song.

By the time she reached the second verse, it seemed she had the entire room hypnotized. Then Madysen and Whitney joined her.

Closing his eyes, he let the music wash over him. Never had he heard such talent. And the harmonies were astounding. They all seemed to have quite a range. From low to high, their voices floated through the scales.

The man next to John leaned over. "I got goose bumps. Don't think I ever had that happen afore."

All he could do was nod. Because the same thing happened to him.

For the final verse of the song, all three girls played their instruments and sang. He'd never seen a violinist sing while she played. For that matter, he'd never seen a cellist do it either. But somehow, the Powell sisters did it. Beautifully.

As soon as the song ended, every man in the room jumped to his feet and clapped. Many of them whistled and threw hats in the air.

Havyn stepped forward and quieted the crowd. Once the men were seated again and relatively quiet, she spoke in a resonant voice. "For this next selection, we'd like to share a song with you that my sister wrote. It's going to be another *a capella* piece, so we'll need you to be very quiet so you can hear."

The same man leaned over to him again. "Uh, what's that mean?"

"It means there won't be any instruments, just their voices."

The young waiter delivered John's order, and he said a quick prayer, thanking God for the food and the opportunity to be there at the Roadhouse that night. When he looked up, Havyn was looking at him as she sang.

His heart beat a little faster, and he forgot all about the food. In his mind he could see himself with Havyn, the two of them walking together—talking . . . holding hands. Stopping along the way to share a kiss. Perhaps many kisses.

Without taking his eyes off her, he sent another prayer heavenward.

Lord, if You wouldn't mind helping me out . . . I'd like to get to know Havyn better, but I'm afraid half the town is already smitten with her. Including me. How do I pursue Havyn, Father? Please show me.

TWELVE

Stepping off the stage into the makeshift dressing room area, Havyn felt as if she walked on the clouds. Tonight had been the best yet. The performance had made her feel alive. But then . . . it was so much more than that. Everything changed when she connected gazes with John.

The dark-haired foreman had been focused on her, and every time she caught a glimpse of him during the evening, he'd been watching her, looking mesmerized. It made her insides flutter. Oh, she'd had men look at her like that before, but something, when John did it . . .

It was different. John's look made her heart soar.

"Ladies, that was remarkable! Outstanding!" Mr. Norris hugged each one of them with one arm. Then from behind his back, he pulled out the can. "You won't believe the tips from tonight. I think you'll be pleased."

Whitney took the can and when she looked inside, her eyes widened. Mr. Norris always counted it and left them a note on top with the amount. "Is this correct?"

He nodded his head. "I even double counted. It's correct."

Whitney showed Havyn the piece of paper, and she couldn't help it—her hands flew to her mouth. "Wow."

Madysen peeked over her shoulder. "Gracious!"

"And there's more." Mr. Norris tucked his hands behind his back. "The men have asked *again* if you would come back every evening. Except Sunday, of course. I have to tell you, my business is doing very well on the weekends when you ladies are here performing. The other evenings, I regret, I don't have anything to compete with the saloons and brothels. I'm willing to pay you more if you'll come during the week as well."

Havyn looked to her older sister. "I love the idea . . ."

"But I'm not sure that would be wise." Whitney held up a hand. "As much as we appreciate it, Mr. Norris, with Granddad laid up, I'm not sure we could keep up with everything. There's a lot of work to do at the farm."

Havyn leaned closer to their older sister. "I hate to point out the fact that in all practicality, if we could bring in extra income it might help out Granddad and the farm."

"While that is true"—Whitney gave an authoritative look—"we have to take into consideration that we will be leaving all the duties of caring for Granddad with Mama. That's a lot for her for such a long time each evening." She lifted her chin and looked back to the owner. "Mr. Norris, may we have some time to think and pray about it?"

"Of course. And I completely understand that. Know that the invitation is open for any time. Just let me know so that I can get the advertisements out. You're a big hit." The owner of the Roadhouse gave them all a big smile.

Whitney emptied the can into Madysen's purse. A mix of gold nuggets and coins settled in the bottom before Whitney handed the can back to Mr. Norris. "Thank you. We appreciate all you've done for our family."

"And I thank you for what you've done to increase my business." With a huge smile, he left them to gather their things.

Havyn studied Whitney's face, then shared a look with Madysen. "I agree that we should pray about it, but I also think it's wise to realize that we could probably use the extra money." They put on their coats and headed toward the back door. "Do either of you know for sure about the finances of the farm?"

A shrug from Maddy. "No."

"No." Whitney shook her head. "Granddad always kept the books, and I have no idea where he keeps the extra funds. It's something I'm hoping he's spoken to Mama about because we need help. Until the salmon run comes, I'm going to have to buy more meat for the dogs. Unless one of you wants to go shoot a musk ox?"

"Have you asked John about it?" *Please, Lord, let Whit be open to John.* "I'm betting he knows where the extra money is."

"Havyn's right, Whitney. He's riding home with us, so that gives us the perfect opportunity. Then maybe we'll be able to sing and play more here." Madysen squeezed Whitney's arms. "We're just trying to help. Plus, I enjoy it. My vote is to agree to Mr. Norris's offer."

"But what do we really know about this John fellow? He showed up one day and Granddad hired him?" Whitney shook her head. "I don't know. It seems a bit odd to me."

How could Whitney be so stubborn about John? "Other than the fact that Granddad was close friends with John's grandfather? And obviously Granddad trusted him. Then there's the undeniable fact that he's a hard worker. Goodness, Whitney, the man has tried to move heaven and earth to help you with your dogs."

Whit shot Havyn an arched look. "I don't *need* any help with my dogs."

"Don't we all know it!" Havyn put her hands on her hips. "Gracious. John has done a phenomenal job with the farm since Granddad had his spell, and half of it he's had to learn on his own. We should at least give him the benefit of the doubt. Just because you don't want anyone else being in control doesn't mean he's shady or untrustworthy. We should respect our grandfather's judgment. Don't you agree?"

Madysen raised her hand high. "*I* agree!"

"We're a little beyond being in school, Maddy. Put your hand down." Whitney rolled her eyes.

"I know that." Madysen buttoned up her coat and put her hat on her head. "But you're not in charge, Whit. We're all adults now, and we *all* help with the farm. We're in this together."

As the sisters exited the building into sunlight that teased the mind into thinking it was still early, John pulled up the wagon outside the door. He tipped his hat to them. "Ladies, you did a marvelous job tonight."

"Thank you." Havyn returned his smile and handed her violin case to him as she climbed into the front seat.

Madysen and Whitney loaded the cello and settled in the back. Havyn shifted in her seat. *Whitney better not cause any trouble.*

John didn't waste any time setting the team in motion. "Everyone seemed to enjoy that. I'm glad I was finally able to come."

"I think I enjoy it more every time." Madysen piped up from the back. "Mr. Norris said he'd like to have us sing every night but Sunday."

John looked to Havyn. "Truly? Wouldn't that be awfully

hard on you? I mean, it seems that would be a strain on your voices to sing every night like that."

"We're stronger than you might think," Whitney declared. "Strong and capable."

Havyn wanted to crawl under the seat. Whitney's tone meant things could turn ugly. Havyn broke in before Whit could say anything wrong. "We're going to pray about it and talk to Mama. I think the financial help would be good for the farm with Granddad laid up."

John tilted his head. "Since I haven't gone over the ledger with your grandfather yet, I don't know a lot about the money side of things, but I can see how taking Norris up on his offer would be a positive."

Havyn studied John's profile. "So you don't know how to pay the workers or where Granddad kept the funds?" At least their grandfather was awake and alert now. That would help.

"No. I'm supposed to bring the ledger to him tomorrow so we can go over all of it. Chuck has some interesting shorthand that I can't decipher. And he told me there's another ledger, I just don't know where."

"Oh, good." Glancing behind her, Havyn fixed Whitney with a look that she hoped silenced her older sister.

It didn't.

"Why hasn't Granddad entrusted you with that information yet?" Crossing her arms over her chest, Whitney raised an eyebrow.

Havyn shook her head and turned forward again. No good could come out of this. *Lord, help.*

"The workings of the farm were your granddad's priority. I have the ledger, but I don't want to mess up his system."

"Who are you, John? We know nothing about you." Whitney's tone was almost accusing.

Havyn hurried to intercede. "What she means is, we were talking earlier and realized we'd like to know you better."

Madysen joined in. "It's true, John. You've been working so hard for our family, it doesn't seem right that you know so much about us, but we don't know much about you."

He looked back toward Madysen and Whitney, and then to Havyn. "You're very kind to ask." He shrugged. "There's not a lot to tell. I come from a wonderful family. I was raised in Italy on the family farm by my parents and my grandfather until I was twelve years old. Then my parents passed away."

"Oh, that's awful! I'm so sorry. What happened to them?" Madysen's voice sounded like she could cry at any moment.

"Measles. I was sick as well, but recovered, as you can see. It was devastating to lose my parents, and even harder to leave my home and everything I'd ever known. Nonno, my grandpa, thought it best to take me far away from the difficult memories and the grief. Besides, there was a lot of unrest in Italy then. Political problems. And the dairy was struggling."

"Dairy?" Whitney asked. "Your family had a dairy? I suppose you always wanted another one?"

John laughed. "I never really thought much about it after we left. I was young, and my grandpa wanted something different. Nonno always had a dream to dig for gold, so we came to America. After we learned English and heard of the gold strike in Cripple Creek, we settled there. That's where we knew your grandfather."

"Oh, so Granddad knew *you* before?" Havyn pointed her words at Whitney. "*And* you grew up on a farm. That's very interesting. No wonder Granddad brought you on." Was Whitney getting the point?

John laughed. "Well, he knew *of* me. I went to school,

so we met briefly. I was young. He and Nonno knew each other well. Even after your family left Cripple Creek, they wrote letters to one another and stayed abreast of the other's family. Before Nonno died, he asked me to come see your grandfather."

"So that's why you came to Nome?" Havyn shot another glance at Whitney.

"Yes, it is. But I used up all my funds to fulfill my grandfather's last wish, so I needed a job right away. Dr. Gordon told me that Mr. Bundrant needed help out at the farm, so I had two reasons to find him."

"That's fascinating." And it was. This man interested her more than she wanted to admit. "Tell me, what do you remember about your farm back in Italy? Did you have cows and chickens?"

"Yes, we did. We also made cheese. Mozzarella. Then there were the sheep. Mama made cheese out of the sheep's milk as well. It was so tasty. I don't remember how to make that. But mozzarella? I could probably still make that in my sleep. It was a job I knew well."

His deep laugh warmed Havyn to her toes. "I bet you must miss it very much."

"I do. But I love America. It's more my parents that I miss."

"That's understandable. I miss our father. He's been gone since I was ten, but even so. The ache is still there not having him around."

A tiny huff from the back seat made Havyn want to turn around and give Whitney a piece of her mind. She knew exactly what Whitney thought of their dad, and could just see the scowl on her older sister's face.

It took every bit of Havyn's restraint to keep her gaze straight ahead.

If John heard the huff, he didn't comment on it. Thank-fully. "Was your father in a mining accident?"

It was a fair question. Especially after she'd asked about his parents. Nevertheless, it struck her heart like a knife. Whenever anyone found out their father died up in Cripple Creek and he was a miner, they just assumed that it had been an accident. But she couldn't very well lie about it. Oh, how she hated this question. "No. He was drunk and got in a fight outside one of the bars. The men left him for dead on the side of the mountain."

"I'm so sorry."

"Don't be." Whitney all but snarled her words. "It's bet-ter this way."

"*Whitney!* How *could* you?" Maddy's voice again sounded as if she were about to cry.

"That's not true, Whitney." The only thing Havyn could do was try to defuse the situation. Why was her older sister so bitter and suspicious? She turned to John. "You'll have to excuse Whitney. She's tired."

"The only thing I'm tired about is how you've set our father up to be a saint. Why do you have to bring him up so much lately? I realize he was our father, but you and Madysen don't know half of what he did."

Havyn couldn't deny the truth of her statement. The awk-ward silence around them sizzled.

Madysen sniffed in the seat behind her.

Another huff from Whitney. "Forget I said anything. You're right, I'm just tired. I'm sorry."

Havyn looked back and watched her older sister wrap her arm around Madysen.

The quiet engulfed them for several minutes.

What would John think of them? Especially after hearing the bitterness in her sister's voice.

His voice came soft and kind. "Death of a family member is always difficult." He reached over and gave her arm a squeeze. Havyn's chest tightened. She gazed upward to look into his eyes. He smiled, then turned his attention back to the horses.

"It was a heavy loss to me." Havyn kept her voice low so Whitney couldn't make out her words. "You'd think it would get easier. But it doesn't."

"Stop the wagon!" Whitney called out. "I think it would be nice to walk the rest of the way."

"Don't go alone, Whit." Madysen laid a hand on her sister's arm.

Havyn pointed. "The dairy is just ahead."

"I know. That's why I want to walk. Maybe I'll rid myself of the foul mood." Whitney jumped off the back. "I'm sorry, John. Thank you for the ride."

"I'll go with her." Madysen hopped off as well.

John held the wagon steady for a moment.

"Whitney has a hard time talking about your father, doesn't she?"

Havyn gave a nod, then bit her lip. "Well . . ." Now that he'd asked, maybe she wasn't being fair. "You're right, Whitney doesn't like talking about our father. And Madysen is so full of compassion, she can't stand watching our sister suffer alone. But Whitney, being the oldest, saw more and understood more about our father's . . . flaws. She loved him. But also is realistic about who he was—a drunken gambler. Madysen was only seven when he died, so naturally she only remembers the good times."

"And you?" His expression said he truly cared.

"Well, I know my dad wasn't perfect and did some pretty awful things. But I've also chosen to forgive him. He was my dad. Does that make sense?"

He nodded. "It's all right, Havyn. Pain makes people act strange sometimes. Losing a father is never easy, and each person grieves their own way." He started the horses back on their course.

Havyn pushed aside her discomfort. "Tell me about your grandfather."

"Oh, he was an ornery old man." John laughed. "But I loved him and he loved me. You have to know Italians to understand what I'm talking about. Family is everything. So when he decided to come to America and raise me here, he poured himself into me because I was all he had left. Most Italians have big boisterous families, but I was the only child of an only child."

"You must have been very close."

"We were. He longed for me to marry and have a family, but he was also determined that we needed to build a family fortune since he'd used up all his savings to get us to America. You'd never meet a harder worker than my grandpa. He was a wonderful man."

They fell silent as the horses turned toward the lane to the barn. John let the lines go lax. "I'm glad we had the chance to talk. This is nice."

"It is." She lifted her face to the evening breeze. "Thank you for your compliment tonight. It meant a lot."

"It was honest. I've never heard anything like you three. How did you get started?"

She felt the smile cover her face. "Our mother is a musical prodigy. I don't think there's an instrument made that she hasn't mastered. When she married our father back in 1877, she made him promise that he would allow her to teach us music. It was her one demand. So we started singing from before we could even really talk. Then, once we were each four years old, we were allowed to pick one instrument to be our main focus. Whitney chose the piano, I chose the violin, and Maddy the cello. We still all had to continue with voice lessons, musical theory lessons, and piano lessons—because all good musicians must be able to play the piano, according to Mama—but then we'd have two lessons a week from her on our chosen instrument."

"That's incredible."

"We tried other instruments too, and spent much more time on music than anything else. But don't get me wrong, our mother taught us reading, math, and history as well. I'm just saying that we spent hours every day on music. Sometimes we still do."

He brought the horses to a stop outside the barn and set the brake. "Well, don't stop, because you are extraordinary."

The evening sun gave them plenty of light, and Havyn enjoyed the way his eyes sparkled. They were so dark it was hard to distinguish the color of his eyes from his pupils. "I'll let you in on a little secret."

"Oh?"

"I love to sing more than anything. As much as I love to play the violin, there's something about singing . . . I simply can't put it into words."

He looked straight ahead for several seconds and a big grin filled his face. "Did you know that the first time you introduced me to your chickens, I had stopped at the chicken yard just before and heard you singing to the flock? Not just any song, either. You were singing 'Santa Lucia' in Italian."

Her face heated as she put her hands over her mouth.

"Don't be embarrassed. It was quite charming. I just never expected an Italian song."

Dropping her hands, she shook her head. "I didn't know anyone else heard me that day. Other than the milkers, and they're used to me singing. Did you know that while 'Santa Lucia' is a song with Neapolitan roots, written by an Italian, Swedish folks sing the same tune but with different lyrics? They call it 'Sankta Lucia' and sing it on December thirteenth while the eldest daughter wears a wreath of lighted candles on her head and serves the family breakfast. Mother taught us that when we were studying the song."

"So it's the same melody as the 'Santa Lucia' that you were singing?"

"Yes, it's quite lovely. But with Swedish lyrics that request Saint Lucia to light her white candles."

"Would you sing me a bit?"

Havyn bit her lip. She couldn't remember the whole thing in Swedish. "Well . . . I only remember a bit of the chorus. '*Drömmar med vingesus, under oss sia, tänd dina vita ljus, Sankta Lucia.*'" She let the notes sound clear in the night air.

"That was beautiful." The man beside her stared into her eyes.

Oh, how she wanted to stay there, caught up in his gaze.

"So my next question is, why haven't you sung to the chickens since?"

"I didn't want to disturb you or for you to think that I was a senseless lady who sang to chickens. Even though . . . I guess technically I am. All except the senseless part."

He gave her a lopsided grin. "Definitely not senseless."

"Thank you."

"And I think you should go back to singing to the chickens. I know it would make *my* day brighter."

The warmth in his voice made a blush rise up her neck. "Thank you for that."

"You deserve as many compliments as I can give, Havyn. You are the most talented person I've ever met."

She narrowed her eyes a bit. "You haven't heard our mother play all her instruments. She could be an entire orchestra on her own if she could be in more than one place at a time."

"While I would love to hear your mother, you are entirely too modest about your own abilities, Miss Havyn Powell. And I meant what I said."

How to respond to that? She looked at her hands in her lap. "Thank you."

"You're most welcome." He climbed down from the wagon and reached up to help her. "One day I'll have to tell you some of the stories my grandpa told me about your grandfather and him. They're pretty comical."

She laughed. "I can only imagine. Our grandfather can be quite cantankerous." She scooted across the seat and took hold of his hand—and stilled. She got caught up in his eyes.

What was happening to her?

"Havyn! Havyn, come quick!"

She startled, as did John.

"Havyn!" Madysen came running.

"What's wrong?" Havyn let John help her from the wagon. Madysen reached them just as Havyn's feet touched the ground.

"It's Granddad. He's had another fit of apoplexy!"

THIRTEEN

D r. Geoffrey Kingston opened the door to his office and walked into the dark space. He took off his coat and hat as his mind went to Mr. Bundrant.

This second bout of the apoplexy appeared to be much worse, but only time would tell. The effects weren't all known yet because they hadn't been able to wake him.

He hung his coat and hat on a hook beside the door and went to light the lantern on the table beside him. Some fresh start. Rather than seeking his own fortune and putting himself first, he wanted to actually heal people—like what doctors were supposed to do. But now . . . everything he tried to rid himself of came back to haunt him. All because of Judas Reynolds.

The money was good though. Very good. So far, he'd made double what he made for being a doctor from selling the fake medicines. And Judas was making a tidy sum himself. Maybe it wasn't so bad.

Kingston walked to his bookshelf and searched for a tome that would help him with Mr. Bundrant. The only way to ease his conscience now was to continue to help people as best he could. That way, he wasn't just taking advantage of people who were always in search of the next great elixir or pill that would cure their ailments, ready to spend their gold nuggets and coins on whatever new medicine he could peddle.

Perhaps if he could build a reputation of actually being the doctor who helped people, then nobody would think that he was a swindler on the side. The fact of the matter was, he knew medicine. Went to school twice for it.

What did it hurt that he provided pills and syrups to people who just wanted something to make them *think* they felt better? It wasn't like he was doing this to anyone who was seriously ill. Of course, if anyone came to him with an ailment, he would treat it with the best of his knowledge and ability. He was a good man. He really was. This little side business with Judas was just that. A side business. It wasn't hurting anyone. And he wouldn't allow it to go too far.

Reading several entries about apoplexy, Geoffrey wrote down some notes on paper. He'd take it with him next time he saw Mr. Bundrant and see if he could help the man make any progress. It all depended on which side of the brain was affected this time. And, if it was the same side as last time, if the damage had increased in severity.

A brisk knock on the door startled him. *It must be a patient.*

He opened the door to an old, grizzled man. "Good evening. How may I help you?"

"I'm afraid it's the whooping cough, Doc. Old Fred down at the saloon started coughin' and coughin', and then he couldn't breathe after it passed. We's seen it afore here, and so we sent him home. I told him I'd come get ya."

"Yes, of course." Geoffrey grabbed his coat and hat. "I treated many cases of the horrible disease before I came." Grabbing a jar of cough syrup out of his medicine cabinet, he nodded at the man at the door. "Please. Take me to him."

Melissa Powell loaded the last of her cloth-wrapped squares of butter and counted them one more time. This ten pounds of butter would bring a pretty penny in town. Their farm was the only source of butter in these parts, unless you counted that horrible oleomargarine, which she certainly did not. Many of the miners, however, used it because they couldn't afford the real thing. The restaurants used the oleomargarine in cooking, but for baking they all still wanted butter and were willing to pay well for it. That put her butter in even higher demand.

A week had passed since her father's second bout. What if he didn't ever wake again? A shiver raced up her spine. Not a thought she wanted to entertain right now. No sense being afraid of the future. She'd just have to take one day at a time.

She hated the thought of leaving him, but she wouldn't subject her daughters to the bartering tactics of one of the men in particular. It was one thing for her to do it, but her daughters?

"I heard you were going to town to sell butter and cream." John joined her at the wagon. "Do you need any help?"

She smiled but shook her head. "No, that's awfully sweet to offer when I know how much you have to do. Whitney's staying with my father, and I don't want to be gone a lengthy time. Besides, this will be a pretty quick transaction. There's not a lot of cream to sell since Mr. Norris already picked up his dairy order, and we used a lot of it to make the butter. Everything will be sold to the two restaurants that have been asking us for whatever we can send their way."

"I've been meaning to ask how much you sell it for. I need to try to keep up with the ledger."

"The butter will fetch over ten dollars a pound."

"Ten dollars?" John's eyebrows shot up and he whistled. "It's only twenty-eight cents a pound in Colorado. At least it was when I left."

"We sometimes get as much as fifteen in the winter. One winter I had ten fellows show up and they carried on a bidding war for my butter. It was the craziest thing you ever saw, but being up here in the shortened days and long nights can do that to a man. You can't get fresh butter, milk, and cream up here unless you have your own milk cow or come to us. Oh, there are a couple of folks trying their hand at producing dairy products, but they don't have the livestock we do."

"Wow. I'll get that in the books. Thank you. I still have a few things I need to ask your father. But nothing to worry about."

"I'm praying he'll awaken soon. The good Lord has seen us through all these years. Papa said he was able to put away quite a bit for our future for when the gold plays out, as it almost always does." She suppressed a cough and cleared her throat. "I should be going. The café is expecting me."

John helped her up to the driver's seat. "I'll unhitch the wagon for you when you get back. I'll be watching for you, so you can return to your father as soon as you can."

Melissa picked up the lines and cast him a smile. "It's kind of you to take care of it. We appreciate all you do around here to keep things going." She snapped the leather lightly against the horse's back. "Step up, Dolly."

The bottles of cream rattled against their metal crate as the horse started for town. Melissa gave a quick look over her shoulder to make sure everything was secured. It looked fine.

Once she was out of earshot of the farm, she tried to take a deep breath to clear her lungs. When spring thaw came, it always released something into the air that caused her more breathing problems. She coughed and coughed, trying hard to rid herself of the wheezing. It didn't do much good.

Gazing skyward, she fought the tightness in her chest. If relief didn't come soon, she'd have an attack. The doctor told her she could even die from such a thing. Taking a glance over her shoulder, she checked to make sure she'd gone far enough from the house, then took a medical cigarette out of her pocket and stuck it between her lips. Next she pulled out a match and struck it against the wooden seat and then lit the cigarette. After several long puffs, her chest loosened and the panic went away.

Since she was going into town, maybe she should stop and see the doctor? Dolly whinnied softly and nodded her head, as if agreeing.

"I don't need to hear from you on the matter." No. Her first priority was to sell her items and get back as quickly as possible.

Melissa glanced toward the water. The Sound was pretty much free of ice now, and any day another ship would appear bringing more gold-hungry passengers.

Lord, I'm going to need my strength, what with Papa sick and the farm needing so much of our time and efforts. I need to stay healthy—to be free to help whoever needs me most.

God knew what she was facing. Everything would be fine. She took another puff and then put the cigarette out so she could save it for later. No use wasting the costly medicine.

She set it on the seat to let it cool off before she shoved it back into her pocket.

But after two breaths, the tightening started again.

———

Warmth floated over his face. Where did it come from? Chuck tried to push through the fog in his mind. Nothing was clear. He couldn't see.

Why couldn't he see?

Voices hummed around him, but they seemed so far away. What were they saying?

The murmurs became a bit louder until he recognized a voice. But whose was it? It was a woman's voice.

"I'm so worried, Whitney. The doctor is supposed to come back today and I still haven't been able to get any response out of your grandfather."

Several coughs followed the words.

"But he's still breathing, Mama. Look. His eyes are even moving under his eyelids. That's got to be a good sign. Right?"

"This time it seems so much worse. I don't know why, but I have a bad feeling."

"Why don't we pray? You know that Havyn and Madysen and John—we've all been praying." The sweet voice belonged to . . . who? He couldn't place it. The other voice had called her *Whitney*. Who was Whitney? He should know. It felt like it was on the edge of his mind, ready to burst forward. Why couldn't he remember?

Their voices hushed and he couldn't understand them anymore. All of a sudden it was like he was floating. Nothing in his body obeyed his commands. Nothing moved. Where was he?

He turned his face toward the warmth—and a flash of

memory hit of turning his face toward the window in the mornings when it was summer. The sun would shine in on his bed. He must be in bed? But why? What was wrong with him?

"Good afternoon, ladies." A man's voice broke through his thoughts. "How is our patient this afternoon?"

"Hello, Doctor. I'm afraid I haven't been able to wake him. But I'm hopeful. He's breathing a bit deeper now. That's good, isn't it?"

"Hmm. Let me examine him and I will let you all know. Would you mind getting me a basin of hot water, Miss Powell? Your mother can help me a few minutes until you return."

"Of course, Dr. Kingston. I'll be right back."

"And bring a few small towels back with you, please?"

"Yes, sir. I'll be right back." The voice was so sweet. Chuck was sure in his heart that he knew who was speaking.

"Papa? Can you hear me?" The first voice that he recognized. She'd spoken a moment ago. She called him Papa. His daughter? He couldn't picture her face in his mind.

"Mr. Bundrant? It's Dr. Kingston. I'm here to check on you and do an examination. So you may feel some discomfort."

A doctor. He must be sick. In bed. But why? And why couldn't he open his eyes? Putting all of his strength and energy into getting his eyes to open, he felt himself moan and heard the sound.

Why did he feel like this? *What* was going on?

"Doctor! Did you hear that?" His daughter sounded excited. And hopeful.

"This *is* good news. Let's see if he responds to any stimuli." The doctor was doing something. Metal objects clanked together somewhere across the room.

"All right, Mr. Bundrant. Let's see if you can feel this."

Something sharp poked his foot. That *was* his foot, wasn't it? It seemed familiar, but it wouldn't move.

Then it poked the other foot. Yes, that was definitely his feet.

He tried to make another sound. Maybe if he put all his effort forth, he could show them he was here and could hear them. For several seconds he pushed. Then, "Mmmmmm-mmmah" escaped his mouth. He felt his lips move. Then something wet and warm dripped down his chin. He could feel that!

"Mr. Bundrant! You know we're here? You feel this?" Another poke.

The only sound he could make was "mmmahhhh." It sounded horrible.

"He feels it! I think he can hear us too!" His daughter sounded . . . delighted.

More descriptive words came back to his brain. Thoughts started to bounce around. He had a farm . . . didn't he? For some reason, he could picture himself milking cows. Throwing hay in the barn. That must be significant. It must be.

"I believe he's beginning to come out of his comatose state." The doctor was speaking.

"Oh, praise God!"

"But don't get your hopes up, Mrs. Powell. I've been doing a good deal of reading in my medical references, and when a patient has suffered not one but *two* bouts of apoplexy, the outcome might be quite limited—disappointing, even."

"I understand what you are saying, Doctor, but he's alive. As long as he is breathing, Papa will keep fighting. You don't know my father very well yet, but he's about as stubborn as they come." Something touched his shoulder. "Right, Papa?

We're going to fight this. We're going to do everything we can to help you get back on your feet."

The words came over him like a calming blanket. The fear that had been at every edge of his mind slipped away. If only he could remember . . .

FOURTEEN

The fireplace roared. Even though the sun was still out, the nights were quite cool. Madysen tucked her feet up under her and waited for her mother and sisters. After dinner, they were all supposed to discuss with John the matter of money. And figure out what to do.

This wasn't the kind of discussion Madysen enjoyed. She'd rather talk about music. In fact, math had been her least favorite subject. But Mama had called the meeting, and so she knew she had to be a part. As an adult and a member of the family, she had to pull her weight, just like everyone else.

Whitney and Havyn walked into the room together. The grim look on their eldest sister's face made Madysen's throat tighten.

"I can't find anything from Granddad anywhere that states he has an account at the bank. Neither can I find any other money or gold."

"Why haven't we asked these questions before?" Havyn looked like she was blaming herself for it all. "I mean, we've relied far too heavily on Granddad for everything ever since Dad died."

Madysen bit her lip. "I know. I'm feeling the same way. He wanted to take care of us, and we got too comfortable with that arrangement. Now, I feel like we've taken advantage of him." A tear stung at the corner of her eye. "He's laid up and we don't know for how long. We need to do more to help."

"I agree." Havyn looked to their older sister.

Mama came in the room. "Well, there is a bit of good news. Granddad moaned a few times, and the doctor thinks he might come out of his comatose state soon." She sat beside Madysen and patted her knee. "The doctor agreed to sit with him for a little bit while we chat."

Grabbing her mother's hand, she squeezed it. "I know this has been so hard. Can I do anything for you?"

Her mother's smile warmed her heart. "Always my merciful one." She put a hand on Madysen's cheek. "Everything you girls have done to help me with your grandfather has been wonderful. I simply need rest." The look on her face said there was more to it, but Madysen decided to wait for now. At least until she could be alone with Mama.

John walked into the room, a ledger in his hands. "This is all I have to go on. It appears that everything is in order. But this only shows the orders, what the farm has provided, and who has paid. There's got to be another one somewhere. One that shows the expenses and payroll."

Mama leaned forward. "So does it show that the farm is doing all right?"

"As far as I can tell, yes. But I have no idea how your father paid for things. When we need supplies—and I have an order that needs to be made—I'm sure I can put it on account. I've done that before, but I can't do that with the workers. The milkers need to be paid, and I don't have any idea how to do that. Your father always took care of that, and he didn't share with me. Since he's the boss, I didn't question it one bit."

Whitney had her hands on her hips. "As foreman, shouldn't you—"

"Whitney, please." Mama held up a hand. "No one is to blame. Your grandfather was a private man. He kept his business to himself—and it's no wonder after all his years in mining towns. But that's no reason to accuse John. He's done a wonderful job." She lifted her chin and took a breath. "We need to figure out something. Dr. Kingston is having to come out several times a week. The medicine he's prescribed is quite expensive." Mama glanced at each one of them. "He asked me earlier about paying his fees."

John's brow was furrowed. "The money that is coming in from all of our customers now could go toward the doctor's fees and the medicine, but that doesn't help us in the meantime to order supplies or pay the workers. Eventually there will be enough for everything, but that doesn't help us now." He frowned.

"Do you know how many workers we have and how many hours they've worked?" Mama tapped her fingers on the chair's arm.

"I was just making a list earlier today, but I left it in my room."

Mama looked away from John for a moment. "Whit, would you mind getting John's list while we talk?"

The look on Whitney's face was like she'd sucked on a pickle. "Sure." She turned to John. "Are you all right with me going into your room, Mr. Roselli?"

He waved a hand. "Of course, it's not a problem. I believe I left it on the little table under the window. It was two pages, if I recall."

That the man treated Whitney with such grace, even after all her little barbs about everything, amazed Madysen.

Whitney turned and left.

A long sigh left Mama's lips. "I'm sorry for all this. I hope Whitney hasn't offended you—she's just used to helping her grandfather run things. It isn't you. It's the situation, I'm sure. I wish I knew—"

"What's important"—Havyn cut off their mother—"is that we all work together to figure out how to keep the farm running and the workers compensated. And Granddad's doctor's bills paid. This doesn't have to all be on your shoulders, Mama."

"That's right, Mama. We're all in this together." Madysen watched her mother's face pale. Something hadn't been right with her lately. She'd been out of breath several times, even had several coughing fits. And she'd lost the color in her cheeks.

Mama nodded. "Thank you. I appreciate all of you . . . very much. John, please, what other thoughts do you have on all of this?"

"Well, since I don't know where he kept the money, I'm afraid I don't know what to say. I could go without a salary for a while. Since my basic needs are taken care of here. I wouldn't mind if we just wanted to keep track of it, and when Chuck recovers, he could pay me."

"That is quite a sacrifice, John. And we greatly appreciate it. I think maybe we should take you up on your offer, at least on a week-to-week basis, until we get things in hand." Mama patted her knee again and then stood up. "The girls and I can cut our spending to the barest of necessities. Then we will need to take matters into our own hands to keep the farm running. Papa never said anything about the farm being in dire straits or out of money. And if you look around, it's clear to see that it is quite successful. I just don't have any idea where he keeps the money."

"Would it be at the bank? Perhaps—as his daughter—you could go in and speak to the manager? See if there's any way to work with the funds until your father is coherent again?" John's furrowed brow displayed his concern. "Wait, I remember he told me he didn't think much of banks."

Mama shook her head. "Papa has never been fond of financial institutions of any kind. So I'm not sure he has much there. If any at all." She stood up and gripped her fingers together. A sure sign this was stressful for her. "This is all my fault. I haven't helped him like I should. I've been so focused on training you girls in music and your education that I've been perfectly content to just let him handle everything. And now I don't know what to do. How long will it take him to recover? Will the farm be able to make it? What if he never gets back to the man he was before?" She put a hand to her brow and rubbed it.

Watching her walk around the room, Madysen could only imagine herself in her mother's shoes. This was so difficult. Mama had been by Granddad's side since he'd first collapsed.

Havyn spoke up. "We'll take care of this, Mama. We will. Between us girls and John, I'm sure we can deal with the farm side of things. You just focus on helping Granddad get better."

"I agree." Madysen stood and went to wrap her arm around their mother's shoulders. "In fact, we've had an offer to sing and play at the Roadhouse every night—except Sundays, of course—and we have been bringing in a lot of tips from that. It could bring in a lot more money if we added four nights a week. I think we're all willing to do whatever we need to, to ensure that the workers get paid and that John can fulfill orders."

"Really?" Their mother's face relaxed a bit. "You'd do that?"

"If it's not too much to leave you alone every night?" This was their biggest concern: leaving Mama alone. What if something happened? What if *she* needed help? What if the worst happened, and Granddad died? She would be all alone. Of course John would be there, but it wouldn't be the same as having her girls.

"Oh, I'll be fine. I can't foresee there being any problems. Especially since Papa's not able to do much right now."

"John will be here," Madysen reminded her.

"I thought maybe John would drive you back and forth to the Roadhouse like your granddad used to." Mama looked at their foreman. "If you don't mind? I know that cuts your days short. I would feel better about them going into town."

"I could make two trips if things get too busy. Although, I'm sure you would rather I stay and be there for your daughters."

Their mother nodded. "Yes, I'd like that."

"But what if you need help?" The thought of Mama all alone made her heart ache. "Could we ask Amka to come and help you?"

The creases in Mama's forehead relaxed. "That's a wonderful idea. I'll ask her tomorrow." She lifted her chin. "But as soon as your grandfather starts to get well, I may need to keep John here with me to keep the cantankerous old man in line."

"Well then, John can just drop us off and pick us back up." Havyn gave a firm nod. "That way we'll have protection from those men who like to keep us lingering at the Roadhouse after our performances, and you can still have his help, if that's all right with John, of course." The way Havyn looked at their foreman made Madysen grin.

"It's not a problem. I already offered." His look back at Havyn left little doubt in her mind: He was smitten with her sister. When things weren't so stressful, she'd have to talk to Havyn about it.

Mama gave a smile. "I guess we have a plan, then. God is good."

Madysen's heart warmed. It was so wonderful how Mama was always able to see the positive, even if that seemed impossible at the moment.

"Well then." Madysen looked at Havyn. "The three of us girls will work each night at the Roadhouse after we've made sure that all of our chores are done around here."

John leaned back slightly in his chair. At least they had a bit of direction now. He didn't want Mrs. Powell to have to bear the burden of all this. It was overwhelming enough to him.

Mrs. Powell smoothed her skirt. "I know we probably still have a lot to discuss, but I find I'm quite weary. I think I'll go check on Papa and then probably just go to bed." She hugged Havyn, and then Madysen. "Please tell Whitney I've gone back to your granddad's room."

They'd set up a cot for her in her father's room, so hopefully she'd get some much-needed rest.

The room was silent for several moments after she left.

Madysen straightened up the cushions and Havyn walked toward him.

"Thank you, John. For all you're doing for our family." She laid a hand on his arm. "We can never repay you for your kindness."

"You're quite welcome." He laid his hand on top of hers, and as their eyes met, he wanted nothing more than to spend the rest of the night right there. With her.

Her cheeks tinged pink and she pulled away. "I'm going to make sure Mama has everything she needs. She looked exhausted. Good night, John."

"Good night." When she'd left, he slapped his hand on his thigh.

"You like her, don't you?" Madysen's voice broke through his thoughts.

"I . . ."

The youngest of the Powell women gave a light laugh. "It's all right. I'm not teasing you. I think it's great." She took a few steps closer to him. "And I won't say a word. I promise."

If Madysen had noticed, had everyone else? His feelings for Havyn were all a bit too new for him to even put into words. What could he say?

Madysen paused in the doorway and looked back at him. "By the way, thank you for sacrificing your salary for our family."

She'd no sooner left than Whitney stomped into the room. "Sacrificing your salary? So you can look like the hero?" She sneered. Her chin lifted, a fierce look in her eyes. "I need to talk to you. Right now." She turned on her heel.

What on earth? He reached out to put a hand on her arm. "What's wrong?"

She yanked her arm out of his grasp. "Not in here. As much as I want my family to know, now is not the time."

"All right." John followed her outside and around the corner of the house. What had he done now?

She held up a paper and his heart sank. The contract. "What is *this*?"

Shaking his head, he swiped a hand down his face. He'd forgotten about it when Whitney went to his room. "That is something we should talk to your grandfather about."

"No. I'm not waiting for that. I want to hear it from you. Is *that* why you're here? You want the farm, is that it?" She grimaced. "All this time . . . and to think, I was beginning to warm up to you. Thought you were here to help. I even was ridiculous enough to think that since you and Havyn seemed to like each other, that you'd be a nice addition to this family." Her voice rose in volume. "And then I find this!" She waved it in front of his face. "How *could* you?"

Words failed him. She was right to feel the way she did. Oh, why hadn't he insisted to Chuck that they destroy the infernal thing? Wait. Did she say she was warming up to him? That was news. She'd seemed as frosty to him as ever.

"Why aren't you saying anything?" The fire in her eyes was accompanied by tears.

Was she going to cry? "Whitney, I'm sorry. This contract was a request from your grandfather when I first got here. He wasn't feeling well and was afraid if something happened to him, you ladies wouldn't be taken care of. He didn't want anyone coming in and trying to steal the farm from you."

"Someone like you?"

He shook his head. "No. I came here because our grandfathers were dear friends. Did you know that they swore to each other to take care of the other's family if something happened to either of them?"

She narrowed her eyes.

"It's true. And I agreed to the contract, yes, because your grandfather pled with me to sign. So I did. Because of my own grandfather. But as soon as I started getting to know all of you, I told him I was uncomfortable with the arrangement. That I didn't need a contract to make sure nothing would be taken from you."

"How do I know you're telling the truth? All I have is your word, and I'm not sure I can trust that."

Several seconds passed as he weighed his words. "You don't know. Other than the fact that I haven't done anything dishonorable."

She tapped the paper against her hand and stared him down. Taking a step toward him, she studied him. "You've probably noticed that I'm not quite as trusting and forgiving as my sisters and mother. As the eldest, it's my job to take care of my sisters. To make sure they don't get hurt. Because it's happened before. I won't let it happen again." She moved back. "But because of everything our mother is going through, I'm not going to talk to her about this right now. Rest assured, though, I'll be talking to my sisters about it."

Havyn. How would she react? "I understand that. But would you allow me to tell them my side of the story?"

"I don't think that's going to matter much to them. Not once they read this." With that, she walked away.

John swallowed against the lump in his throat. This would change everything. And to think that he'd really felt like he and Havyn had a chance.

What would she think now?

FIFTEEN

T here's something I need to tell you both."

Havyn frowned. Whitney sounded so serious. That couldn't be good. A sinking feeling in her stomach didn't help matters. "What's going on?"

"And why did you bring us out to the dog kennel?" Madysen waved an arm toward the yipping puppies. "You *never* want anyone else out here with your dogs."

"That's exactly why I brought you out here. So no one else would hear."

Whit wasn't one for dramatics. That was Madysen's area of expertise. "All right, then. Now you've really got me worried."

Whitney pulled a piece of paper from her apron pocket. "I found this when I went to John's room."

Havyn reached for it. Her heart sped up. Why did Whit look like it was something ominous? As she opened it up, Madysen leaned in beside her.

At the bottom of the page were two signatures. One, her grandfather's. The other, John's. She went back to the top of the page and started reading.

As the words sank in, she forced herself to keep breathing. And not cry. It *couldn't* be what it looked like . . . could it? The dogs barked and whined around her. Cows lowed in the distance. Everything was normal. Except her world. It felt like it'd been tipped.

Madysen straightened up beside her. "So what's got you all upset about this, Whit?"

The look on Whitney's face went from angry to incredulous. She stuck her chin forward. "Don't you get it? John's here so he can get the farm. By marrying one of us."

Havyn had no words. She just stared at her sisters.

Madysen's brow furrowed. "It's not as bad as all that. This clearly states that Granddad put this agreement on paper so that we would be protected. See?" Madysen leaned back in and pointed to a line.

"I saw that"—Whitney pointed to another line—"but it *also* states that John is to marry one of us, and then *he* will own the farm."

Like a dog with a bone, Whitney wasn't going to let this go.

"Oh." Madysen was quiet for a moment. Then she shrugged. "But it's not like any of us were going to inherit it anyway. We're women. And don't you *want* to get married one day? I know I do. And I don't exactly plan on staying here."

Havyn whipped her attention full-on to her younger sister. "Wait . . . *what*? You don't want to stay?"

"No . . . I mean, I love you guys. But I dream of seeing other places. Traveling. Playing the cello on a bigger stage than the Roadhouse in Nome, Alaska." Her voice softened the longer she went on. "I didn't mean to hurt you."

Tears slipped down Havyn's cheeks. Maddy leaving? It

broke her heart. Not to mention the contract that was still in her hands. Why, oh *why* did Whitney have to tell her about that awful thing?

Whitney stepped closer to them. Hands on her hips, she was back in older-sister-take-charge mode. "The real problem here is John. We can talk about your dreams later, Maddy, but I think we need to admit that John needs to go. He's not here for us. Or for Granddad. Or . . ." She laid a hand on Havyn's arm. "Even for you, Havyn. He's here for the farm."

Madysen put her hands on her hips too. "That's where you're wrong, Whit. I've seen the way he looks at Havyn. He cares about her. He cares about all of us, and I refuse to believe anything different." She stood with her jaw set. "Besides, you didn't hear him offer to sacrifice his own salary so that we could pay the workers. I doubt a man that was only interested in taking the farm from us would do something like that."

"Maddy—"

"I'm not finished. The contract is in place, whether you like it or not. I believe Granddad drew it up because he was worried about us if something happened to him. I've seen nothing out of John but good. So don't be so quick to judge him."

Whitney paced a few steps to the left and then returned. Her gaze hit Havyn like a branding iron to her soul. "Why are you so quiet, Havyn? Why aren't you defending John, like Maddy? We've all noticed the looks and sparks between you two. If you fancy him, then why aren't you saying anything?"

Heart pounding, she swallowed. "Because . . . I don't know what to say."

"That's a bad excuse and you know it." Whitney pushed for a reaction.

Like she always did.

"No . . . it's not. I'm thinking about it. I've read the contract. And I refuse to charge John with an offense before I've heard his side of the story."

Whitney narrowed her eyes. "Fine. Go talk to him, then. He's not going to deny it."

"Of course he's not going to deny it—his signature is on the page." Did Whit think she was stupid? Heat crept up her neck, but now was not the time to lose her temper. "But you're both right . . . I like John. I have for a while now. I just don't know what to do with this, and I don't intend to overreact or lose my temper before I know the facts."

Whitney's eyes sparked.

Uh-oh.

"I'm not overreacting or losing my temper, and I resent the notion that you think that! I'm not attacking John just because you like him—"

Havyn stopped her cold. "No. But you *are* attacking him."

Her older sister came close and took her hands. The contract crinkled. This time her voice was calm. "Only because I care about you. And I care about this farm."

Havyn squeezed her sister's hands. "We all do, Whit, but Granddad obviously knew what he was doing. I think you're still upset that he didn't put you in charge. Maybe that's why you're attacking John."

Whitney pulled her hands free. "Maybe you're too blinded by your feelings to see the truth."

"Maybe you both need to stop before you say things that you'll regret." Madysen placed herself between Havyn and Whitney. "We need to pray for guidance on this matter.

If Havyn wants to talk to John, then she has that right. But we don't need to get rid of him. Granddad hired him. And obviously saw the need to legally protect us with that contract. So until he wakes up, we shouldn't override his decisions. This is *his* farm and we would do well to remember that."

Whitney stomped toward her dogs. "But what if he doesn't wake up, Maddy?" The dogs' yipping grew to a roar and they started jumping and trying to get her attention. "*One* of us has to think clearly. I don't want this man stealing the farm that is rightfully ours!"

Was that John's intention? No. He didn't come here with any knowledge of the farm. There had to be another explanation.

There *had* to be.

Or her heart would shred into a million pieces.

An entire day had passed and John hadn't spoken to any of the Powell women. Not that they had avoided him, but he'd made sure to give them plenty of space. He'd rummaged around in the kitchen when they weren't around and found enough leftovers to get by. Then he'd worked. A lot. And waited for the moment when Havyn would give him a look that showed him she knew.

So far, it hadn't happened.

And that was torture!

What if she despised him for what he'd done?

John shook his head. Best to keep his mind on the work. Though he still hadn't paid the workers, several of the native workers had asked for time off. It was the traditional period for seal hunting, and although the influx of people

to the area had caused the native men to have to go farther
to find the animals, they still needed time to stock up their
families' food supplies.

Now was as good a time as any to give them what they
asked for. Especially with the financial state of things.

Earlier, he'd worked up a schedule to allow for the men to
alternate their hunts. That would allow him to get the milking done and save the farm some money at the same time.
Next the salmon would be running, and he could offer the
same kind of schedule.

Whitney had made it clear they would need salmon for
her dogs, as well as for their own food supplies. Not that she
would be happy if *he* did anything to help her.

The Powell sisters' different personalities were a wonder.
Where one was fiercely independent, another was beautifully merciful.

They might look a good deal alike, but they were each
unique. With strong personalities, and a million good quali-
ties. Any man would be blessed to partner with one of them.
The fact that Chuck had offered the contract to him was
a great compliment, but John doubted that the Powell sisters saw it that way. Or that they realized their value. And
now . . .

He might not ever have the chance to show them. Especially Havyn.

Enough! He grabbed a shovel.

With the first two workers gone on their hunt, John had
to muck out the milking barn. And it was quite a job. The
backbreaking work took hours that he normally would have
had for the long list of other things he needed to do.

Unfortunately, all that work gave him too much time to
think.

About Havyn.

What she was doing? Had Whitney told her sisters about the contract, as she'd threatened? What must they all think of him now?

Lord, should I have not signed that contract? Was it the wrong decision? I didn't want to hurt anyone. I didn't come here to stay. You know that. But these women don't. And I'm afraid they'll hate me.

Especially Havyn.

The only thing that encouraged him this morning was the fact that Mrs. Powell told him Chuck had opened his eyes for a bit. There still didn't seem to be any communication or movement, but every little bit had to count. Perhaps the man could make a full recovery. But what if he didn't? Not only that, but with the shortage of workers, John could no longer help Mrs. Powell care for her father's private needs. No doubt that created difficulties for the poor woman.

As he shook his head of the doubts and gloomy thoughts, his mind drifted back to Havyn. She'd been a light in his life. Ever since their little chat, he'd found her singing to her chickens in the afternoons. At least . . . until today.

Standing up straight, he stretched out his back. This job was grueling. Maybe he could reassign this chore to one of the other workers. Not that he was afraid of hard work, but at this rate, he was working about sixteen hours a day. Add in the time it took to eat and then to get cleaned up at the end of the day, and it was time to go to bed so he could start over again the next day.

Wasn't a good schedule for getting to know someone. Much less, to court someone. Not that Havyn felt the same way that he did. At least, not anymore.

What was he thinking? It was awfully selfish of him to even have thoughts about her at a time like this. So why couldn't he get her off his mind?

"John?" Mrs. Powell's voice interrupted his thoughts.

He strode to the entrance of the barn. "How may I help you?"

"I wanted to speak to you, and the girls are with Papa at the moment, singing to him, hoping that it will help him to wake up again."

"You don't get much time to yourself right now." He leaned on the shovel he'd been using and studied her. She looked . . . pale. "I'm sure it's difficult to carry the burden of caring for a loved one by yourself." Even though Whitney said she didn't want to burden her mother by sharing about the contract, there was a chance she'd told her anyway. "What do you need to speak to me about? Is everything all right?"

She crossed her arms over her chest and began to walk around the front of the barn. "Yes. I mean, they're not because Papa's laid up, but you know what I mean. My intent was to thank you for coming at the time when you did. Had you not been here when he collapsed . . ." She choked on the last word. "I'm sorry. But had you not been there, I don't know what we would have done. It's just like God supplying the ram for Abraham and Isaac. Not that we want to sacrifice you." She shook her head. "I'm making a mess of this because I'm so weary. The girls are wonderful at helping around the farm—I know you know that—but they couldn't do the job that you are doing right now. No matter what Whitney thinks she's capable of." A smile crossed the woman's face. "We're a stubborn lot. And my girls are willing to do whatever it takes, but I hope you understand . . ."

"Ma'am, there's no need to thank me, nor do you have to explain. It's an honor to work on this farm. I've got a great deal of respect for your father. *And* for each of your daughters."

She reached out and touched his arm. "John. Please. Let me thank you. Things haven't run this smoothly since Papa was much younger. What I'm trying to say is that I haven't had to worry about things getting done. The finances are a bit difficult to deal with, but you have helped so much." This time she started crying. In earnest.

Sobs shook her shoulders.

What should he do? How did he comfort a woman who was unsure whether her father—her rock—would live or die? "Mrs. Powell. I'm sorry. I wish I could do more."

"You've done a lot already, John. That's what I'm trying to say—even though I'm flubbing it up." She pulled a hankie from the waist of her skirt and dabbed at her eyes and cheeks. "All of this was to say thank-you. That's it. I just wanted you to know how much we appreciate you, and Papa told me several times that he thought of you as family."

That made John smile. "Thank you. That means a great deal. Nonno talked of Mr. Bundrant quite often. Apparently they were each other's sanity while they worked in the mines in Cripple Creek. I'm just sad that I never had the chance to meet any of you before now."

"It's been a privilege to have you here. I hope you know that." She gave him a watery smile. "I'm sure this hasn't been easy on you either. Being away from your home."

"Oh, that's no difficulty at all. For years my only family was my grandpa. He sent me here, and I came. Then your father hired me on, and I'm feeling like this is home now." As soon as the words left his mouth, he froze.

He *meant* that. Nome *had* begun to feel like home. It was wonderful—and also like a stab to the heart. Because if he couldn't stay . . . if he had to leave Havyn . . . would anyplace ever be home again?

"That eases this mother's heart, knowing that you are comfortable here." The dark circles under her eyes showed her weariness. "I know it's been a lot of work, and it will probably continue to be that way for a good while, but thank you."

He focused on her. "You're most welcome."

She turned to go and then stopped. Turning back, she tilted her head and smiled again. "You're a good man, John. You didn't have to sacrifice your salary either, but you did. You know, it wouldn't bother me at all if you took a liking to one of my girls. It's a privilege to have you be part of our family."

Another stabbing pain. Two days ago, those words would have made his heart soar. But now? He had no response for her other than a slight nod. Did she know that he had feelings for Havyn? Could it be that obvious? Madysen obviously noticed.

No. He couldn't torture himself anymore with these thoughts. When she left, he threw himself back into his work and tried to think of anything else.

An hour later, John heard approaching footsteps. No. Running . . .

Someone was running. Something was wrong.

John set the shovel down and went to the door. He looked toward the sound and saw Havyn, her hair flying out behind her as she ran toward the barn.

"John! Please, help!"

"What's wrong?" He ran toward her.

"It's my chickens . . ." She stopped and he caught up with her. Tears stained her cheeks.

"What's happened?"

"There's a whole group of them . . . dead!"

Sixteen

Tears clogged Havyn's throat as she grabbed John's hand and dragged him to the chicken yard. She didn't care about any stupid contract! He was the only one who could help her right now. She sniffed and sniffed, but her nose was stuffed from all the crying.

As they reached the gate, she opened it and led him through.

It probably wasn't appropriate to hold on to a man's hand, but she couldn't help it. He had been so supportive of her love for her chickens.

When they reached the northeast corner of the fenced-in chicken yard, she couldn't help but gulp again at the sight. "Look. I don't know what happened. But it's too awful to even put into words."

"Oh, Havyn . . ." He scanned the scene. "I'm so sorry."

She followed his gaze. She didn't want to look, but she couldn't help it. Because a tiny piece of her mind said she might have dreamed it all up. But no.

Chicken feathers were strewn about the area. Deep red splotches stained the dirt.

John squeezed her hand and gave her a sad but reassuring look. "Wait here for a minute?"

"Sure." She swallowed hard.

When he let go of her hand, she wanted to grab his hand again, but stopped herself.

John took several steps forward and crouched to look at what was left behind.

Havyn chewed on the edge of her thumbnail. Could he tell what happened? The rest of the chickens wouldn't be in danger, would they?

A few moments later, he stood and walked to another area.

For the next several minutes he continued his perusal, and then he walked back toward her. "I hate to say it, Havyn, but I think a predator made it over the fence. Which is quite the feat, because your grandfather built it pretty high."

"I know. That was my thought as well, and it just breaks my heart."

"Unless . . ."

"Unless what?"

He glanced up at the sky. "It could have been several hawks. I've seen some large ones around here lately. If they found a good roost up in one of those trees over there and watched the chickens for a while, they could have swooped in and done quite a bit of damage. How many chickens are missing?"

"Twenty-seven hens." Even giving voice to the number made her think of each one of her pets.

"That's a lot for hawks." John rubbed his chin. Then he put his hands on his hips and surveyed the whole area. "Why don't we check the fence line and see if we've missed something."

She nodded and followed him, her heart breaking with every pile of feathers they passed. She knew which chicken they belonged to. Maybe Mama was right when she said Havyn shouldn't get so attached to her chickens. But she loved them so much!

Why did love have to hurt like this?

For half an hour, they checked the entire fence. Well, to be truthful, John checked the fence. Havyn simply followed him around in a daze, hoping and praying they could fix whatever happened so it couldn't happen again.

"Havyn, look!" John's voice penetrated her fog.

Her gaze followed where he pointed and she saw a gap in the chicken wire. "Could an animal have done that?"

He was crouched down in front of the hole, his elbows on his knees. Shaking his head, he let out a breath. "I don't know. This looks like it was deliberately pulled up. But why?"

"So someone could steal my chickens?" Her voice squeaked. "But who would *do* such a thing?"

John shrugged. "Starving people might have done this to grab a chicken or two, but it looks like they opened it up for other predators. And not the human kind."

The thought made her shiver.

He walked back over to her side. "Are you all right?"

"No." She flung herself into his arms and hung on tight. "It's not going to be all right for a long time. I love my chickens!" She cried into his shoulder.

First Granddad and now this.

John stiffened, but after a moment, he wrapped an arm around her. "I know you love them. Believe me, we all know."

She pulled back and wiped at her face. "But don't you see? Now we'll be down in egg production, and we need every little bit that we can muster to pay for Granddad's medicine and to keep this place running."

"Aw, Havyn. We'll figure something out. I know how devastating this must be. Don't you worry about the money. God is going to take care of us, and He knows how much this hurts you."

"I know He does, but what if it happens again?"

"It's not going to. At least not like this. I'll fix that gap right now, and I'll try to get creative with other ways to keep predators out."

He gazed down at her, and she couldn't stop staring. His dark brown eyes had flecks of gold in them. And the look in those depths . . .

Her knees suddenly seemed . . . weak. "Thank you, John." Cheeks warming, she stepped back. What on earth should she do with these feelings John caused inside her?

She looked down at the ground. "I guess I'll need to clean up this mess tomorrow. I'm sure the other chickens will be traumatized for some time."

John nodded. "Why don't I fence in a smaller area for a bit? To help them feel safer. They'll huddle up together right now anyway."

"Oh, could you? That's a great idea." Then she shook her head. "I can't ask that of you, John. You've got entirely too much on your plate as it is. Besides, I know how to build a fence. Granddad taught me. So let me do this. I'll get started on it tomorrow."

"Are you sure?"

Glancing at his eyes again, she wanted to beg him to help her. Not because she needed his help, but because she *needed* his companionship. Every waking moment.

Then reality settled in. She couldn't ask any more of him. That would be selfish. What if she was the only one who had these feelings? What if Whitney was right, and John just

202

wanted the farm and not her? "Yes, I'm sure. But thank you for offering." She started back toward the house.

He stepped in pace beside her. "You're welcome."

"I guess I better break the news to my family."

"That's probably a good idea."

"I just wish they understood."

Out of the corner of her eye, she saw him shove his hands into his pockets.

"It's one of the things I admire about you," he said, then cleared his throat.

"What?"

"How much you care for your chickens. And all the little stories that you tell at dinner about them." He opened the gate for her. "You're one special lady, Miss Havyn Powell."

While her heart wanted to soar, a niggling at the back of her mind wouldn't leave her alone. Why was he here? Why had he signed that contract?

Why was it that, out of everyone here, she'd run to *John* first when she'd found the massacre?

She picked up her pace and almost ran to the house. Her emotions were all over the place. She didn't know what to think or feel.

God, why are You doing this to me?

Geoffrey arranged the new shipment of medications on the shelves in the cabinet. Amazing how they all looked almost like the real thing. Reynolds was good, he'd give him that.

"I see you received the next order."

Speak of the devil. Why did the man always do that? "Do you *not* understand the concept of knocking, Judas?"

"Watch your tone, Dr. Kingston." The man arched his brows and clasped his hands behind him. Pacing the room, he looked around. Pulled a book off a shelf, thumbed through it, put it back. Clasped his hands again.

"Is there something I can do for you?"

"I simply came for an update."

"On what?"

"Your patients. Our partnership." Judas narrowed his eyes. "How *are* your patients?"

Was he always going to have to do this? This wasn't why he came here. . . . "They're doing fine. Thank you for asking."

"Business is going well?"

"Yes. Quite well."

"I hear the new elixir is popular." Judas looked at the medicines on the shelf.

"Yes." Was Reynolds expecting praise for ordering stuff that was nothing more than sugar, alcohol, and cherry bark?

"Why don't you sound more . . . congenial about our arrangement? Aren't you making plenty of money?" The man's smooth words had an edge to them.

Geoffrey emptied the box. "It's been a long day. I apologize."

"Not a problem." Reynolds stuck his hands in his suit pockets and sat on the settee that was for the waiting patients. "I'm hoping to speak to you on a matter."

"Oh?" He sat in his chair and glanced around the room. He'd always wanted an office where he felt like a real doctor. Someone out to heal the sick and do good.

"How is Chuck Bundrant doing?"

"He's progressing." Geoffrey folded his hands in his lap.

"That's it?"

"Judas, I'm not supposed to share details about any of my patients and you know that. Or you should."

Leaning forward, Reynolds propped his elbows on his knees. "But that's not how we are going to do things. We have an agreement. You do what I ask, I don't tell anyone about who you really are."

Geoffrey couldn't change the past. Nor could he change what this man knew. Better make the best of the situation and play nice. "He had another bout of apoplexy, but he is recovering."

"And Mrs. Powell?"

"What about her?"

"Hasn't she been seeing you?"

Did the man know everything? "I'm surprised you know that, but yes."

"What ails her?"

"Asthma." Unable to sit still, he stood and went to the shelves and pretended to rearrange the books. "Why are you so interested?"

"Everything about that family interests me."

Something in the way he said it made Geoffrey's skin crawl. The Powell women were so sweet. What was Judas after?

"Just keep me apprised. That's all I ask." Reynolds stood and headed to the door.

All he asked. Right. "I'll do my best."

"Good, good. I'm looking forward to a long and prosperous partnership, Dr. Kingston." He opened the door and looked over his shoulder. "Oh, how's the whooping cough issue?"

"Not good, I'm afraid. I've got five cases. One pretty severe."

"Well, then. Let's hope for the best." With that, Reynolds exited.

Geoffrey walked over to the door and locked it. At least

for a few minutes, he needed silence. A visit from Judas always made him feel like he should wash his hands. What was the man up to?

No. He didn't care. He was already in too deep with Judas Reynolds as it was. So this was the life he'd come to Nome for? Shaking his head, he went to pour himself a strong drink.

As long as nobody died for a while, he'd be fine.

SEVENTEEN

Havyn stood in the parlor with her sisters. They were gathered at the grand piano, Havyn standing, her sisters sitting on the piano bench.

Madysen played a few notes on the upper keys. "Up for a duet, Whit?"

Their older sister closed the lid. "No. I'm sorry. In fact, the reason I asked you all to come in here is quite serious."

Havyn grimaced. Oh, not another serious conversation. Too much of late was heavy and downright depressing. "Please don't hound me about John and the contract. The more I think about it, the more I'm inclined to think that Granddad was smart in doing what he did—"

Whit held up a hand. "It's not about that. And Havyn, I'm really sorry about the chickens. I know how much they mean to you. That's got to be devastating."

Tears stung Havyn's eyes. "Thank you, Whitney. But I know this isn't about me." She lifted her chin. "Go on."

Her older sister's shoulders rose and then fell. "It's about Mama."

Madysen put a hand to her throat. "What is it?"

"I don't know. But she hasn't been breathing well lately. I think something is seriously wrong."

No! "Have you asked her about it?"

Whitney pursed her lips—a sure sign she was struggling—and grabbed on to Madysen's hand. "I asked her once . . . she snapped at me and said she would not discuss it. That nothing was wrong with her and our focus should be on the farm and praying for Granddad."

"It must be bad." Maddy's voice squeaked. "Mama doesn't ever hide anything from us."

Whit paused before replying. "Let's not jump to conclusions. I just thought that we all needed to be aware. See what we can watch for, how else we can help her . . . I don't know, but I know something isn't right." Whit sounded weary too. "She has an interesting odor to her nowadays . . . some strange herbs. But maybe that's something she's been using for Granddad? I don't know. . . ."

"Thanks for bringing us in on it. We needed to know." Havyn walked behind her sisters and squeezed their shoulders. "Let's each find a spot in the room to get down on our knees and pray. Since we've got to leave for the Roadhouse in less than an hour, it would do us all good to quiet ourselves before the Lord and cast our burdens on Him." Havyn wasn't sure where the calm in her voice came from, but she was thankful for the words being laid on her heart.

They dispersed to different parts of the room. Whit stayed at the piano bench. Madysen went to the fireplace. Havyn walked over to a large window and let her gaze roam the horizon.

Lord, it hurts. Granddad, John, the chickens, and now Mama. But I know You, as my heavenly Father, are waiting for me with open arms. So I come to You now with a heavy heart . . . a heart that feels broken by all of this. . . .

She fell to her knees and let the tears fall. *God, I don't know what to do. I don't know how to see what You have for me. What can we do for Mama? What can we do for Granddad? I have so many questions, and so much hurt. I need Your strength, Your wisdom, and Your mercy. Help us, Lord. Please. Help us to seek You.*

Her heart quieted.

God knew. He understood better than anyone what was going on. So she rested in the comfort that He would carry them through. No matter what they might face.

He *would* see them through.

Friday nights at the Roadhouse were as exhilarating to Havyn as they were exhausting. The crowds were the largest on Friday and Saturday evenings, with standing room only and men bumping into one another all over the place, trying to get as close as they could to the stage.

But even as exhausted as she felt from giving her all for a few hours straight, performing lifted her spirits in a way nothing else seemed to. Especially after a day like today.

As she prepared for bed, she couldn't help thinking about their handsome foreman. If things were different, and Granddad was on his feet, she'd have more time with John. Of course, if Granddad were well, then she could ask him about the contract and clear it up once and for all. But for now, she would have to settle for working with John, seeing each other at meals, and the occasional times he could get away to stay for a performance at the Roadhouse.

Whitney seemed to be over her initial anger at John, but how long would that last? Until they heard the truth from their grandfather's lips, Whit would be untrusting. So the question was, could *Havyn* trust him? Or would she always doubt? And how was she to know if he even cared about her?

A slight tapping made her stop in the middle of her room and listen. Was she imagining things, or was that someone at her door?

Tap tap tap.

It was definitely a knock. Throwing her dressing gown over her nightgown, she went to the door and opened it a crack.

Madysen stood there fully dressed, eyes teary, cheeks flushed, and a lantern in her hand.

"What is going on?"

Her little sister pushed her way into the room. "I need your help. And please, keep your voice down. I don't want to wake Whit or Mama."

Havyn led her to her bed and they sat on the edge. "Of course. What do you need?"

"Sheep."

She closed her eyes and shook her head. "I'm sorry. Did you say . . . sheep?"

"Yes."

"All right." Havyn swallowed. What sheep had to do with anything had her stumped. "Would you mind explaining?"

Her younger sister scrunched her face up. "Do you know Old Fred?"

"You mean Old Fred in town? The skinny man who hangs out at a different saloon every night?"

"Yes. Well, he died of the whooping cough yesterday."

It didn't surprise Havyn that Madysen was sad about an old man dying. But still. They hardly knew him. At least, Havyn didn't. "I'm so sorry. I know how much you hate loss. Did you know him at all?"

"No. Not a bit." She sniffed and wiped at her eyes and nose.

"Then, I guess I don't understand. What's got you so upset?"

Her sister tilted her head. Uh-oh. A clear sign she wanted something big. "Fred is dead. He ordered sheep from Mr. Reynolds. Said he was going to start a sheep farm. And at the Roadhouse tonight, I overheard Mr. Reynolds say that since the old man died, he was going to sell the animals to the local restaurants to be slaughtered." She grabbed Havyn's hands. "Don't you see? We have to save those sheep!"

Havyn formed an *o* with her lips and gave a slow nod. "Now I understand. But what exactly is your plan?"

"I want to bring the sheep here."

What? Havyn tried to keep the shock from her face, but she couldn't help it. "And exactly *how* will we do that?"

"We're going to herd them here. I know where Mr. Reynolds has them penned up."

"But, Maddy, that's stealing."

Her little sister stood and stomped her foot. Her whispered words rose in volume. "We know Mr. Reynolds. He's a good man. If we tell him later what we did and show him how good we are at taking care of them, I'm sure we can figure out how to pay him for them later. I doubt he wants to see them slaughtered."

"Maddy, I don't think this is a good idea. Why don't we just ask him for them?"

"We can't! He's got someone picking them up first thing tomorrow."

Havyn looked at the clock. It was far too late to pay a visit to Mr. Reynolds tonight, no matter how fond he was of them. She chewed on her lip. "Perhaps you're correct. I mean,

Judas Reynolds has been a friend of our family for a long time. And you're sure this is the only way to save the sheep?"

Maddy nodded.

"I'll need to get dressed, but I'm assuming you have a plan to get them here? Do you know anything about herding sheep?"

"Oh, *thank you*, Havyn!" Maddy threw herself at Havyn and hugged her. "Look, I've got my pockets filled with grain."

"And that's going to work . . . how exactly?"

"I think so. At least, I hope so. I'll drop little bits here and there to get them to follow. I just know that we have to save those sheep. I kept thinking about Rahab and how she lied to rescue the spies in the Old Testament. We're rescuing these sheep just like Rahab."

Havyn tried not to laugh at her sister's train of thought. Shaking her head, she threw on a work dress and shawl. "All right. You do realize it's going to take us forever to herd sheep all the way out here to the farm."

"Probably a couple hours?"

"At least." Havyn sighed. "We each better grab a rifle. We'll be prime bait herding a bunch of tasty treats for predators."

Madysen's eyes widened. "I hadn't thought of that."

"Well, you should have. But now we'll just have to deal with it." Havyn cast a longing glance at her bed, then turned back to Maddy. "So since I'm going to lose sleep tonight over these sheep, I suggest you come up with a plan for what we are going to tell Mama tomorrow about why we are exhausted and falling asleep in our oatmeal."

They left her room and tiptoed down the hallway and out of the house. The twilight offered plenty of light to see where they were going. Thank the good Lord it was summer and not pitch black.

Once they were outside, Madysen linked arms with her sister and whispered, "I'll just tell them that I tried counting sheep and it didn't work. . . ."

Havyn put her free hand to her forehead. "Oh, ha ha. I think you need to come up with something better than that."

"Well, at least it's partially true."

"Keep trying, Maddy. It's going to be a long night."

Two hours later, they were covered in mud and still had more than halfway to go. The sheep kept wanting to run in circles around them. One would stop, and they all would stop. Then Madysen would offer handfuls of grain to those nearest and they'd start moving forward as she walked away.

Why had she agreed to help Madysen with this?

Baaaaah!

Another sheep decided it was time to run in a circle, and off they went, circling the sisters. Jumping and running.

Baaaah! Baaaah!

Exasperated and more tired than she'd been in a long time, Havyn finally threw up one of her hands and gave Madysen a stern look. "This is not working."

Maddy put her hands on her hips. "Well, what do you suggest? It's not like I'm an expert sheepherder over here. And if you haven't noticed, they're a lot faster than I expected."

"What did you expect? That they would be like cows and mosey their way along?"

Her sister's eyes narrowed. "Don't get all snippety at me. Just because you get grumpy when you don't get your beauty sleep doesn't mean that you should take it out on me. We're doing this for the sheep, remember?"

"Oh, believe me. I remember." Havyn took the strap of her rifle and put it over her shoulder, then stomped off toward a tree, mumbling under her breath the whole time. "Dumb sheep. They just go wherever they please, following the leader, and making noise as they go along."

Picking up two large sticks off the ground, she realized what she'd just said. It was all true. On top of that, they smelled. And they bit too. If she weren't so agitated and tired, she'd actually be amused at the thought that God used sheep as an example of people several times in the Bible.

Wasn't that the truth? Stinky, dumb biters. Yep, that pretty much summed up humans. In their flesh, they tended to treat one another that way.

She took a moment to watch the sheep as they circled her sister.

They hadn't been herding the sheep. The sheep had been a group of childlike, chaotic, wild followers without a leader.

A leader.

Hey . . . wasn't there something from a Sunday School class when she was little about that? One sheep in the flock wore a bell around its neck and was called the bellwether. If the bellwether went astray, the entire flock went astray because they followed the leader. The teacher used this to teach them that positions of leadership were important, and God held leaders at a higher accountability.

Now Havyn studied the sheep in earnest. One in particular seemed to hold the attention of the others. When she stopped, the others stopped. When she went left, the rest of them followed. Could it be? Was this sheep the leader?

"I wish we had a bell."

"What?" Madysen fought to keep a sheep's nose out of her pocket.

"I said, I wish we had a bell. I think that one sheep is the leader. Have you noticed how the others tend to follow her?"

"I haven't noticed much of anything but sheep muzzles and bleating."

Havyn went back to her sister. "How much grain do you have left?"

"One whole pocket full."

"Good, because I have a plan."

"Great, I'm exhausted."

"Well, you're the most important part of the plan, so don't give up on me."

"I'm not sure I like the sound of this."

Havyn pulled a face at her sister. "I didn't like the idea of stealing a flock of sheep in the middle of the night either, yet here I am."

Madysen nodded. "Point taken. What do you want me to do?"

"If this sheep is the leader, as she appears to be, we only need to make sure *she* keeps following you. Keep giving her the grain—no one else. Instead of pushing her away because of her greed like we were doing, we need to let her lead."

"Do you really suppose it will work?" Madysen gazed down at the sheep that was even now nudging her pocket.

"I don't think we have much of a choice but to try it. I believe this will give the leader reason to follow you, and the rest of the sheep will follow the leader. I'll bring up the rear to encourage any stragglers." She waved the sticks.

Maddy smiled. "I like how you think."

"Good. Let's get these sheep home. Preferably before the family wakes up."

EIGHTEEN

Splashing water on his face from the basin by his bed, John worked the sleepy fog out of his mind. After he'd gotten back from the Roadhouse last night, he'd still had chores to do in the milking barn. But it had been worth sacrificing a bit of sleep to hear Havyn sing again.

Well, truth be told, he had been able to hear all of the Powell girls sing, but his attention had been on one particular sister. Just thinking of her made him smile.

A knock on his door made John jump. No one ever came to his room. Except for Chuck. And it couldn't be him.

He grabbed a towel and dried off his face and neck as he went to the door.

"Hello?" He pulled it open, and his eyes weren't quite prepared for the sight. "Havyn? Are you all right?" Her hair was in a mass of messy waves strewn about her shoulders. Mud and what appeared to be a few dead leaves dulled the deep red color. Her dress was also covered in mud and something that didn't smell too ladylike. Even in that state, she was beautiful.

"I'm fine. But I need your help."

He nodded. "Of course. What can I do?" Did he hear the bleating of sheep?

A wince crossed her face. "Madysen overheard Judas Reynolds talking last night. Apparently Old Fred died of the whooping cough. Fred had ordered sheep from Judas. I have no idea why." Her shoulders lifted as she went on. "But since Fred was dead, Judas said he had no choice but to sell the sheep to the restaurants to be butchered. Madysen couldn't stand the thought of that. Why, I don't know. She doesn't seem to mind when we eat a pig or one of the cows. But apparently, she has a soft spot for sheep now."

She spoke so fast, John had a hard time keeping up.

"Last night she came to my room and somehow convinced me that we needed to go get the sheep and herd them here." Havyn held up a hand. "And before you scold me and say that's stealing, I already know that. I told her as much, but I must have been too tired to think straight."

He opened his mouth to speak, but she beat him to it.

"So now, we have spent the entire night herding a bunch of crazy sheep back to this farm. Sheep that don't belong to us. And we have to tell Judas before he finds out and comes to arrest us. *And* we have to convince him to let us buy them from him." She lifted her hands in the air and then let them fall again. "I give up. I'm way too tired to think straight."

He blinked several times to make sure she was finished. "So you'd like me to go speak with Judas?"

"No . . . well, maybe. I don't know. But I had an idea. If we have a plan in place for how we intend to increase profits with these sheep, then when we tell Mama and Whitney in a few minutes, hopefully they won't go through the roof."

"Ah, I see. And do you have a plan?"

She cringed and squinted at him. "You said you could

218

make mozzarella in your sleep. I was kinda hoping that you would teach us how to make cheese. And then perhaps we could all learn how to make sheep's milk cheese too?"

The idea wasn't a bad one. With all the butter, cream, and milk they sold, they'd had a lot of requests for cheese. No one else in Nome made cheese, so the prices were dear for it at the mercantiles. A local cheese producer would be ideal. But it was also a lot of work. Which meant they would need to hire more people. And pay more people. But he'd think about that later. "I think you're onto something brilliant. Of course I'll help."

She let out a sigh. "Thank you. I didn't know where else to turn. I just knew we needed to start bringing in more money right away. And now somehow we have to pay Judas . . ."

"Don't worry about it. We've got a plan."

A smile lit up her face. "Thank you again." She looked down at herself. "I better go get cleaned up before Mama sees this. It will be hard enough telling her about the sheep." She turned to go and then turned back. "Do you think you could go with me to see Judas? As soon as possible? That might help us manage the situation. Then we can come back . . . and I'll break the news to Mama and Whitney."

"I'd be happy to." The fact that she had come to him encouraged him. Maybe he could still win her heart after all.

An hour later, he and Havyn stood in front of Judas Reynolds's massive desk. The man sat in a fine leather chair and appeared to be considering all that they'd told him. His expression softened and he shook his head. "And you say, it was young Madysen that concocted this little scheme?"

Havyn took a step closer to John. Like she needed—wanted—him by her side. "I'm so sorry, Mr. Reynolds. Yes.

She overheard you talking about the sheep last night, and you know her soft heart. Gracious, you've known us for many years now—remember that stray dog she tried to convince you to keep? Anyway, I don't wish to take advantage of a longtime friendship, but please, will you work with us on a payment plan to purchase the flock?"

John wouldn't have been able to resist Havyn's passionate plea. Now if only Mr. Reynolds would agree.

The shipping owner laughed. "I'm so glad you came to me. This morning, I thought I'd been robbed. Now . . . there's no need to plead. You should know that I would do anything for your family. It doesn't surprise me at all that one of you sweet Powell girls would want to rescue the sheep from being slaughtered. What do you have in mind?"

"Is there a way to pay a little each month? With Granddad ill, we need to be wise with our finances." Havyn fidgeted with her hands.

"Yes, I can appreciate that." Reynolds stood from behind the desk. He was a tall and powerful-looking man. And not just in stature. "I'm sure we can come up with a suitable plan. In fact, I'll give you until next month to start payments. You'll have to feed the poor animals after all."

Reynolds was so compassionate and helpful! He was a very wealthy man. He couldn't have gotten to this place without being shrewd. Then again, maybe the good Lord had blessed him for being generous. Whatever the case, John was grateful.

He stuck his hand out. "Thank you, sir. As foreman at the Bundrant Dairy, I appreciate this even more."

Havyn stepped forward and smiled as she put a hand on Reynolds's forearm. "Yes, thank you. You've relieved a great deal of concern on our part. Now we need to break the news to Mama that Madysen is now the proud owner of sheep."

Mr. Reynolds laughed again and escorted them to the door. "It's a pleasure doing business with you." He patted John's back. "I'll let you know when I have your order."

"Thank you." Thank goodness the man didn't say what the order contained.

As John led Havyn out to the wagon, he could feel her eyes on him. "What did you order?"

Uh-oh. Now how would he get himself out of this? "Something for the farm."

"Oh. That makes sense."

Whew! At least he didn't have to make up a fib.

After he helped her up into the wagon, he walked around the back to the other side. He needed to get the conversation onto something else and fast. She didn't need to know that he'd spent all the earnings he'd made before Chuck collapsed on chickens.

For her.

Before he'd gotten to know the Powells, that money had been to buy his passage back to Seward. But now? The thought of leaving Nome didn't appeal at all.

If only Whitney hadn't found the contract. Would she ever trust him? If she didn't, well . . . he didn't want to think about the consequences.

Picking up the reins, he put the horses into motion. Havyn reached over and touched his arm. "Thank you, again. For all you did to help." She yawned. "I'm sorry. Staying up all night was probably not the best idea."

"Especially since you need to perform tonight." He studied her, frowning a bit at the way her shoulders slumped.

Another yawn. "You're right. But we better discuss what

we're going to say to Whitney and Mama when we get back. As long as we have a plan in place, I think we'll be able to convince them it was a good idea."

"I agree. But I would like to discuss something with you first."

"Sure. What is it?"

"I'm sure Whitney has talked to you by now about the contract I signed with your grandfather."

She stiffened beside him. "Oh . . . that. Why exactly did you sign it, John?"

Lord, give me the right words. "Your grandfather asked me to. He was certain something was wrong with him and wanted to make sure that nothing happened to you all and the farm."

She picked at her thumbnail. "I said as much to Whitney, but you must know she is convinced that you're trying to steal the farm from us. *Is* that what you're planning to do?" Her face had turned toward him and he couldn't resist the pull to look her in the eyes.

Slowing the horses, he met her gaze. "I have no intention of stealing your family's farm."

"Why did Granddad make you sign that document stating that you would marry one of us? You didn't even know us!"

A question he'd asked himself over and over. But Chuck had been so insistent and had made a strong case. . . . "He was convinced that was the only way to protect you women and the farm. By having a man's name on the documents."

"Oh."

"Havyn, I spoke to Chuck just before he collapsed and told him how uncomfortable I was with the whole arrangement. I told him that love was sacred, and I hoped to fall in love one day and then marry. *Without* some contractual obligation."

Her chin lifted a bit higher as she turned forward. "Oh." Several seconds passed.

What was she feeling? Her expression gave him no clue.

"We need to get back and talk to Whitney and Mama. They're sure to have noticed the sheep by now."

"Right." Maybe she needed time to process it all. He flicked the reins to urge the horses on. "You know, your grandfather only had your family's best interest at heart."

"I know he did."

"When he gave me—" Oh! Why hadn't he thought of it before? "Of course!"

"What?"

"Your grandfather just saved the day again." He flicked the reins even harder. "Let's go!"

Havyn sat in silence the rest of the way home. Not that she had a lot of choice. John was all fired up and in a hurry to get back. So she held on to the seat and bounced along with the wagon. Hoping he didn't know her thoughts. Frankly, she didn't have the energy to pursue what was going on in his mind. He'd all but said that he wasn't interested in her. He wanted to fall in love. Granddad's contract made him uncomfortable.

How could she have been so stupid?

Everything had been going so well . . . even Maddy and Whit had commented about the connection they'd seen between her and John. So where had she gone wrong? Did he really not care?

Her heart sank. She'd just have to carry on as if his words hadn't stung.

At the house, she left John by the fenced-in area where they'd left the sheep and went in search of her mother and sisters.

It would be nice to take a nap and have a nice long cry. But that wasn't to be.

When she'd gathered them all together outside, she walked them over to the pen. John looked to her as if for direction, so she cleared her throat and gave a dry but detailed account of all that had happened.

Mama paced the full length of the pen. "Sheep. You brought us sheep. But not just any sheep. *Stolen* sheep?" She looked at Madysen.

"I didn't mean for them to be stolen, and now they're not. Havyn and John said they took care of everything with Mr. Reynolds." Maddy had a most determined look in her eyes.

"But what if he *hadn't* been willing? We'd be having this conversation with you in jail. Honestly, Madysen, with all the other problems we have, I don't need to have to worry about one more."

Madysen's eyes filled with tears. "I'm so sorry, Mama. I didn't steal them on purpose. Well, I did take them on purpose, but stealing them wasn't how I planned for things to turn out. I always intended to talk to Mr. Reynolds about them, I was just afraid that I wouldn't be able to get to him in time. He said he planned to sell them first thing."

"Madysen." Mama gave an exasperated sigh. "I know that you intended this for something good, but you can't go around deciding these things. Adding animals to this farm means that you're adding jobs. The idea of making cheese is wonderful, but it's additional work. And none of us know how to make the cheese except John, and he's already working around the clock."

"If I might interrupt." John spoke for the first time. He was leaning up against the fence, hands in his pockets.

Everyone turned to him, and Mama nodded.

He straightened. "I believe the least of our troubles will be making the cheese. For now, we need to make a place to keep these sheep, and figure out how we're going to feed them. We can't just let them roam and graze in this small space for long. Someone will need to be with them if they aren't penned. Then there's the concern about predators."

"Madysen, this will be your responsibility more than anyone else's." The fire in Mama's eyes said it all. "I have always loved your kind heart, but this time you just may have taken on more than even your heart can bear."

Whitney went over to Madysen and put an arm around her. "I'll help you with them. Besides, what's done is done. Now we need to figure out how to make them turn a profit."

"Won't their wool be worth something too?" Madysen swiped at her cheeks.

Mama put a hand to her forehead. "I need to get back to your grandfather. Amka can only stay for a little bit today. And with the workers needing to be paid, I'm afraid this is just too much for me to think about right now." She headed for the house.

"Mrs. Powell, if I might offer one more thing?"

She turned back and looked at John. "Yes?"

"Your father gave me this, and I thought we could use it to help pay the workers." He held out a gold nugget the size of his palm.

Whitney was the closest to John. "He *gave* that to you? When?"

He looked between Mama and Whitney. "When he asked me to take care of the farm."

Havyn could have smacked her sister. Mama didn't know anything about the contract, and they'd agreed to keep it that way for a while.

Mama placed a calming hand on Whit's shoulder. "John, if he gave it to you, I'm sure it was for a very good reason. I don't need to know why . . . that's your private business. But if you are willing to use that to help us out during this time, I'm sure Papa will repay you when he's well enough. I can't tell you how much we appreciate it. Thank you." With a nod, Mama lifted her skirts and hurried back to the house.

"Yes, thank you, John." Though Whitney's arms were folded across her chest, the words were sincere. Well . . . that was progress. "I still don't understand about the contract, but I think I can speak for all of us when I say that your sacrifice for us is noble." She turned on her heel and headed toward the dog pen.

Maddy stood by the fence, looking at the sheep. Turning around, she looked at John and then to Havyn. "I guess I need to learn how to make cheese out of sheep's milk, and study up on wool. . . . You think I can make a go of this?"

"Well, we'll have to start small. I can teach you what I know about making cow's milk cheese, but I have a feeling there will be a lot to learn." John smiled. "We'll take it one step at a time together. All right?"

"Thank you both for helping me. I know it wasn't smart. But thank you anyway." Maddy reached out and squeezed John's arm.

"Any time." John tipped his head at Madysen, then stepped toward Havyn.

She held her breath for a moment. Everything about him drew her. And that hurt even worse.

"I was hoping we could talk later today?" The look in his eyes was deep . . . pleading.

No. It was probably about making cheese. Sheep. The farm.

Whatever. "Sure. Tonight on the way to the Roadhouse would be good."

The light in his eyes dimmed for a moment. "Oh, yeah. That will be fine." He looked down at the ground and cleared his throat. "I have a lot of work to do. Better hop to it."

Havyn watched John walk away. What man was willing to sacrifice his salary and now a gold nugget sure to be worth a good deal? The contract no longer bothered her. Even if he *had* been interested in her, it wouldn't. Because . . .

John Roselli was a good man.

Her heart twinged. If she just knew what to do with the growing feelings she had for him, she'd be okay.

Maddy walked over, shaking her head. "Why didn't you offer to talk to him another time, Havyn? If he wanted to talk to *all* of us, he would've suggested the ride to town himself."

"I don't know what you mean." She'd just have to shut the door to her heart. It was the only way to survive.

Her younger sister leaned her head back and groaned to the sky. "Can you *really* be that daft? He asked to talk to you. *Just* you. Everyone can see that he cares for you, Havyn, so why are you shutting him out?"

Maddy walked off, her hands waving at her sides as she mumbled. Probably about how exasperating it was to have an older sister ignorant in the ways of love. But she didn't know what John had said. She only had the fairy tale in her mind.

What was Havyn supposed to do? Hadn't he said that he was uncomfortable with the contract? Because he wanted to fall in love naturally?

Seemed pretty clear to her. Even though *she'd* begun to fall in love with John Roselli, he wasn't interested in her.

And that broke her heart.

Nineteen

Turning his face to the right, Chuck felt the warmth from the sun touch his cheeks. A bit of clarity seemed to push through the fog in his mind. It was summer. He could tell by the way the sun felt. There was nothing like the sunshine of Alaska in the summer.

With some concentration, he was able to open his eyes. Memories of the past few weeks came in. Him feeling like he was stuck in a fog in his mind. All the poking and prodding and how he tried to make a sound. The new doctor's voice. The other voices—Melissa and the girls. He recognized them all now.

Blinking several times, Chuck took a few deep breaths and looked around the room. It took so much energy to move his head, but he was able to do it.

To his left, a cot had been placed close to the door. Melissa was sound asleep on it. Had she been with him the whole time? It seemed like she had. The poor thing. She must be exhausted. She winced and coughed several times. Seemed like he remembered her doing that more lately. Was the summer air bothering her?

She settled back into a state of rest. She no doubt needed a break. It wasn't fair for her to have to sit by his side all the time.

God, why can't You heal me? Can't You see that they need me?

Memories of hearing the girls singing, talking, and laughing came back to him. They'd been in here too. Begging him to wake up and come back to them. He'd woken up many times, but it had taken the past few days of serious concentration to get his mind to function and remember.

So many things flooded in. Thank heaven he was thinking clearly again, even though he couldn't remember everything that had gone on since he'd collapsed with Havyn. How long had he been bedridden?

The doctor poking him came back. They hadn't been able to get him to move. Well, that simply had to change. He was going to get better. He had to. His girls needed him.

Putting all of his energy into it, Chuck tried to lift his right hand. Nothing happened. Then he tried to lift his left hand. His fingers moved. That was a good sign, wasn't it?

If he couldn't lift his hand, how was he going to write? That was his only way of communicating right now, because his tongue didn't seem to work. He'd just have to work at it more. But every time he tried to move his hand, only his fingers moved. And even that slight movement took all his energy.

Relaxing his worn-out body, Chuck tried to think through everything. He couldn't leave his girls like this. He couldn't. It was a good thing he'd brought John on, but there was so much he hadn't told him.

Fact was, he *had* to get better. To tell them where he kept the money, how he paid the workers. Come to think of it

230

. . . how were they managing? How long had it been since he collapsed? How far behind were they in paying the workers?

His heart picked up its pace. His girls didn't know about the gold . . . that there was plenty stashed away. They must be worried sick.

As his mind went through all the ways he'd failed his family, another memory came rushing to the forefront of his mind. Christopher.

What if they found out about the secret he'd held all these years regarding that man?

His heart sank.

Please, Lord, don't let them find out. At least not before I have a chance to explain.

———

The Roadhouse church was packed this morning, which made it stuffier than usual. Havyn fanned her face. She hated the heat.

Scanning the room, she sang along with the congregation. Mr. Norris was so generous to let the pastor preach in the Roadhouse on Sunday mornings. Not only was it big enough to house their growing congregation, but there was a piano there for the girls to take turns playing for the service.

Every bench and chair had been utilized. Mr. Norris had arranged them in rows, pushing the tables to the side for the maximum seating capacity. It suited them well—maybe better than some of the other tent churches. Not that all that many people in Nome concerned themselves with church. Still, Mama always talked about how they should shine a light in the darkness of their town.

The singing was over and Havyn sat down. Maybe the

sermon would be short today. She had so much to do at home. Animals didn't stop having needs on Sunday, after all. She'd found plenty to do this past week, which helped keep her mind off John.

Well . . . sort of.

In any case, she didn't need time to herself. Because then her mind just strayed to a tall, dark-haired, handsome Italian. She fanned herself with her gloves. It was so stuffy. Couldn't someone open the windows? She looked toward the window, willing someone to open it, but John turned his face from the front and caught her attention. His smile was genuine, and all of a sudden she longed to ask Maddy to change places with her.

No. She'd sat in the middle of her sisters for this very reason. She *had* to stop thinking about John. Turning her face back to the front, she fanned herself some more.

She drew a deep breath. Her complaining needed to stop, even if it was just in her mind. She needed to do a better job of being content. She could get up and come to church. Poor Granddad loved the services, but he was stuck in bed. And poor Mama had chosen to stay home with him. Things could be so much worse.

"'Rejoice in the Lord always: and again I say, Rejoice.'" Pastor Wilson stood behind the pulpit, his Bible in his hands. "Did you all hear that? The apostle Paul is admonishing us that in all things—because that's what *always* means—we need to rejoice." Their pastor smiled and looked around the room. "Now, I'm not going to name names, but how many of you have been complaining lately?"

Havyn squirmed. She wanted to hide underneath the bench. Had he read her mind? Had God told him she was complaining in her heart? Heat crept up her neck, and she took long, deep breaths. Blast her complexion! She turned red so easily. She probably looked like a tomato right now.

Pastor Wilson continued. "The rains have left us with increasingly muddy roads, the sickness has been insufferable for many, and let's not forget about the mosquitoes."

The congregation moaned and laughed together.

"But we see right here, in the fourth chapter of Philippians, that we are instructed to rejoice. Not just when we feel like it. Not when things are going well. It clearly says, 'Rejoice in the Lord *always*.'"

Several *amens* sounded from around the room.

"I'm not going to belabor the point, but don't forget that, all right?" Pastor read some more verses. "Folks, we have been neglecting one of the most powerful resources we have. And if you don't know what I'm talking about, it's a little thing called prayer."

More affirmation filled the room.

"And what is the benefit—the result of prayer? The peace of God. Do you see that? Do you understand how important this is? I hope you do, my friends. It's hard to complain when you're praying and praising."

Ouch. She hadn't done much of either lately.

"'Finally, brethren, whatsoever things are true, whatsoever things are honest, whatsoever things are just, whatsoever things are pure, whatsoever things are lovely, whatsoever things are of good report; if there be any virtue, and if there be any praise, think on these things.' Now, let's take a moment to examine these verses. It's pretty simple when it all comes down to it. The last part of the verse says, 'think on these things.' That's a command, folks. Just like rejoice always. It's not a suggestion. It's not an if-you-feel-like-it-today kind of idea. It's imperative. So what is it that we are supposed to think on? Look at the list. What's first on that list? True. What is truth? Well, that's easy. The only pure truth that we have is Jesus Christ. This world is full of lies and half-truths. But God—He remains steadfast. He *is* truth." Pastor walked away from the pulpit for a moment and shoved his hands into his pockets. "This isn't intellectual mumbo-jumbo here. This is for you and for me. The common man. Right here, right now. Take this list and examine it. Copy it down and hang it in your homes. I think if we could master this list right here, we could be doing mighty things for the Kingdom. Don't you?"

John echoed several other *amens*. It thrilled Havyn's heart to hear his voice in church. It took every fiber within her to not look down the bench at him just so she could see his face—

What was *wrong* with her? Fanning herself with her gloves again, she focused on the pastor. *Lord, I need Your help. I like John. A lot. But he made it clear . . .*

Their conversation in the wagon ran through her mind again. Maybe he wasn't saying that he wasn't interested in her . . . maybe . . . no. She couldn't go there. As much as she wanted to get her hopes up, she couldn't allow it. "Amen." John's voice brought her out of her thoughts.

Havyn focused back up front. *Pay attention.*

Pastor looked around the congregation for several moments. It seemed he was trying to make eye contact with every single person in the room. He stepped back behind the pulpit and looked down at his Bible for another second. The congregation was hushed.

"We often quote this verse to encourage ourselves that we can do something that might be hard, don't we? And I'm not saying that's wrong. But I am wanting you to look at this passage carefully. Paul has just talked about being content in any circumstance. Then he says, 'I can do all things . . .' Don't you think it's interesting that this verse is right here, not in a passage where some great giant is being defeated? But it's right after he talks about contentment. Personally, I think it's because God knew that we would struggle with being content. That we would struggle with rejoicing always. He knows that we are a big bunch of complainers."

No one said a word. The pastor's words sank deep into her heart. Peace wasn't about her being able to accomplish tasks or do hard things that she didn't like. It was about her contentment. Was she content with what God was doing in her? Was she content with just being John's friend? Or whatever God had in store for her future? The questions made her swallow hard.

Havyn's mind went to all the times that she'd struggled with complaining—when she hadn't rejoiced. When Whitney was a little too bossy, when Madysen forgot to do something . . . again. When Mama insisted they practice until it was perfect.

Heavenly Father, I know I'm sorely lacking in rejoicing always. Would You please help me? I long to be content in every situation. To cast aside worry. To have Your peace. As we're facing so many unknowns with Granddad, I need Your help to make this change in my life and for it to be a permanent one. And, Lord, could You please help our grandfather to heal? We need him. And we love him. In Jesus' name, Amen.

As she lifted her head, everyone began to stand. It must be time for the last song. Whitney went to the piano and pounded out the introduction to the Doxology. It made Havyn smile.

"'Praise God, from whom all blessings flow . . .'" Havyn thought about the words for the first time in a long time.

"'Praise Him, all creatures here below . . .'" She smiled at the thought of her chickens. Maybe all that clucking was them praising God. Wouldn't *that* be something?

"'Praise Him above, ye heavenly hosts. Praise Father, Son, and Holy Ghost. Amen.'"

One of the men came to the front to give announcements of upcoming events and needs.

While he spoke, a new feeling pressed on her heart. She bowed her head again. She might not have been complaining out loud about John, but she definitely had been in her mind. She'd been mad at God for allowing her to care for him, and then having him reject her. But why? John had done nothing but be nice to her. He'd asked her several times to talk and she'd brushed him off. Just because she wanted something more didn't mean that God hadn't blessed her with John's friendship. Was that not good enough for her? If she didn't get what she wanted, was she just going to throw away any connection with John?

Lifting her chin, she risked glancing at him. He'd given up so much to help her family. Without a single complaint. It was time she put her selfishness aside and allowed herself to be John's friend. Heavens, Whitney had even dropped the subject of the contract and thrown herself into helping with the sheep.

Lord, help me to accept whatever You have for me. Even if it means just being John's friend.

With a new spring in her step, Havyn followed the others out of the row of chairs and benches and into the aisle. There was so much to be thankful for—so much to rejoice about.

Judas Reynolds stopped them about halfway to the exit. "I'm so very sorry to hear that Chuck still isn't up and about yet. I've instructed Dr. Kingston to let me know if there's any special medication I can order. I'll make sure to get it as swiftly as possible."

"Thank you, Mr. Reynolds. That means a great deal to us." This man had been so generous with them over the years. Another gift God had given them.

"You're most welcome. Your grandfather is a good friend. And we need your dairy to be fully operational. It's a much-needed commodity in our fine town."

Whitney stepped forward and nodded at him. "We appreciate all you've done."

"How goes entering into the world of cheese making?" He tilted his head as they all moved toward the door.

"Well, we haven't started yet, but we will let you taste our first products. We have a long-term plan and need to learn and get it all in place." John nodded at their friend.

"Good, good. I'll gladly take you up on that." Tipping his hat, he nodded to each of them. "Have a lovely afternoon."

After they each spoke to the pastor, they loaded up into the wagon. Havyn hadn't sat in the front with John for quite a while, but today, she climbed up, determined to stop wallowing. Madysen poked her head up into the front seat. "John, do you think you could teach us how to make cheese today?"

He angled a look at Maddy. "Really? You'd like to try it this afternoon? But it's Sunday."

"I know, but we're so busy every other day. I think it would be fun." Maddy gave him her best wide-eyed look. "Please?"

John hesitated. "I've been reading up on making cheese from sheep's milk, but I'm not sure I feel confident enough about it yet."

"Then why don't you teach us how to make mozzarella first? You said you could make it in your sleep, right?" Havyn put all her pride and doubts aside and shot a smile his way.

He looked at her for several moments.

Havyn nudged him. "It *would* be fun to all be together, not worried about everything else."

He shrugged and then smiled. "I'm up for it, if all of you are."

Havyn looked back at her two sisters. "Whit?"

"It actually sounds like fun. And wouldn't that be a nice surprise for Mama? Granddad loves cheese too . . . I wonder if he would like it?"

Maddy clapped her hands. "All right, then. Let's do it." She leaned back and started up a conversation with Whit about the sheep.

Havyn's gaze went back to John.

He was still staring at her.

"What?" Did she have something on her face? She swiped at her cheek.

"I was beginning to think that you didn't like me anymore. It's nice to see you smile."

Had she been that horrible to him? "I'm sorry, John." What could she say? The truth was the best . . . but how did she do that without giving away how she felt? "I think I was just wrestling with something and I wasn't listening to God."

"Well, I'm glad you've worked it out. Because I've missed you." The way he looked at her sent a shiver skittering up her arms.

Oh, if only he meant it the way she wished. Because that one simple phrase from him made her face the facts.

She was in love with John Roselli.

TWENTY

John tied an apron around his waist as Whitney, Havyn, and Madysen gathered everything he asked for. They had met in the kitchen after a hearty lunch and decided to surprise Mrs. Powell and Chuck with their first collaboration. That is . . . if it turned out. It had been years since he'd made mozzarella.

Sending a quick prayer heavenward, he picked up the bucket at his feet. "All right. I've got a bucket of fresh milk here, with the cream skimmed off. We should be able to make some fine cheese out of this."

Out of the three sisters, Whitney looked the most skeptical. No surprise there.

Hopefully, today would help her to see that he wanted the farm to thrive. And not so he could steal it away. When Havyn softened toward him after church, hope sprang back to life. Not that he wanted to rush into anything—he'd have to tread carefully. But it was good to see all three sisters smiling at him. At least for the moment.

Oh well. Best to just get started. "All right, I need you

to put this milk in that big pot over there and bring it to a temperature where it feels warm to the touch."

Whitney surprised him when she was the one who started.

Havyn looked to him. "What do you want us to do?"

He handed her a small glass filled with rennet and water. "Mix this up. When Whitney says the milk is warm, have her take it off the heat and then you add this mixture."

"I can handle that." Havyn gave him a broad smile.

Was he seeing things? He could swear that was a special smile just for him. No, best not to get his hopes up.

No matter how much he wanted to.

Madysen poked him in the shoulder. "All right, what next?"

"After Havyn adds her part, we're going to wait several minutes. At least five. If it looks like it's set up, then I want you to cut it up in the pot."

"Seriously? You want me to cut milk?" She put her hands on her hips. "I'm not dense, I'll have you know, John Roselli."

He held up his hands. "I'm not teasing. Just watch."

"All right." Her tone of voice made it clear she didn't get it.

Havyn giggled. "Three redheads in the kitchen . . . and you trying to teach us? Oh my, this is going to be interesting."

"Hey, I've got this under control. In fact, if the first batch goes well, then I will expect you all to work on your own batches at the same time. Imagine if we could get that much cheese made in under an hour."

"Hey, you're on." This from Whitney, at the stove. "If it's this easy, I think we can handle it." She stuck her finger in the milk. "This is ready." She moved the pot from the stove to the worktable.

Havyn poured in her mixture. Whitney and Madysen gathered around and watched the pot.

"It's not going to happen in seconds. Give it a few minutes." He couldn't hold back a smile as he watched them. The clock on a shelf above the stove ticked. "Normally, you'll be working with other curds while you wait for this process. So I promise, it won't be this boring next time."

The girls all quirked an eyebrow at him, and he laughed. "Did you ladies practice that look?"

When they glanced at each other, they burst into laughter too. Havyn lifted a finger. "I have an idea. Why don't we go sing a song for Granddad? That would take up the rest of the time."

They scurried out of the room, and John heard the refrains of "O God, Our Help in Ages Past." The harmony was impeccable, as usual, and he hummed along. He checked on the pot—the curds were coagulating. Just like they were supposed to. Thank goodness! It wasn't like he had a recipe written down. All he had to go on was his memory.

Hurried footsteps sounded down the hall, and the sisters rushed back into the room.

Whitney peered into the pot, then turned a wide-eyed gaze on her sisters. "Well, would you look at that!"

Madysen picked up the knife and started cutting the contents of the pot.

"Make sure you cut all the way through it. But don't make the pieces too small." John watched from the other side of the worktable.

Whitney looked up. "What's next?"

"Put the pot back on the stove and stir it every so often as we heat it up a little bit more. Until it's hot to the touch, but not burning."

With a serious nod, she took the pot back to the stove. All three girls hovered over the pot.

Madysen gave a little squeal. "It's ready!"

"All right, move the pot back over here to the worktable and let it sit another few minutes."

Havyn looked at her sisters and they all scurried out of the room.

This time, they sang "O For a Thousand Tongues to Sing." As it soared to the rafters, John closed his eyes, savoring the sound.

"'He breaks the power of canceled sin, He sets the prisoner free; His blood can make the foulest clean; His blood availed for me.'"

Laughter and footsteps headed toward him again.

He lifted the sieve they'd gotten out and handed it to Havyn. "Your turn. Hold this over this other pot here while Whitney and Madysen scoop the curds into the sieve. Make sure you keep it over the pot, because it will drain more whey off it as they add the rest."

With a nod, Havyn took her position. The other two grabbed wooden spoons and started lifting the curds out of the whey. When they were all done, three pairs of brown eyes stared at him, awaiting the next step.

"Whitney, take that other pot that's filled with water and bring it to just under a boil. But don't let it boil."

She nodded and went to it.

"Havyn, you keep holding the sieve over the whey, while Madysen squeezes any excess whey out of the curds and presses them together to form a clump."

The younger two worked together, and pretty soon a roundish clump of curds sat in the sieve.

Whitney turned to look at him. "The water's ready."

"Bring it over here. Gently lower the curd into the water, and we're going to let it sit for a couple minutes. But this time, don't leave. This will go fast."

They all nodded and watched the ball that sat in the water.

John watched the clock. Then he went over to the pot and used a large spoon to scoop the curd out. It was quite hot to the touch, which meant it was about right.

He took a small bowl of salt and looked at the girls. "Now you need to rub about a teaspoon of salt over this ball of cheese and start folding it over itself, stretching it, and keeping it warm. Why don't each of you try it."

They passed it back and forth between them, while John went to the icebox for a piece of ice.

"Does it feel smooth and elastic?" He took the ice and put it in a bowl of water.

Havyn had it in her hands at the moment. "Hmm . . . maybe not yet?" She passed it back to Whitney. Then it went to Madysen.

After folding it a few more times and reshaping it, she held it up and examined it. "I think we did it!"

John took the ball of cheese from her and smiled. "Job well done. Look. It's beautiful." He took the cheese and plunged it into the bowl of cold water.

"Can we taste it?" Whitney looked even more excited than the other two. Which was saying a lot. Anticipation seemed to sizzle in the room.

John grinned. "It just needs to sit for a few minutes. So why don't we clean up and get ready to make some more?"

The women scurried around and prepared to start again.

It didn't take long for everything to be ready. John pulled the cheese out and placed it on a wooden board. He took a knife, sliced off four pieces, and then sliced the rest.

The room was silent as everyone took a bite.

As soon as he popped his piece into his mouth, the familiar

flavor filled his senses, and he was transported back to Italy. It was just as he remembered. Even better, actually.

"That is the best thing I think I've ever tasted!"

John looked at Whitney. Did she just compliment him?

She clapped her hands. "Let's do it again."

"Mmhmm . . . yum." Madysen snagged another piece.

Havyn's face captured his attention. "Amazing. I can't believe we made this. And in so little time."

"You like it?" He couldn't take his eyes off her.

"I love it." She turned to her sisters. "Let's get some more pots. We can each make our own batch this time. This is going to be a hit in town, so we better make a lot!"

Laughing at their exuberance, John looked around the kitchen. "Hey . . . I tell you what, you ladies make more cheese, and I'll get the ingredients together to make my mother's lasagna for dinner."

"Lasagna?"

"Lasagna?"

"Lasagna?"

Their different pitches made the word sound funny.

"Don't worry. It's got lots of that cheese in it. You'll love it."

———

Melissa sat at the table with her girls for the first time in weeks. John had offered to sit with Papa while she ate with her daughters. That young man was so generous.

The last few days she'd been so weary. And this niggling cough seemed to be getting worse. She'd have to talk to Dr. Kingston about it. He was supposed to come back tomorrow. Maybe some tea with honey would help for now.

She took another bite of the delicious Italian dish John had made. She wanted to savor and enjoy this time with her girls. They'd been regaling her with the stories of the sheep herding, and then the cheese making this afternoon. They finished each other's sentences and kept the storytelling going for the better part of an hour.

Oh, how wonderful to sit here and smile and laugh with these beautiful blessings God had given her. If only Christopher could have seen them grow up into the strong women they were. Life with him had been pretty miserable, but she chose to think about the happy times.

"Mama?" Whitney's voice grabbed her attention.

"Hmm? I'm sorry, my mind wandered for a moment."

"I was asking what you thought of John's lasagna."

"Goodness, wasn't that about the best thing you've ever eaten?" She pressed her napkin to her lips. "And that cheese. I'm so glad you all know how to make it now, because I think I could eat that on almost everything."

"Me too!" Havyn agreed from across the table. "It's divine."

"I have to admit that was pretty incredible. And I enjoyed the process too." Whitney took a drink of her water.

Melissa tilted her head and looked at her eldest. "It appears you've softened a bit toward our foreman?"

She peered over her glass. "Oh, I haven't been that bad, have I?"

Madysen and Havyn tossed their napkins at their sibling.

"All right, so maybe I've been a little tough on him. But this *is* Granddad's farm we're talking about."

Her girls all shared a look. Whatever it meant, it was good to see Whitney letting go a bit. She'd had such a tough time since Christopher died. Building that hard little shell around her and seeking to protect her sisters at all costs. Melissa often prayed for a way to help Whitney, but the last thing her eldest needed was her mother trying to fix her. Because she didn't need fixing. She just needed to forgive.

The clock in the other room chimed. "Well, I better help get this cleaned up so I can get back to your grandfather."

"Not so fast." Madysen came over to her chair. "We want to play some music with you. It's been far too long since you've been in here, and we all know that you need it for the soothing of your soul."

"And we will clean up the kitchen, so don't even think about arguing with us." Havyn walked over to her.

After a few minutes of being at the piano, Melissa had tears in her eyes. Oh, how she'd missed this. Whitney slid next to her on the bench and they played a duet. Havyn started singing the song they'd written together, and pretty soon they were all singing along. Their voices blended like only family could.

Then a tickle started in her throat. It built until she couldn't swallow it down any longer.

All of a sudden, a spasm hit her chest that made her cough over and over and over again. Each cough harder and tearing at her throat. Her vision blurred as tears filled her eyes and she gripped the side of the piano.

"Quick, get her some water!" Whitney's voice echoed in her head.

But the coughing continued until Melissa feared she'd never be able to take another breath.

All sound around her disappeared but the pulsing of her heart pounding in her ears. The cough tightened her chest and pressed into her like a knife. Again. And again. And again.

When the coughing spell finally stopped, she struggled for air. Sucking in as hard as she could.

Nothing happened. A horrible croaking sound came from her lips. But no air had entered her lungs.

Everything began to swim. The girls were shouting, but she couldn't understand them.

God . . . is this the end? Is asthma going to kill me? Please take care of my girls. They've already lost one parent. I can't imagine how hard this will be. And who will take care of Papa?

Pressure built in her head. And then—

Her chest released its grip and air flooded in.

She closed her eyes and took several deep breaths. The roaring in her ears stopped, but she was so weak she could only collapse into Whitney's arms.

"Mama?"

She needed a bit of rest. That was all . . .

TWENTY-ONE

Geoffrey Kingston urged his horse to move faster. John Roselli, the foreman at the Bundrant Dairy Farm, had sent a worker to summon him because Mrs. Powell had collapsed after a coughing fit and hadn't woken up since. The worker looked scared.

If Geoffrey didn't watch it, this infernal plan with Reynolds was going to kill people. How could he have been so stupid? The man had reassured him that he'd supply the real medications as well as the fake ones. What Geoffrey hadn't realized—or maybe he hadn't bothered to check—was that the last box of the *real* Kinsman's Asthmatic Cigarettes he'd ordered were actually *Kinman's* Asthmatic Cigarettes. The packaging was an exact replica other than the missing *s*.

And the product wasn't real.

He thought he'd given Mrs. Powell the real medication—because that was what he'd asked Judas to send—but to discover it was *all* fake? What was the man trying to pull?

Now Melissa Powell was sick. Had Judas done that on purpose? Or had it been *his* fault?

When Bundrant's daughter came to him a while back, it

had been difficult to give her the diagnosis of severe asthma. Especially with her father's ill health. He still couldn't fathom why she'd asked him to keep her secret from her close-knit family. Unless, of course, she didn't want them worrying about her in the midst of all that was going on with her father.

As he rode up to the family home on the farm, he hoped he'd be able to help her. But what if he couldn't? What if he wasn't good enough? He climbed off the horse and wrapped the reins around the hitching post.

"I'm so glad you're here." Miss Powell—Whitney, was it?—stood on the porch. "Her lips have turned blue and the coughing fits are getting worse."

Coughing fits? That didn't sound good. Either her asthma was more severe than he'd thought, or . . . no . . . Please no. Not another case. He couldn't let his mind go there yet. "Lead me to her, please."

The house was quiet. Every other time he'd been here to visit Chuck, there'd been lots of music emanating from the parlor.

But today, a hush fell over the rooms.

Whitney led him to another bedroom, where one of the other sisters sat with their mother. She stood when he entered. "She just coughed for over a minute and then couldn't breathe. It sounded awful."

The panic and worry in her wide eyes told him more than he wanted to know.

His stomach dropped. Could his suspicions be true? How would he cope with an epidemic? There'd already been a death. The other physicians would find out. . . . He'd be kicked out of town. "Where's your other sister?" Placing his bag on the end of the bed, he pulled out a wooden stethoscope.

"Havyn? She's with Granddad." Whitney's red-rimmed eyes pled with him for help.

So the other curly-haired sister in front of him must be Madysen. He met her worried gaze. "Has Havyn been in here when your mother has had a coughing fit?"

The two sisters shook their heads. "No. I don't think so. I sent her to stay with Granddad last night. We haven't talked about today yet, but we were all together last night when Mama started coughing. Why? Is there a problem?"

He listened to Mrs. Powell's breathing. "I don't wish to alarm you any further, but I'm afraid she may have developed whooping cough. There are several cases of it in town. Which means that you've all been exposed. It's not something we want your grandfather to come down with, so we'll need to come up with a plan of prevention."

"Will Mama be all right?" The younger sister stepped closer to him.

"I hope so, but considering the condition with her lungs . . ." He'd just betrayed a patient's confidence, but it couldn't be helped.

"What condition with her lungs?" Whitney's words held a bite to them. She crossed her arms over her chest and stepped closer. Her take-charge stance was . . . imposing.

He stepped back to gain his bearings. *He* was used to being in charge. He was the doctor, after all. "I hate to be the bearer of such bad news, but she's been dealing with severe asthma."

"What exactly is asthma?" The younger one's voice squeaked as tears streamed down her face.

"It's . . . uh . . . a condition where the bronchial system is in distress." Why was he so nervous all of a sudden?

"What exactly does that *mean*?" Whitney's voice brooked no argument.

"Well . . . it's a bit difficult to explain. But her airways constrict and it's difficult for her to breathe."

Madysen gasped, and Whitney stepped even closer. She narrowed her eyes at him. "Are you telling me that she's had this for a while and you didn't think it was important for us—her *family*—to know?"

Now up against the wall, he held up his hands. "She made me promise to keep it a secret. She didn't want anyone having to worry over her. I gave her the only medicine that I knew to help, and have been checking up on her."

"Where's this medicine?" The oldest Powell daughter had her hands on her hips. Her cheeks burned fiery red. "Why aren't you giving it to her now?"

"I don't know where your mother keeps it, but I have some more in my bag. I just don't know if we'll be able to administer it."

"Whyever not?" Whitney's voice rose.

"Because she has to smoke it. That's why. And right now, your mother is unconscious."

"We'll wake her up. If that's the only way, then we will do our part to help." She turned to her sister. "Come on, Madysen. Help me get her to a sitting position. We've got to get her awake."

"Her lips are so blue. What does that mean?" The younger one's voice sounded weepy.

Geoffrey dug in his bag. No time now to mince words. "It means she's not getting enough air."

"Oh, please help her, Doctor."

"Mama, we need you to wake up." Whitney patted Mrs. Powell's cheeks.

As he dug around, he found a box of Kinman's—the fakes. There *had* to be a box of the real medicine left. If he ever needed it, it was now. Underneath the rest of his instruments, he found another box. Holding it up, he saw the label read *Kinsman's*.

At that moment, Mrs. Powell began a horrible round of coughing.

"Keep her upright."

Whitney rubbed her mother's back. "It's all right, Mama, we're here."

The woman's eyes were open, but they were glassy.

Geoffrey took out a match to light the cigarette. "Mrs. Powell, I know this is very difficult, but I need you to stay alert. As soon as you can breathe again, we're going to give you something for your asthma."

The woman looked up at him and continued coughing. Her face turned a deep shade of red. When the coughing spasm finally passed, he counted to twenty before she was able to inhale. Her breaths came in short gasps, and her eyes rolled back.

"Stay with us, Mrs. Powell. Stay awake."

Leaning against her youngest daughter, she gave a barely perceptible nod.

He lit the cigarette and held it up to her lips. She sucked a tiny bit and then blew out. Then she sucked again, this time with what seemed more strength. After the fifth inhale, her lips were no longer blue but returning to a normal color.

She closed her eyes. "Thank you."

Madysen snuffed out the cigarette. "Can we use this again?"

"Yes. And I'll leave the rest with you, just in case." He handed Whitney the box. "Now, I'm afraid this is only a small portion of the problem that we are facing. It indeed sounds like your mother has whooping cough. That means that you will need to be very careful. Try to keep your faces covered when she's coughing so that you don't get it. Keep things as clean as possible in her room, and make sure she doesn't cough around your grandfather. In his weakened condition, whooping cough could be deadly."

Another gasp from the younger sister. "Will Mama make it?"

Geoffrey stared at the patient on the bed. "I think she will be fine, but it takes a long time for whooping cough to run its course. I've often heard of it described as the one-hundred-day cough. And it has the potential to get much worse because of her asthma. So make sure you are using plenty of steam in the room. Hot towels on her chest. Hot tea to drink. If you notice she's having trouble breathing—and not just during a coughing attack—treat her with one of the asthmatic cigarettes."

"Yes, Doctor." At least Whitney didn't look like she wanted to hit him any longer. "Thank you for coming. Will you check on Granddad for us?"

"Of course." Geoffrey walked out of the room and closed the door. He walked down the hallway toward Mr. Bundrant's bedroom.

Twelve cases of whooping cough. What if more people died?

The middle daughter greeted him at the door. "How's Mama?"

How he hated having to deliver bad news. "I'm afraid she's very sick. Your sisters can fill you in on it later, but she has severe asthma and has now developed whooping cough." He moved past her to Chuck. He really didn't need to deal with one more emotional woman.

The older man's eyes were open and Havyn had him propped up on several pillows.

"How are you today, Chuck?"

A moan came out.

"Good. You're awake and responding. That's very good news. Let's try some of our exercises."

After some work, he and Havyn were able to ascertain that the apoplexy had indeed hit the right side again. But with some effort, Chuck had moved his left arm and left leg.

Geoffrey turned to Havyn. "He's going to need a lot of help with the exercises. Every day. Several times a day. The sooner we get the left side of him working, the sooner that side can help support the right. I've brought some more medicine for you to give him each morning and night. It should help him to recover a bit faster." He looked back to Chuck and handed the bottle of elixir to his granddaughter. "We need you to be strong now, Mr. Bundrant. Your daughter is very sick. I know your granddaughters and all your workers at the dairy are relying on you. I'll come back in two days."

The older man moaned again and lifted his left hand an inch. Good progress. At least until he had another bout.

Geoffrey picked up his bag and led Havyn out of the room. "Your grandfather has had two pretty significant bouts of apoplexy. Do you know if he had any symptoms that led up to this point?"

Her face paled.

"I'm sorry to put you on the spot. I know it's difficult when a loved one suffers so much. But I just wish we would have known . . . something. Dr. Gordon mentioned him working too hard and needing rest, but nothing that suggested apoplexy. If we'd known, perhaps we could have taken measures to prevent this. Or at least prevented it being this bad." He shook his head. "My apologies. It's not like we can do anything about it now." Patting her shoulder as he walked out, he gave her a smile. "I'll be back. But send for me if your mother's condition worsens, all right?"

"Thank you, Doctor."

Her words sounded strained. No wonder. Their family seemed to be crumbling.

As he rode back to his office, his thoughts volleyed back and forth.

One minute, he was tormented by the thought of giving out all that fake medicine. Then the next, what did it really matter? He was helping lots of people.

But Mrs. Powell was a genuine and wonderful woman. Shouldn't he feel bad that her asthma had worsened? Because of him?

No. He straightened his shoulders. It wasn't his fault.

Judas was to blame.

When he made it back to his office, a familiar figure strode toward him. Great.

"Dr. Kingston, I'm glad I caught you." Reynolds's voice sounded all too fake.

"What can I do for you, Judas?"

"Let's go inside, shall we?"

Geoffrey opened the door and put his bag on the desk. Crossing his arms over his chest, he stared down his business partner.

"I just came by to drop off this." Judas pulled a leather drawstring bag out of his jacket pocket. "Things have been very profitable." He put a hand on Geoffrey's shoulder and placed the bag in his hand. "*Very* profitable. This is yours. You've earned it. I look forward to a fortuitous relationship for many years to come." Judas gave an oily smile, nodded, and walked out.

Geoffrey wanted to take a bath after the man had touched

him, but when he opened the sack, the sight of all those gold nuggets made him smile. He walked over to his desk and poured them out.

More than a year's salary for most men. In one little bag.

He put a hand to his brow and stared at the nuggets for a moment. Was it really all that bad working with Judas? After all, he'd helped a lot of people. And Reynolds had a great reputation around town.

Clearly, his association with the man was to his advantage. Especially if he could make this kind of profit regularly.

He picked up each of the nuggets and put them back in the bag. Hang it all, his conscience was getting all bent out of shape for nothing. The best thing he could do was better himself. And that took money.

Besides, he'd done his duty. He'd gone through his certificate program twice. He'd earned this right.

From now on, he wouldn't worry about the medicines Judas delivered.

It was worth it.

TWENTY-TWO

The fresh air did nothing to assuage Havyn's grief. She and her sisters were all dragging. They'd been taking turns with Mama and Granddad. Whitney had to take time out to care for her dogs, and then Havyn had her responsibilities with the chickens. Then Maddy and the sheep. And somehow they had to keep the farm running. Thank heaven the workers were dedicated to their family. And . . .

They had John.

Little had been said about paying the employees, but John must have taken care of it.

The excitement over their new cheese business was no more. Yes, it would be a great way to make money, but now they didn't have the hands to do it. And they would need more money than ever to pay for Mama's medicine, the doctor, and the extra hours the workers were having to put in with all the extra livestock. *God, what are we supposed to do?* It was good to have the extra money from the Roadhouse, but would they be able to keep it up? They were all running ragged.

Pastor Wilson's sermon came back to mind: rejoice always. But how was she to rejoice at *this* moment?

The pastor's words replayed in her mind. *"Here's the tricky part. The part where I'm going to ask you to examine yourselves. Are you content in all circumstances? Are you just as willing to rejoice when things are difficult as when they are easy? This is the point here. And it's driven home by verse thirteen. A verse that many of us know by heart. 'I can do all things through Christ which strengtheneth me.'"*

In her weariness, she couldn't even cling to it. She couldn't be content right now. She was a failure.

Every step she took seemed heavy with the worry she carried. Worry for Granddad. Worry for Mama. Worry for the farm. Now worry for her own walk with the Lord, because she obviously wasn't handling things well.

Then there were Dr. Kingston's words. Had she been wrong to keep Granddad's secret? What if all of this could have been avoided?

All of her life she had thought that keeping secrets was a good thing—a way to keep others from experiencing pain. Of course, there were those few secrets that were pleasurable, but most were ways to keep the terrible things of life hidden. Surely that wasn't wrong. Telling those secrets could only generate pain and sorrow.

Of course, that wasn't the case with Granddad's secret. If she had told Mama about his collapsing maybe he wouldn't be in such a bad situation now. Maybe he wouldn't have even had the attack of apoplexy. *Could* she have stopped it?

"Lord, I don't know what I should have done. I was honoring Granddad's desire that I say nothing, but now I see that may well have caused more harm than good." She glanced heavenward. Why did it feel as though the words were just bouncing back? She *knew* God was there for her. She *knew* He heard her prayers. So why did she feel so alone? In the past, when times like this came, she would talk to Mama. Mama always had a way of soothing Havyn's spirit and pointing her in the right direction. But she was far too sick to talk to.

When Havyn was almost to the gate of the chicken yard, she spotted John exiting the milking barn.

John.

Maybe she could talk to him. Seek his counsel. Changing directions, she went to him. The only person she wanted to talk to right now.

He spotted her and smiled.

Oh, how that smile did things to her insides. She wasn't afraid to admit it anymore. John had become her rock, and she appreciated it. Even if he thought of her as just a friend.

"You look like there's a storm brewing in that pretty head of yours."

She nodded, but words wouldn't come out. In fact, all she wanted to do was cry. She battled to keep the tears from pouring down her face.

A battle she lost.

"Oh, Havyn. I'm so sorry. I didn't mean to tease you." He took her elbow and led her over to a bench the men often sat on when working on the milking equipment.

She shook her head. "No, you didn't do anything wrong. I appreciate you. More than you know."

"What's wrong, then?"

"Everything."

Taking a deep breath, she stared into his dark eyes and wished she could get lost in them . . . just forget all the worries of the world. But she couldn't. "The doctor confirmed on his last visit that Mama has whooping cough, and he told us that she's been suffering from severe asthma for a while. She never even told us. Why didn't we know? We could have helped her." She choked on a sob. "And then there's Granddad. He's struggling to get well, but he told me a while before it all happened that he was worried about apoplexy. At least, Dr. Gordon had been. I found Granddad one time in the barn, collapsed, and he confided in me, then told me not to tell anyone else. I kept his secret, but Dr. Kingston told me that if they had known earlier, they could have prevented the attacks from happening." Staring down at her lap, she watched the tears drip. "It's all my fault."

John lifted her chin with his finger and made her look at him. "This is *not* your fault. None of it. So get that out of your head right now. Just because you kept your grandfather's secret doesn't mean that you are responsible for his illness."

"Don't you understand? All these years, I've been the family's secret keeper. Because I'm trustworthy. But what if my keeping all these secrets is wrong? What if it ends up amounting to lying?" She looked back down at her hands. Her father's secret came back to mind. Was she wrong not to tell Mama or Granddad?

"You can't beat yourself up over this, Havyn. It won't do any good, because you can't change the past."

She nodded but couldn't get the picture of her dad out of her mind.

"Havyn. Look at me. Please." His voice had gotten soft and pleading.

She did as he asked. There was such compassion in his gaze. And something more . . . something deeper that she didn't understand.

"I know this isn't easy for you and I'm so sorry you've

carried so many burdens all your life. Burdens that probably weren't yours to carry. But you've got to forgive yourself. If you've held something back that you shouldn't have, then make it right." He paused and stared at her, his gaze intense. "I think it's admirable that you're the secret keeper."

It made her laugh. "You do?"

"Yep. Can I tell you a secret?"

"Of course. I'll keep it along with the rest."

"It just makes me adore you even more." He slid a finger down her cheek.

For a moment, everything vanished. It was just her and John.

And it was beautiful.

"You adore me? But . . . I thought you didn't feel comfortable with Granddad's contract?"

He leaned back and his eyes widened. "Ah, so *that's* why you stopped talking to me for a while. You thought I meant . . ." He shook his head and looked away for a moment. She waited until he turned back to her. He cleared his throat. "Let me clear this up right now. I was uncomfortable with the contract not because I didn't care for you, but because I wanted to fall in love naturally. And when I did, I wanted the one I chose to know that I loved *her*. Not what her grandfather had to offer."

As his words sank in, she sucked in a breath. "So . . ." She bit her lip. Was he saying what she thought he was? "You adore me?"

The tenderness in his smile warmed her from head to toe. "I do. I adore your spirit and your love of family and, of course . . . your love of your chickens." He scooted closer to her and took her hand in his. "You have a spirit that invigorates me and makes me look for the beautiful things of life.

After speaking with you, I feel refreshed, and when I hear you sing or play—I'm transported to a place where problems cannot reach me. You are one of a kind, Havyn. A special and beautiful lady and I'm a better man for knowing you."

Her spirit soared. "I can't tell you how wonderful it is to hear you say that, John. You've become special to me as well."

"I'm glad to hear it. That's a good start."

"A good start for what?" She shook her head and continued before he could reply. "Wait. No. I can't be selfish right now. I'm worried about my family. How are we going to manage keeping up our performances at the Roadhouse, taking care of the farm, taking care of Mama *and* Granddad, plus trying to make cheese now? We owe the workers, we owe Mr. Reynolds. We owe the doctor." Her breaths came faster and faster.

John grabbed both of her hands and held them. "Slow down. I'm here, and I'm going to do everything in my power to make sure that everything gets done. Don't you worry about the finances. I'll take care of it. Okay?"

"But we owe you too, and it won't be that long before we head back into winter. We need to order straw and lots of hay and grain. We need to build new pens and sheds for the sheep. There's so much to do to prepare for winter. It's never easy up here. Without Granddad and Mama, the workloads will be impossible."

"Stop worrying about it, Havyn. I won't leave you to face it alone, nor will God. You know that. God has provided for you over and over. I've heard you say as much."

"I do believe that, but . . ."

"But what?"

"What if He stops? What if Granddad dies? What if we

lose Mama? What if . . . ?" She couldn't continue, because John put his finger against her lips.

"Life is full of what-ifs, and I've yet to see even one of them resolve anything or make a bad situation better. I care about you, Havyn . . . and I care about the others. I'm going to do whatever I can to help get you all through this. If there is loss—we'll bear it together. If there is gain—we'll rejoice. Together. The Bible says two are better than one. You're one and I'm one and together we make two. We'll be there for each other and that will strengthen us both. Agreed?" He slipped his arm around her shoulder.

She leaned into him. "Agreed." With a nod, she put her head on his shoulder.

He tightened his hold on her. "There. Isn't this better?"

"Yes," Havyn whispered. "Much better."

After he finished cleaning the milk barn, John readied the wagon to take supplies to the Roadhouse. Mr. Norris oversaw the delivery and paid John per the regular agreement.

"I could definitely use more of everything." Norris nodded. "With the girls singing every night, my business has tripled. Can't keep enough food in stock. I guess there are a lot of men out there who are just looking for a good hot meal and some pleasant entertainment."

Climbing back up to the wagon seat, John agreed. "It beats getting robbed at the gambling tables or being given watered-down whiskey and beer. I'll see what we can do about increasing your supplies." He wasn't sure how, but God would provide. John just had to have faith.

He slapped the lines and headed to Reynolds's Shipping and Freight. He didn't want to leave the girls alone too long.

Whitney was caring for their mother but had plans to go with some of the native people to fish. The amount of food she needed for her dogs was outrageous, especially during winter. So they had to dry it and smoke it so it would store for the winter months.

Madysen did what she could for their grandfather while Havyn was caring for her chickens.

And that was what brought him to the freight yard today. Judas sent him a message that the chickens had arrived. It was exciting to think that he would surprise Havyn. She needed something good right now. They all did. And John would do just about anything to make her smile. What's more, he didn't want to leave Havyn.

Ever.

What did that really mean? While the thought of marriage had crossed his mind, this was the first time he believed it could happen. Sure, they worked together and saw each other every day, but he didn't want to rush anything. Especially after the fiasco of Whitney finding the contract. Which he wasn't sure the eldest Powell daughter had gotten over.

It was times like this that John wished his mother were still alive. If she were, he could talk to her about his feelings for Havyn and ask about the proprieties of courtship and engagement. But she wasn't, and Mrs. Powell was far too sick to bother.

At least right now he could focus on the farm. Keep things running. Keep the workers paid and income coming in. And try to keep the Powell women from overdoing it and getting sick themselves. These were his priorities for the time being. The best thing he could do for Havyn was provide. Show that he loved her by his actions.

He pulled up to the shipping company. Would the chickens

he'd ordered make Havyn happy? They were already laying eggs, so they would be a perfect addition to their flock.

He set the brake and jumped down.

Judas Reynolds came out the main door and greeted him. "Glad you made it, John."

"I'll have to get them loaded up quick, sir. Still have a lot of work back at the farm."

"And how are our sick folk?" Reynolds joined John at the back of the wagon.

"Hard to say. Mrs. Powell doesn't seem any better. Dr. Kingston says whooping cough has been going around."

"Yes. I think we've managed to ward off a full-blown epidemic, but it's taken several lives."

"I worry that it will do the same with Mrs. Powell. She's not very strong. Not like her girls."

The shipping owner smiled. "Yes, those Powell girls are something else. The very picture of health and vitality. Quite the beauties too. I can't imagine why they aren't married."

Well . . . this was an awkward turn of conversation. Definitely not one he cared to have with Mr. Reynolds. "I need to hurry."

"Well then, let me help you get loaded." Reynolds gave him another broad grin. "Just bring your wagon to the back. I've left the chickens in the crates since they just arrived today."

"Thank you." John jumped back up in the wagon and followed Judas behind the huge warehouse. When he rounded the corner, his eyes went wide. "That's a lot of crates."

"I admit, I might have ordered more than you asked for." He held up his hands before John could protest. "I wanted to make sure you had enough. And to account for transit deaths. We lost five on the way up, but that will be my loss."

He motioned to one of his men, then looked back to John. "I know how high the demand is in town for eggs, so we need your supply to match it."

"But I can't possibly pay you for the extras right now. What I gave you was all I had. It's impossible for me to come up with double the money."

Reynolds looked to his man. "Load these in Mr. Roselli's wagon."

"Sure thing, boss." The large, well-muscled man stacked several crates on top of each other and headed for the wagon.

"Look, John, the money isn't a problem. I trust you. I know you'll be able to pay for them eventually. Let me do this for you now to help you all get back on your feet. Whitney even told me that you are starting to make cheese. I'll help get the word out. That will boost your sales."

The man really was generous to a fault. "Sir, I don't even know what to say. But thank you."

"You're most welcome. You just keep the dairy and poultry yard running for Chuck. He's a good friend. And we're all praying for his speedy recovery—Mrs. Powell's too."

"Thanks again. I will pass that along as well."

As he drove the wagon back toward the farm, John thought about Judas Reynolds. It was a wonderful thing to have a man like him in their community. Since coming north, John had often heard it said that the only way to survive in Alaska was for every man to be selfless and be there for one another. It was clear Mr. Reynolds took this to heart. No wonder his freighting company was so successful.

TWENTY-THREE

Fifty?" Havyn stared at the crates. "Fifty new layers? Oh, John, that's wonderful! How did you ever manage it?" She threw her arms around him.

"I should have gotten twice as many if this is the reward." John held her close.

His words made her heart pound. She pulled away. "Sorry. It's just everything has been so bad and this is wonderful. I can hardly believe you did this. How could you afford it?"

He shrugged and shoved his hands into his pockets. "Let me worry about that. It's just great to see you smile like that."

She went to the back of the wagon. "It looks like some of these crates have five hens and others four . . . some even six. I would imagine they're desperate to be out. Would you help me with them?"

"Just tell me what you want me to do." He shot her a grin.

Her stomach did a little flip.

"Havyn?"

She blinked. "Hmm?" The chickens. "Oh, right. Let's put them in the short run, where we put the baby chicks. With it running alongside the main yard, the other hens can get

269

used to the new arrivals and vice versa. And I'll have an easier time naming them."

"You're going to name fifty new hens?" John scratched his head.

She laughed at the look on his face. "Well, we can't have them nameless. I mean, what would I call them when we converse?"

He chuckled. "How thoughtless of me."

The sparkle in his eyes did that thing to her stomach again. Oh, she was hopeless. "You're excused this time since you aren't a full-time chicken man, but next time I'll expect you to remember the importance."

"I will, I promise. Now let me go get a crowbar and we can get down to business. I wouldn't want to keep Henrietta waiting." He pointed to a chicken in one of the top crates.

She couldn't have covered up her surprise if she wanted to. Havyn put her hands on her hips. "How do you know her name is Henrietta?"

"That's simple." John shrugged. "She told me." He turned to the crate. "Didn't you, girl?"

The chicken squawked.

"That's right. You tell her . . . apparently, she doesn't believe me."

The whole crate erupted in chatter.

John held up his hands. "I hear ya, but if you all talk at once, I can't understand."

Laughter spilled out of Havyn. At that moment, she knew. God had answered her prayer.

———

Though tired beyond belief, Whitney couldn't seem to fall asleep. Their financial situation was just so . . . unsettled. It was all fine and dandy that John had paid everyone so far, but she couldn't allow him to give up his salary much longer. That was like he was a member of the family . . . and she wasn't ready for that yet.

The longer she thought about it, the more the contract made sense from Granddad's point of view. And John had been honest, hardworking . . . loyal. But something made her hesitant about him.

Granted, it was nice to have a foreman. And she had to admit that he wasn't as bad as she first suspected. But that didn't change things. It was her duty. Her responsibility.

Mama moved in her bed.

Whitney sat up and checked on her. Please . . . not another coughing fit. When they hit, it sometimes took hours for Mama to be able to breathe regularly again.

Her mother's eyes opened. "Whitney . . ." Her voice was raspy and breathy.

She moved to her mother's bedside. "I'm here."

"You're so beautiful."

"Thank you, Mama." No matter how strong she tried to be, hearing her mother's weak voice made tears spring to her eyes.

"Christopher needs to see you."

Everything spiraled downward. "Mama, he's gone."

"But he needs to see you. How well you've turned out. No need for another family. Three beautiful girls . . ." Her eyes shifted to the ceiling. "Oh, Chris . . ."

Was she seeing their dad? No. No. She couldn't be—she couldn't be that sick. "No, Mama, stay here. Please."

"Did Papa lie? Or did you fool us all?" Her eyes remained glued to the ceiling.

Whitney looked up to check if anything was above their

mother's head, but she didn't find anything but the painted plaster. "Mama, I don't understand."

Her mother's eyes turned toward her again. "Don't worry, sweetheart. It'll all be okay."

With a nod, Whitney gave her mother a smile. "I know. You're going to be all right. You just need to rest. I love you."

"Love you too." She closed her eyes. And then another coughing spasm hit.

Whitney lifted her mother to a sitting position and held her while the cough wracked her frame. The spasms shook her body, taking every last bit of Mama's energy and breath. Then the coughing stopped and Mama tried to breathe. She sucked in, but her throat made an agonizing croaking noise. She went limp in Whitney's arms.

The suffering her mother was going through made Whitney want to scream. But instead, tears sprang to her eyes.

Mama took a breath.

Thank goodness the spasms had stopped. She watched her mother take another deep breath. Mama's brow was covered in sweat. *Lord, I don't know how much longer she can go through this. It's so hard to watch. Please help her. And please heal Granddad too.*

Exhausted after the episode and her own lack of sleep, she checked on her mother's breathing and then went back to the pallet she'd made on the floor. Sliding her feet under the covers, she lay on her back. What had Mama been saying about Dad? It didn't make sense. She must have been dreaming. Or had the sickness warped her mind?

If something happened to Mama, she wasn't sure what that would do to all of them. Oh, she and Havyn were strong and would grieve, but they would keep moving forward. But

Madysen? Such a loss could break her spirit. She relied on their mother the most. Who could ever fill those shoes?

None of them. Their mother was one of a kind.

Whitney shook her head. These morbid thoughts weren't healthy. She closed her eyes and tried to relax. But as soon as she closed them, she was transported back to Cripple Creek—to the last time she saw her father.

She and Dad were out in the street in the middle of the day. Arguing. Because he'd decided that instead of staying home with them and helping them build the birdhouses like he'd promised, he was going back to the bar. And it was barely noon.

At twelve years old, Whitney was tired of seeing how Dad's drunkenness affected his decisions. The family. Others around him. He never worked anymore, and he gambled away their food and housing money almost every week. Every time he promised to work he never followed through.

So she let him have it. Right there in the middle of the street. She was so mad, she didn't care who heard her. Someone had to be the grown-up, and it might as well be her.

Because of him, they lived in a tiny little shack. Because of him, they never had any money for anything pretty or nice. Because of him, the other kids in town made fun of them. That's why Mama kept them home from school and taught them herself. So they wouldn't have to hear any of it.

Hurt had flashed through her father's eyes as Whitney yelled at him. Telling him that he was a horrible father and husband. That he should just go away so they could live with their Granddad. He at least cared about them and wouldn't gamble away all their money.

Dad hadn't said a word. Just shoved his hands in his pockets, lowered his chin, and walked away.

Whitney never saw him again.

She rolled over on her pallet. For thirteen years, she'd carried around the guilt of her last words to her father. Would she have said those things to him if she'd known he was going to die that day? Probably. Because she had a temper. And was headstrong.

But she also would have hugged him and told him that she loved him.

She'd carried the secret of what she'd done all this time. She could never let Mama or her sisters find out.

The memory in the street flashed right back to her. She remembered feeling triumphant that she'd stood up for her mother and sisters. But as soon as they learned that Dad died, that feeling never came back.

Shame and sorrow replaced it.

Mama had been nagging her for years to work on forgiving. Was that even possible? How could she forgive her dad for all that he'd done to them?

Mama's voice echoed in her mind . . . *"Talk to God about it, sweetheart. He understands forgiveness like no one else."*

It was time she did just that. For Mama's sake.

God, it's me again. You know I've had a hard time forgiving my father. And in truth, I don't want to forgive him. But I know I should. Could You help me work on that? I don't even know where to start. For Mama . . . and my sisters. Please.

In the stillness of the night, Chuck lay in bed, working on moving his left arm and left leg. He felt completely useless.

Determination filled him. Today, Havyn caught him up on everything that was going on at the farm. Then she mentioned that Melissa wasn't improving. As his granddaughter chattered her way through how they were taking care of her, Chuck wanted to leap out of the bed and run to his daughter. But he couldn't. All because he was crippled in this stupid bed.

Doc Kingston said he could overcome it, get his movement back. And Chuck clung to that. It had taken so long for his mind to clear of the fog. And then even longer to string words together in his brain that made sense. But as his memory returned, so did his clarity of thought. But he still needed a way to communicate, since he couldn't get his mouth to work. Which meant he needed the use of his hand. So far, he'd gotten pretty good at lifting his arm a few inches and moving each of his fingers. But every time they gave him something to hold, he couldn't do it.

So here he was. Lying in bed in the middle of the night, exercising.

He could do this. He knew he could. It just took determination, willpower, and strength. He had the determination and willpower—now he just needed to work on strength.

All his failures came rushing back to his mind every time he thought about his family. He'd left them in a bad position. That was unacceptable. He'd started a letter to them after the first time he was bedridden because they needed to know so many things. That there was plenty of money. That he wanted them to be taken care of for the rest of their lives. That he loved them. So he'd begun a confession of it all.

But he'd placed it back in the box with the pencil and paper they kept for him. No one knew it was there, and he couldn't tell them. Where was the box anyway? Somewhere under the bed or in the room . . .

Blast! He *had* to regain movement. He had to communicate with them. So they wouldn't worry.

The only consolation he had was that John was here. He was a good man.

Weary from lifting his arm up and down an inch, he thought of his girls. Even though he'd done everything to take care of them and protect them . . . it hadn't been the right thing to do.

Perhaps he would go to his grave without them ever knowing the truth.

But it nagged at him. Maybe that was God. Telling him that he needed to come clean about the past.

The thing was, he didn't think he could do it. What would they think of him? The thought of any one of his girls despising him for what he'd done . . . he couldn't take it.

No. His secret would stay hidden. Hopefully forever.

TWENTY-FOUR

The early-morning sun always invigorated Havyn. Which was a good thing because it was her turn to sit with Mama, and she tended to cry every time she saw her lying there, still and pale. So she went around the room tidying things up.

Amka now came in the evenings so that two of the sisters could go perform at the Roadhouse and one could stay. They traded off nights so they could still bring in income, but the audiences would get to see them all over the course of the week. Really, it was nice to have a break.

Sure, they were all tired, but nothing could be done about it.

She stifled a yawn and found the package of the asthmatic cigarettes on the table beside the bed. But where were the others that Dr. Kingston said Mama should have? Maybe she could find them.

She tapped her foot on the floor. Looking around the room, the only place she could think of would be under the bed. So she got down on her hands and knees. Sure enough! She found two medium-sized boxes. Sliding them out, she looked up to make sure Mama was still asleep. She hated going through her personal things, but it had to be done.

The first box contained mementos from their childhoods. Pictures or cards they had made her. And, it appeared, a few love letters from their father. Havyn put it all back, not wanting to invade her mother's privacy. Maybe one day, Mama would share with all of them about the treasures she kept in there.

Lifting the lid of the second box, Havyn saw a box of the asthmatic cigarettes sitting right on top. Without looking at anything else, she took the package out and replaced the lid. Then she tucked both of the boxes back where she found them.

Mama started to cough as Havyn stood back up. Struggling to breathe, Mama choked on the coughs.

Havyn rushed to her side and helped Mama sit up. The doctor said it would help, and most of the time it did. But this time, her mother gagged and choked and sputtered while the coughing spasm continued. It was heartbreaking!

It seemed to take forever for the coughing to stop, but once the spasm finally released, Havyn could tell their mother was still in distress. Once again, her lips had turned blue. It happened all too often lately.

Havyn rushed for the matches and the cigarettes. Since she had the package from under the bed in her hands, she took one from it. Lighting the thin cigarette, she tried to coerce her mother to suck it in. A tiny puff. Another. But Mama's wheezing worsened.

Maybe this pack was too old?

She raced around the bed to get the ones that Dr. Kingston had left. Lighting another, she put it to her mother's lips. "Breathe, Mama. I need you to breathe. Please."

After several puffs of the cigarette, Mama relaxed a bit more and fell asleep. The blue tint to her lips began to fade.

Both packages of the cigarettes sat on the bed. As Havyn examined them, she noticed a difference. The one from Dr. Kingston was spelled different than the other.

An awful feeling filled her. She went to the doorway and called out for Madysen, who was with their grandfather.

Her younger sister came running. "Is everything okay?"

"I need you to go get John and Whitney. Right away."

Madysen looked worried, but she ran for the others.

In a couple of minutes, they were all gathered in the hallway between the bedrooms.

Havyn held out the packages. "Look at these."

"What's wrong? So one of them is misspelled." Whitney shrugged her shoulders.

"That's what I thought at first too." Havyn took them back and opened the packages. "But I gave Mama one of these and it made her breathing *worse*. Then when I tried the other, it helped." She pulled a cigarette out of each pack. "Smell them."

John was the first. His eyes widened as he passed them to Whitney. "They're different."

"Exactly." Havyn paced back and forth in the small hallway.

Whitney studied her for a moment. "What are you thinking?"

"I'm not sure. But something is definitely wrong. One of those is the correct medicine, and one of them is not."

John stepped closer to her. "Do you think Dr. Kingston knows that one isn't medicine?"

"I don't know. That's the problem. But we've been taking that man's word on everything. We've paid bills for his visits, plus all the medications. It's gotten quite expensive." She held up the pack with the missing *s*. "And these were from him. He gave them to Mama before she got worse."

Whitney looked at each one of them. "Why don't we send a telegram to Dr. Gordon. Tell him what's happened, and that Mama is very sick. Maybe he will have some suggestions for us."

"I think that's a good idea." Madysen nodded. "Dr. Gordon will know what to do."

"All right then, why don't I go get the wagon." John looked to her older sister. "Whitney, are you done with the dogs?"

"Yes, for now."

"Good. Then you and Madysen can stay with your mother and grandfather. I'll take Havyn into town, and we'll send the telegram. Hopefully Dr. Gordon will be able to send us a response quickly. While we wait, we can go see Mr. Reynolds and see if he knows anything about all this. If we don't hear back from Dr. Gordon straightaway, we'll come back and try again tomorrow."

"That sounds like a good plan." Whitney's face was solemn. "Please hurry."

John walked away and Havyn looked to her sisters. "I have a very bad feeling about all this. Now I'm even more worried about Mama."

Madysen hugged her. "Every time I sit with her, it makes me cry."

"Me too." Havyn hugged her sister back.

"I'll go in with Mama. That way Madysen can stay with Granddad a bit longer. Is he awake?"

Madysen nodded. "He keeps moving his hand, but I don't know what he means."

Whitney put a hand on Madysen's arm. "That's all right. Just try to keep his spirits up, and maybe soon he'll be able to write again."

Madysen walked toward Granddad's room. Whitney turned to Havyn. "I'm glad you noticed that about the cigarettes. Where'd you find the other box?"

"Under Mama's bed. I just started looking everywhere."

"Well, I'm glad you found them. I'll go sit with her. Which ones are the good ones?"

"These." Havyn took the cigarettes out of the Kinsman's box. "I'll take the packages and the bad ones with me so they don't get mixed up."

She walked down the hall and out to where John had the wagon waiting. Man, he was fast.

He helped her up into the wagon. "I'm so sorry about all this, Havyn."

At the moment she couldn't say anything. Tears swelled her throat, but she was so thankful for this man. God had brought him at just the right time.

An hour later, they were at the telegraph office. Havyn had penned a lengthy—and costly—telegram to their family doctor in Walla Walla. Once they were assured it was off, they walked over to Reynolds's shipping office.

Judas met them at the door. "How are you two doing today?"

Honesty was always the best policy. Havyn didn't even smile in return. "Not all that great. Would you mind if we discussed something with you?"

"Come on into my office."

John held the door for Havyn and she entered.

Taking a seat in a plush chair, she sat ramrod straight.

"Mr. Reynolds, I—we need to ask your advice on a delicate subject. So I need to ask you to keep this in confidence."

"Absolutely. You have my word. How can I help?" The man leaned back in his chair.

"My mother was given a package of asthmatic cigarettes by Dr. Kingston a while back. Supposedly to help treat her asthma—which is quite severe."

"All right." Mr. Reynolds nodded.

Havyn pulled the two packages out of her bag. "When she came down with whooping cough, Dr. Kingston left another packet at the house. We were using that one for when she had attacks, but when I found this package—" she paused and pointed to the misspelled one—"I used it for Mama. Only problem was, it made her worse. So I used a cigarette out of the other packet. It *did* work. And it made me examine them more closely."

He reached over and took both of the packages. "Well, would you look at that. They're exactly the same."

"Except one of them is missing an *s*," John pointed out.

Mr. Reynolds nodded. "Ah, yes. I see that. Which one is the good one?"

"The one that says *Kinsman's*." Havyn stood up and showed him the variances. "If you smell them, you can tell the difference. I left the good ones at home for Mama."

He sniffed the boxes and set them down. "So we have a problem on our hands, don't we?"

She looked to John. He nodded. "Yes, sir. That's why we came to you. As a trusted friend of the family."

"You haven't gone to the sheriff yet?"

"No, sir. We didn't want to accuse the doctor just yet. But what if there are more people being given the wrong medicine?" John let out a long sigh. "People could die."

"This is indeed horrifying." Judas took the cigarettes out of the fake package and then handed the packages back to Havyn. "Why don't you take those home, since you need the correct ones but know what to look for in case there's another box around the house. I'll see if I can order some more on my own, so you have them for her. Let me do a little digging into how this could have happened."

"Thank you." It was wonderful to have such a good friend.

"In the meantime, I'll check into this. Quietly." He stood.

"Thank you, Mr. Reynolds." John held out his hand.

The men shook and Havyn prayed that perhaps Dr. Gordon had received their message and had sent a response by now. "Thank you."

"You're most welcome. Anything I can do to help. You just let me know."

John put his hand on her elbow and led her out of the shipping office and back to the telegraph office.

Only a half hour had passed. Charlie shook his head as they entered.

Havyn's heart fell. If only they could hear from Doc Gordon soon. But what if he wasn't even there? What would they do then?

John escorted her out and helped her up into the wagon. "Don't worry. I'll come back first thing in the morning after chores and check. All right?"

"All right." She let out a deep sigh. "Go ahead and read it. Because there might be something that needs addressing right away. I would hate for you to come all the way back to the farm, only for us to have to go right back and send another telegram."

"I can do that."

"Thank you, John." She reached up and kissed his cheek. "For everything."

———— ◆ ————

John rose an hour earlier than normal so he could get all his chores done before he left for town. Since it was just him, he could take a horse and make the ride that much faster. Although he missed the time with Havyn. At this point, he shouldn't be thinking about that, though. Lives were on the line.

When he reached the telegraph office, there was a telegram waiting. Opening it up, he scanned to make sure it was from Dr. Gordon. It was.

But the news wasn't encouraging. The good doctor didn't think that Melissa staying in Nome was a good idea. He was going to wire a friend of his in Seattle and tell him about Mrs. Powell's case.

The big problem would be getting Melissa Powell there.

After reading through the telegram several times, John realized he didn't have many options. Somehow, he needed to find a way to pay for her transport to Seattle. And one of the girls would have to go with her. That would be *two* tickets.

At this moment, they didn't have the funds to do that.

But they couldn't risk Mrs. Powell's life.

God, what am I supposed to do?

His gaze went to Reynolds's shipping company. As much as John hated being in debt, he loved Havyn and her family more.

Taking long strides, he went straight to Judas's office.

The man welcomed him. "Any news on Mrs. Powell?"

"That's actually why I'm here." He tapped the telegram

against his palm. "Dr. Gordon said we need to get Melissa to Seattle. On the next ship out. He's got a doctor friend there that can treat her."

"Is it that bad?" The older man looked quite concerned.

"I believe so. She's gotten worse the past few days."

"Well, what can I do to help?"

"Sir, I'm a man of my word and I do not like to be in debt, but I'm coming to you again for a large favor. I need a loan. Somehow, I've got to get Mrs. Powell and one of her daughters to Seattle."

Judas picked up several sheets of paper off his desk. "This is the shipping schedule. Looks like the next boat to Seattle is in a week."

"Will you help me, sir? With the loan?" He didn't want to beg, but at this point, he would do just about anything.

"I'm sorry, John, I didn't realize I hadn't answered you. Of course I'll help. Just go to the ticketing office and tell them to send the bill here. I'll take care of it."

"Thank you. Is there perhaps some work I could do around here to help repay the loan? It would have to be late at night, after I'm done at the farm, but I don't mind."

Mr. Reynolds rubbed his chin. "You know, now that I think about it, I could use a man to sort inventory in the warehouse to get it ready for the next day. You could do that after you're done at the farm."

"I'll do it. Thank you. I could even drop the ladies off at the Roadhouse and work while they are there. Then I can return and finish at the farm later." John stuck out his hand and Judas shook it. "I'll start tonight if you'd like."

"I'll get my foreman on it and he'll leave you a list of things to do."

His heart a bit lighter, John left the shipping company. It

wouldn't be great news to have to share with the Powells, but at least there was a plan in place.

And, if it came to it, he could go without sleep for a few days. Even if he could just get an hour here and there, he'd probably be fine.

He'd sacrifice everything for this family he'd come to love.

TWENTY-FIVE

A knock on the door startled Geoffrey. Not another late-night emergency. Taking care of drunks that had beaten each other up during a brawl was getting old. Maybe he should start sending them away.

As he stood to answer the door, his conscience got the better of him. If he wanted to be known as the good doctor in town, then he'd have to treat everyone. All the time.

With a sigh, he opened the door.

Havyn Powell entered, her sister Whitney right behind her. "Dr. Kingston, I wasn't going to say anything to you, but I want you to look at this." She threw down two packages of asthmatic cigarettes. One the real one he'd left with them when Mrs. Powell was struggling to breathe. The other—a fake.

"Is there something wrong?" He put on his best quizzical look.

If he thought the fire in Havyn's voice was burning, he wasn't prepared for the older sister's scorch. "One of these is not medicine, *Doctor*." Hands on her hips, she looked ready to do war.

Havyn took another step closer. "Why do these smell different? Did you not notice the misspelling on the packaging? What about all the medication for Granddad? Is it fake too? Are you cheating us?"

Geoffrey peered over their shoulders.

Judas Reynolds now stood in the doorway. A deep scowl on his face. "Miss Powell, is there a problem?"

The sisters turned and started talking over one another to Judas.

He held up a hand. "Is this true, Dr. Kingston?"

The sisters looked over their shoulders at him.

"I . . . uh . . ."

Judas let out a lengthy sigh. Rubbing his forehead, he *tsked*. "Ladies, as a dear friend of your family, I am appalled at what has happened to you. Rest assured that I will get to the bottom of this. And I will ensure that you are refunded your money." He leveled a narrowed gaze at Geoffrey.

He could almost feel the weight pressing down on him.

"And you, sir. If you have done anything inappropriate in any way, I will have your license revoked and have you thrown in jail. Do I make myself clear?"

Geoffrey nodded.

Judas escorted the two ladies out the door.

Several moments later, he returned, slamming the door after he entered. "Are you out of your *mind*? Why on earth did they have a fake package *and* a real one?"

He stumbled over his words. "I . . . I don't know."

Judas marched over to the desk and leaned over it. His face was inches from Geoffrey's. "Let's get one thing clear. You *will* figure out a way to explain this little mix-up without a mention of my name, or I will see to it that you are exposed for the fraud that you are, *Herbert*. And if you make one more mistake, we're done. Which means—*you're done.*"

The chickens chattered and followed Havyn around like little puppy dogs. All the new chickens were finally in the group with the others. And so far, so good. There'd been a few little hen-pecking fights. But for the most part, they all got along. There was enough space for all of them, so that helped.

No matter how much she tried to sing to them or carry on a conversation with her girls, it wouldn't come. Too much weight seemed to be on her shoulders.

What if Mama died? She'd been their anchor for so long. What would they do without her?

Regret pulsed through her. How many times had she missed an opportunity to hug her mother? Or to tell her that she appreciated her? They were together every day, and yet Havyn felt like she'd taken her mother for granted. Why was it that she realized how much someone meant to her when the thought of them leaving overwhelmed her?

She'd been pouring her heart out in prayer for weeks, but God seemed silent. If only she could do something to change their circumstances, but it was out of her hands. Besides, God was Almighty God. He could handle this.

But could she?

The verse from Philippians came back to mind: "*I can do all things through Christ which strengtheneth me.*" How many times had she thought of that verse when she faced something difficult? And prayed for some superhuman power or to be able to accomplish something ridiculous. After Pastor Wilson's sermon on it, it made so much more sense. No matter what circumstances she faced, she could be content. Christ would help her.

In fact, at this very moment, she was wandering around the chicken yard melancholy and full of worry. *Okay, God. I think I'm finally getting the point. I need to be content. And knowing that I can do all things through Christ, who strengtheneth me, I'm calling on that help so that I can be content. I want to be able to rejoice always. I can't do it on my own. But You can do it through me.*

Peace filled her heart and mind. And when she looked down, she could smile at her hens. There was much to rejoice about. The farm was doing well. John had expanded their milk, butter, and cream production. Then he'd added the cheese making. She had no idea how it was all getting done, but there were lots of orders coming in. Was he making cheese in the middle of the night? Did he have anyone helping him?

Once again, her thoughts overwhelmed her.

Stop it. Be content. Rejoice.

She took a deep breath. Amazing how easy it was to go right back to a worry-filled frame of mind.

She turned her thoughts back to her family. Granddad was finally improving, but he was so frustrated that he couldn't communicate with them. Hopefully soon he'd be able to hold a pencil again, but at least he could move his left arm and leg.

They had the opportunity to play music every night—that was a big reason to rejoice. God had given her the gift of music and she wanted to use it for His glory.

Movement in the next field caught her attention. John was herding some of the new calves.

John.

Just the thought of him brought cheer to her heart. He'd been so wonderful and supportive. Helpful in every aspect of life. And now he was working extra for Judas so that they could pay passage for Mama and Madysen to get to the hospital in Seattle.

Love swelled in her heart for the man.

Love.

Was that really what this was?

They hadn't courted. Hadn't done anything but work together and share the daily life on the farm. But he already had her heart. And he probably didn't even know it. That was what was so special about it. He sacrificed of himself day in and day out, never asking for anything in return. It proved to her that he'd signed that contract for the best interest of her family. And if he chose her, then she would be proud and thankful.

As her feelings swelled within, a spontaneous thought came to mind.

She set the feed bucket down and left the chicken yard. With determined steps, she made her way over to the next field, opened the gate, and walked through it. After she'd latched it back, she took a deep breath and strode over to John.

It didn't matter that they hadn't fallen in love the normal way. It didn't matter that he hadn't asked to court her.

What mattered was that she was about to tell the man she loved exactly how she felt.

———

Judas sat in his chair and watched the doctor fidget in front of him. What a fool.

"I don't know what to do to fix this situation, Mr. Reynolds.

I've been wracking my brain for ideas, but nothing sounds believable. You have to admit, this is partially your fault—"

He came out of his chair. "Excuse me? You're the one who gave *both* boxes to a patient."

Kingston shriveled in front of him. "What's the big deal? I'm new here. But they trust you. . . . Can't you tell them it was some sort of mistake? That you contacted the manufacturer since you're the one who orders everything?"

Judas put a hand to his brow. This guy had a lot to learn if he was going to survive here.

"That way you can be the hero, and I can look ignorant of anything being amiss."

Well, that was not a bad idea. He paced behind his desk, then set his palms on the desk in front of him. "I'll let you off this once, but let this be a learning experience. I'll handle the family."

"Thank you, sir." Kingston headed for the door and then turned around. "I noticed you've been helping out that family a great deal."

"And?"

"Well, it just made me curious . . . that's all."

Little rat. Judas knew that game. The man was trying to find an edge somewhere. "There's nothing to be curious about. I'm a businessman. I help people out, they owe me. Simple as that."

"Right." Kingston looked at him for a moment and then shrugged. "Well, I guess I'll be going." He reached for the doorknob.

"Don't let it happen again, Doctor." Judas straightened his vest and took his seat again.

The man gave a slight nod, opened the door, and left.

Several moments passed as Judas thought through the

quandary. On one hand, having the doctor here was good for business. Especially since he had so much to hold over the man's head. On the other hand, Kingston could be a liability—even possibly a threat to Judas's cover.

So far, no one knew what he was up to. He wanted to keep it that way.

Tapping the desk, he weighed all the options. Should he allow the doctor to stay . . .

Or get rid of him?

Twenty-Six

A light breeze blew across Havyn's face, and several locks of hair escaped her braid. She took a deep breath and smoothed her apron as she headed toward John.

Her heart fluttered and she couldn't help but smile as she got closer. This was not like the love she'd read about in books. It hadn't been some grand romance, or love at first sight. It wasn't like what she'd seen from Mama and Dad. This was . . . what was it?

It was real. Exciting, yes, but more of a warm, cozy feeling. Like she *belonged*. Even though they hadn't shared how they felt about one another, she knew. Deep down. Even after all the doubt.

And she couldn't wait to see what God did through it.

She thought about what she would say. And she went blank. How did she tell him that she loved him? Especially when there had been no foundation prior to this point. Well, none except for a good friendship and shared responsibilities.

The wail of a cow made her frown.

John rushed over to the animal. Havyn lifted her skirts and ran toward him. The sound was horrific.

The cow lay down, and John knelt beside it.

She slowed her steps and tried to walk up quietly so she wouldn't spook the animal and cause it to kick John. "Do you know what's wrong? Can I help?"

He rubbed the side of the cow. "I don't know. She just started wailing and then went down."

"She looks bloated." Havyn knelt and ran her hand down the full length of the cow. "John, I think she's calving. Look at the way her body is heaving."

John shook his head. "She wasn't one of them on the list. I thought we'd had all we were going to have for a while. She's a young one, so this is her first." John rubbed his chin. "Stay with her. I'm going to get a rope and see if we can't take her into the calving shed. That way we won't have to deal with any of the rest of the herd."

Several of the cows had already gotten closer. Probably because of the wailing.

John rubbed the muzzles of a couple of cows, then headed to the barn. While he was gone, Havyn started to sing to the cow. In a soft, hopefully soothing voice.

John returned. "What's that?"

"It's a German song." She continued it as John slipped the rope over the cow's head. *"Ich selber kann und mag nicht ruhn, des großen Gottes großes Tun, erweckt mir alle Sinnen. Ich singe mit, wenn alles singt, und lasse, was dem Höchsten klingt, aus meinem Herzen rinnen.'"*

John and Havyn coaxed the cow to stand and together led her to the birthing shed. John tied the cow to one end of the pen. "It's a beautiful song. What does it mean?"

Havyn thought for a moment. "If I remember correctly,

it describes not being able to be still because of God's great works. The singer joins with everything, singing and praising God from the heart." She smiled. "For some reason, the song comforts the animals."

"I can see why, especially when *you* sing it." He looked at her. "I know it comforts me."

Their gazes locked, and Havyn's heart pounded. Was it . . . did she see love in his eyes?

The cow gave a pitiful sound and broke the spell. John checked the animal. "Sure enough, looks like she's about to give birth." He moved to the back and arranged things.

"We'll call the baby Surprise." Havyn couldn't help laughing.

"We don't name the calves like you name chickens." John shook his head. "We don't have time."

"I think everything deserves a name." Havyn went to the cow's head and rubbed her between the ears. "Like this cow looks like an Esmeralda."

John chuckled. "Really? I knew an Esmeralda once, and she looked *nothing* like this cow." John lined up some ropes. "Your grandfather showed me how to pull the calf if I have to, but I might need your help."

"All right. I'm ready. Was she pretty?"

"Who?" He frowned and glanced back over his shoulder at Havyn.

"Your Esmeralda." Havyn tried not to sound jealous, but she felt that way.

"She wasn't *my* Esmeralda, but yes. She was very pretty. Beautiful blond hair and blue eyes."

What if John preferred blondes with blue eyes? Havyn bit her lip.

The cow's sides heaved, and this time tiny hooves emerged

from the birthing canal. John smiled and stepped back. "Well, she may be new at this, but it looks like she's getting it done right."

"Can I do anything to help you?"

"Not at the moment. But if I have to pull the calf, I'll need you. I haven't had to do it since I first arrived, so I hope I get it right."

"I helped Granddad many times with pulling calves. We'll do it together." Havyn stepped up. "I think we'll make a good team."

He paused and looked at her for a moment, then grinned. "I think we make a *great* team."

An hour later, Havyn couldn't have agreed more. Sure enough, the calf had gotten stuck. But they'd done it.

She didn't even care that she was covered in straw and muck. Havyn shot John a smile. "I'm so glad you're here. I don't know what we would have done without you. Not just now, but all these weeks."

He looked at her, his dark eyes full of an emotion she couldn't decipher. "Havyn . . ." He let out a long breath. "I know you have so much going on with your family, and with your mother sick, your grandfather laid up, and all the responsibilities around here. But there's something that I have to tell you."

All she could manage was a nod. She wiped her hands off on her apron to keep them busy. Her stomach felt like it was turning flips inside her.

"I know I don't have any right to tell you this . . . we haven't courted or anything. And you might think this is completely improper, but I can't hold it in any longer. I have come to care for you a great deal." He reached for her hands.

There they stood, in the stinky calving shed, possibly the most unromantic of places, still wearing the filth of the birthing, while the new mother cow tenderly cleaned her calf. Havyn's heart pounded in her chest. "The whole reason I came over was to tell you something similar."

"Really?"

"Yes. In fact, I was determined to tell you because my feelings overwhelmed me. I put the feed bucket down and marched right over. You are an amazing man, John Roselli, and I . . . I love you."

"You *do*?" A huge grin spread over his face.

"Don't act so surprised. My sisters have noticed. I thought for sure that you had too."

"I admit, I had hopes. But after Whitney found the contract, and then you wouldn't talk to me for a while . . . I was just thankful when you started speaking to me again. Then I didn't want to ruin our friendship."

"Let's not talk about all that mess. I don't care that you signed a contract. I trust you. My love for you is real. I think it's the best kind of love, because we built it on friendship. Don't you?"

"I do." He pulled her closer. "Havyn Powell, I love you too. You have captured my heart completely, and I want to spend the rest of my life with you. As soon as I can, I want to ask your grandfather for your hand in marriage."

A light laugh bubbled up. "That would make me the happiest girl alive." She threw her arms around his neck and hugged him.

Strong arms wrapped around her waist and held her for several seconds. It was the most incredible moment of her life. Feelings she didn't even realize she could have filled her being. Now she understood the love Mama held for Dad—

why she had put up with so much and kept loving him. This feeling . . .

Was glorious.

She pulled back a few inches and stared into John's eyes. So many things filled her heart and mind, and that was okay. Even if she couldn't put it into words now, they had the rest of their lives.

He lowered his forehead to hers. "Would it be terribly inappropriate if I kissed you?" His breath fanned her face.

She gave a tiny shake of her head and held her breath.

When their lips met, she felt more loved and cared for than she ever had in her life.

He pulled back. "I've been dreaming of that for a while." He put his hands at the sides of her waist and stepped back. "Even though I'd like nothing more than to kiss you for the next hour, I better take care of this mama and her calf."

Biting her lip, she stepped back too and felt a blush rise up her cheeks.

"I'll see you at dinner."

"See you then." She nodded and watched him turn back to his work. "John?"

"Yes?" He looked over his shoulder.

"I love you."

His smile made his eyes shine. "I love you too."

———

Weariness filled his limbs, but John's heart was flying high. Even hours later, he couldn't get the image of Havyn's lips out of his mind. Not only had Havyn expressed her love for him, but that kiss! No wonder men lost their heads over women.

He left Judas's warehouse and walked to his horse. These

long hours working into the wee hours of the night were exhausting. But it was worth it to make sure that Mrs. Powell got the treatment she needed.

Three o'clock in the morning now. By the time he got back, he might be able to get an hour's sleep before the chores of the day needed to start. At this point, an hour sounded glorious.

As he lifted himself into the saddle, his thoughts raced back to Havyn.

It was a good thing Chuck approved. John had gone after dinner to tell Mr. Bundrant. Asked for his permission. The light in Chuck's eyes had answered. Now there was no need for a contract of any kind. John *wanted* to be part of the family. He would help run the farm at Chuck's side, and the family business would flourish. No more need for Chuck to worry about things if something happened to him.

Looking up at the starry sky, he prayed for their future. He and Havyn hadn't talked about a timeline, but he assumed they would wait until Melissa and Madysen returned from Seattle. Which could be next spring, if the treatment took several months. And then they'd have to wait for a ship.

He really didn't want to wait so long, but it couldn't be helped. It was the right thing to do. Maybe by then, Chuck would be up on his feet and stronger. John loved being the foreman, but it was a lot to take care of on his own. He prayed the older man could recover so that John could learn more from him.

As he approached what he thought of as the saloon district, he nudged the horse to a faster pace. Sleep awaited him, and he doubted anyone would hear the sound of his horse's hooves here.

Wait. What was that?

Something was happening in the middle of the street in front of him.

John slowed his horse enough to go around them.

Then he heard the voices. One pleading. One shouting.

A man held a gun, which wasn't an unusual sight in Nome. Especially around the brothels and saloons. Men got drunk and called each other out to fight.

Didn't they realize it was the excess of liquor that made them do things like this?

Shaking his head, he lifted a prayer heavenward. Should he stop and help?

Probably best not to get in the middle of a brawl. John passed them—then did a double take. The man with the gun pointed at his chest was Dr. Kingston.

John pulled his horse to a stop and dismounted.

"You've been selling us medicine for our daughter that didn't work! And you know it, Doc." The man holding the gun sounded like he was choking back tears. "You *killed* her. It's your fault."

"I . . . I don't know what you're talking about." Dr. Kingston held his hands up. Even in the dimly lit street, John could see his face was ashen.

"How many more people have to die, Doc? Huh? How many? Why did you have to kill our daughter? She ain't done nothin' to you."

Praying every step, John approached as softly as he could. "Sir, I'm sorry about your daughter, but shooting the doctor won't help anything."

The man looked over his shoulder at John but kept the gun leveled on the doctor. "Yes, it will. He's been making a tidy sum off of selling fake medicine to good folks. People who needed him to help. And now my daughter is dead." The man's grief was overwhelming. He turned back to Dr. Kingston. "So now it's your turn to pay. All your fancy clothes and things can't help you where you're going."

"Please!" The doctor winced. "Please don't shoot. I'm sorry! I'm sorry!"

"It's too late for that. . . ." The man's voice fell and his shoulders slumped. And then he fired the gun.

An hour later, John stood with the sheriff in the jail. His heart ached for the father now behind bars. A man whose daughter had died only hours before. A man who'd taken the law into his own hands in the midst of grief and would now have to pay for his crime.

And John grieved for the doctor. What the man had been doing was wrong, but did he know the Lord? What if he hadn't ever had the chance to hear the Gospel? All the times John had seen the man, not once had he even thought to share his faith with him. And now he was dead. What did that say about John? Could he have done something more to prevent the doctor's death? Should John have confronted the doctor privately about the fake medicine and told him that it was possible to clean up his life?

"Thank you, Mr. Roselli, for your statement. Having a witness helps in these situations." The sheriff held out his hand. "I'm sure you must be ready to get home. I'll come out to the farm if I need anything else."

John shook the man's hand. "What will happen to him?" He pointed his head toward the jail cell.

"It will go to trial. The judge might be lenient because of the circumstances, or he might conclude that it was premeditated and choose to hang him. Either way, it's going to be horrific for the family."

"The man was obviously grieving the loss of his daughter." Even though John had witnessed the man kill another human being, he couldn't help but feel sorry for him.

"Yes. But he still chose to get drunk and then shoot a man." The sheriff shook his head. "These are the kinds of cases I hate. I'm glad the judge will have to carry the weight of this and not me. It's too easy to be clouded."

"I agree." John put his hat back on his head and looked to the sheriff. "I'll be going now."

"Thank you for your time." The sheriff scribbled on the papers in front of him.

John mounted his horse and headed toward the farm as light began to streak across the sky. So much for getting any sleep. He'd have to try to get a quick bit of shut-eye maybe after lunch. If there was time.

As he pushed his horse to trot, John's stomach churned. God had called all of them to go and make disciples. But John hadn't done much of that. At all.

Oh, he'd lived a good life. For the most part. But he hadn't felt an urgency to share his faith. And yet, he was surrounded by a lost and dying world.

All these years, he'd worked in gold-mining towns. He'd despised the way most of the men lived, and yet, what had he done about it? The mission field had been right in front of him and he hadn't done a thing.

The conviction weighed heavy on his chest. Things needed to change in his life. That was for certain. Maybe he should meet with the pastor.

Because he never wanted to see anything like that happen again.

About a mile from the farm, a man was walking alongside

the road. Who would walk out to the farm, especially this early? There wasn't much of anything else out here.

Pulling his horse up alongside him, he shouted out a greeting.

The man stopped and turned, a smile on his face. "Good morning."

"Good morning. Can I help you with something?" John eyed the man. There was something familiar about him, but he couldn't place it.

"I'm headed up to the Bundrant Dairy." The man shoved his hands into his pockets.

"I'm the foreman there. Is there something I can help you with?"

"No. I just need to see Mr. Bundrant and the Powells."

"Oh, you know them?"

"Yes." The man sighed. "I do."

"Well, I can let them know you're coming. But Mr. Bundrant is not having visitors right now, and neither is Mrs. Powell." John leaned over the saddle horn. Who was this man?

"Is there anything wrong?"

"Mr. Bundrant has been laid up for some time. Apoplexy. And Mrs. Powell is quite ill."

"Oh."

"Perhaps you should come at another time?"

"No. I need to come now." The slump of the man's shoulders made John pause.

Why? John narrowed his eyes. Why did the man look so familiar? "All right. But I can't guarantee that you'll be allowed to see anyone, sir."

"They'll want to see me."

John stared at the man for several moments. "Okay, then.

I'll see you up at the farm. The name's John if you need anything."

The man nodded. "Thank you. I'm Chris."

John urged his horse back into motion. Had the man been on the ship with him? No. That wasn't it. And John hadn't met him in Nome. So why did he seem so familiar?

Maybe someone from Cripple Creek? It was the only thing that made sense.

Then a picture of the man playing with a little boy came to mind. Throwing him up into the air and catching him. A lady hanging wash on a clothesline.

John tried to place it—

And the memory came back. In Cripple Creek. Actually, a small area outside the mining town. He'd been riding back up to the mining town, and in the woods on the way a woman had offered him water.

The memory took root, and then the rest came back.

One night John had been outside one of the saloons looking for his friend Ben. John heard he'd gotten involved with gambling, so he went to find him. But instead, he'd come upon that man. The man playing with his little boy just a few days prior. Several men encircled him.

"You think you're the big man in town, don't you, Chris?"

There were more words, and then one of the other men threw a punch. Next thing John knew, all of the men were hitting and kicking Chris.

He'd only been fourteen, but he'd rushed to the man's aid. Not that it had done any good. The men had already done too much damage.

John shook his head of the memory and looked over his shoulder. The man he'd just seen walking toward the farm had died that night. At least, that's what was declared minutes later.

So what was a supposedly dead man doing looking for Chuck and the Powells?

John's gut twisted into knots, and he spurred his horse forward.

He rode the rest of the way up to the house and hoped to find something to eat before he headed out for some of the chores. Maybe he could sneak into the house without disturbing anyone. But then there was that man coming to visit. Probably better to let someone know a visitor was on his way.

John's mind refused to cooperate and sort through the matter. He was famished and exhausted, and nothing seemed to make sense.

He hopped off his horse, scrubbed a hand down his face, and put the reins over the hitching post. Walking in the back door, he heard crying and then muffled voices.

Had something happened? He made his way toward the sounds. Torn between not wanting to intrude and wanting to be there for Havyn, he cleared his throat to let them know he was coming.

When he entered the dining room, the sisters were at the table with hankies in their hands.

His heart sank. "What's wrong?"

Havyn got up and made her way to him. She looked up at him with red-rimmed eyes. "It's Mama. She's gone."

TWENTY-SEVEN

John stood rooted to the spot. The room emptied as Whitney took her sisters to go tell their grandfather. He'd wanted to go to Havyn. To hold her and comfort her. But he'd held back a second too long. And then Whitney whisked her away.

And poor Chuck. What would this do to him? How had this happened? To such a wonderful woman . . .

God, why?

Couldn't God have intervened to help her make it a little longer? Until they could get her to Seattle?

Blinking several times, he moved his feet and walked back outside.

He'd failed.

Failed to help Chuck get his daughter to the hospital.

Failed Havyn.

Failed Whitney and Madysen.

It was all too much. He wiped a hand down his face. The Powell ladies would need him more than ever now.

Losing his parents had ripped him apart all those years ago, and it still hurt. And then, when Nonno died, John only survived with his faith and doing the next task at hand. Putting one foot in front of the other. One day at a time.

He grabbed the reins to his horse and saw that man—Chris—walking up the lane. With a heavy sigh, John walked down to him. He'd completely forgotten about him.

"I'm afraid you won't be able to see anyone today. There's been a death in the family."

The man's face went ashen and he staggered a step. "Not Melissa, was it?"

What an odd reaction. "I'm afraid so. I'm sorry. But perhaps in a week or so, we could meet in town? I'll be glad to tell Chuck that you came by."

"No." The man began to weep and held up a hand.

Who *was* this guy? And why was he so upset?

Chris pulled himself together after a moment. "Don't say anything. Not yet. I . . . I need to go." He turned and started back the way he came, his shoulders slumped and shaking.

This made no sense. Why had his path and this man's crossed again? And how did he know this family? The questions nagged at him, but there were weightier things that needed his attention.

He would throw himself into the work of the farm, taking care of Havyn's chickens and then Whitney's dogs and Madysen's sheep—so they wouldn't have to worry about it today. Then he'd do everything else that he could to ease their load. If he didn't sleep for days, so be it.

By the time he'd taken care of the chickens and dogs and sheep, it was well past lunchtime. His rumbling stomach attested to the fact that he'd missed breakfast, but he couldn't think about that right now. If he went into the house and disturbed them all because he was hungry, that would be selfish.

If only he could see Havyn . . . He'd thought she would

have come to him by now, but it wasn't doing any good for him to wallow in the fact that he wasn't needed. At least not for comforting.

But he *wanted* to comfort her.

He went back to the milking barn, then stopped and stared. The workers had not only done all the milking, but they'd mucked out the barn too. What a huge help. He'd have to thank them when they came back for the evening milking.

"John?"

He turned at Havyn's scratchy voice. "Havyn . . . oh, sweetheart, I'm so sorry."

She ran into his arms and he held her as she cried.

They stood there for several minutes, rocking back and forth. He rubbed her back. She sobbed against his chest.

"I love you, Havyn. I'll do anything you need me to do."

She nodded against him. "I can't believe she's gone." Sucking in a trembling breath, she pulled back and looked up at him. "It doesn't seem real." Havyn let go of him and swiped at her cheeks. "There was so much more I wanted to say to her. But I did tell her last night that I loved you. She gave a little smile, so at least she knew I was happy." Tears streamed down her face. "I just wanted her to be here . . . for all the important events, you know? I don't want to do all of this without her." She sank to her knees and then sat in the dirt.

John knelt before her. "When I lost both my parents, I didn't know how life could go on without them. And then Grandpa moved me halfway around the world. I had to learn a new language and make new friends. It was the most difficult time of my life, and yet I can see how God used it to help me grieve and move on. Not that I think you need to move on . . ." He should just stop talking now. He was such a bumbling idiot!

311

Havyn hugged herself. "When Dad died, it was . . . different. It's not that we were relieved he was gone, but it wasn't this bad. Mama has always been our rock. Always there. Steadfast. Strong. And when Dad died, we also had Granddad. It wasn't too long before we moved away as well. I think it was good for all of us. A fresh start, you know?"

"Yes, I felt the same way."

She nodded. "But we can't do that now. We have a wonderful farm that's well established. Besides, it would be incredibly costly to move anywhere from here. And now, with Granddad not well . . ." The last word came out choked. "I just wish I understood what God was doing." She wrung her hands and looked up at him with pleading eyes.

"I don't have any answers for you, Havyn. I wish I did. But I do know that we will get through this. Together."

Another nod. She stood, straightened her shoulders, and let her hands fall at her sides. John stood too, slipping his arm around her.

She leaned against him. "Whitney sent me to ask you to go into town and cancel the tickets for Mama and Madysen. If we can get that money back to Mr. Reynolds, that would be a good thing. And if you could stop and speak to Pastor Wilson. You should find him in the tent behind the Roadhouse. All the arrangements will need to be made."

"I'll go do that right now." He went to the barn door. "Is there anything else you need?"

"Please pray."

"You got it."

The ride into town was exhausting, with the weight of everyone's grief pressing on him. He went to the ticketing office, and then returned the money to Judas.

"She's . . . dead?" Reynolds's face went ashen. "Dead?"

John nodded. "I don't know much more than that."

"That shady doctor! I'm sure it's because of the fake medicine." Judas stomped toward the door. "I'm going to go talk to the sheriff right now. That man is guilty of murder."

John stopped him. "You must not have heard yet. Dr. Kingston was killed in the street this morning."

Judas sank into his chair. "What a horrible thing. No, I hadn't heard. What happened?"

"A father of a patient shot him." John's strength and energy were fading fast. "I have to go talk to the preacher. I'm sorry I can't tell you more." He headed for the door, but Reynolds called out.

"John, don't worry about working for me anymore. The Powell girls are going to need you. We'll work out the other debt . . . later." Reynolds shook his head. "It's not important right now."

"Thank you." What else was there to say? John headed for the Roadhouse. Complete weariness took over him as he went the few blocks. He reached the tent. "Pastor Wilson? Are you here?"

"I am, come in."

John entered to find the man on his knees, with a Bible on a stool in front of him. A single lantern hung from the top tent ridge. "I'm sorry to disturb you."

"It's no problem, John." He got to his feet. "What can I do for you today?"

"I'm afraid I have some bad news to convey. Mrs. Powell passed on this morning. We'll need to arrange a funeral and for her burial. I came on behalf of the family to ask if you wouldn't mind coming out to the farm." He stood there, holding his hat in his hands, his mind suddenly blank.

"I can leave immediately." The pastor walked toward him and put a hand on his shoulder. "I must say, I was hoping it was happier news. For a moment, I thought perhaps you were coming to ask me to do a wedding rather than a funeral."

John felt his eyes go wide. "I wish that was the case—Wait. How . . . how did you know?"

"Oh, it doesn't take a genius to see the spark between you and Miss Havyn."

"Oh." John blinked several times. "I hope to talk to you about that soon, Pastor, but it will have to wait awhile. I appreciate your prayers."

"You've got them, son." The pastor put on his hat and headed out of the tent. John followed. "I'll go fetch my horse and head right out to the farm."

"Thank you." John gazed toward the blue sky Melissa Powell would never see again. A million thoughts raced through his mind. The majority of them questions. It's not that he doubted God was in control, but it didn't make sense. And it hurt.

Melissa Powell was one of the most amazing people he'd ever met. Her death was a great loss.

A man cleared his throat, and John turned.

Chris stood there. His shoulders still slumped, his face haggard. "I'm sorry to disturb you, but I need to talk to you."

John furrowed his brow. "This is a difficult time for the family, Mr.—?"

"I know, and I'm sorry."

"Look, whoever you are, I just think it would be best if you waited awhile."

"I've been waiting for too long as it is, Mr. Roselli."

"How do you know my name?"

"I asked around." The man looked to the ground. "The thing is . . . my name is Christopher Powell."

What? Havyn's father? "I'm not quite sure I understand. . . ."

"Melissa was my wife. Whitney, Havyn, and Madysen are my daughters."

"But Christopher Powell is dead."

"That's what we wanted you to believe." The man shook his head, still looking at the ground.

Something didn't add up. "I'm sorry, sir. But I have a hard time believing you are Christopher Powell, because I remember you from Cripple Creek. I remember seeing you with another woman as your wife and with small children. And I remember vividly the night I saw you in the street and a bunch of men had it in for you. That was 1891, if I recall. I saw you with a little boy earlier, and then . . . Well, I thought you were dead. I was there. I tried to stop the men." John shook his head. Was this some kind of bad dream?

Shock covered the man's face. "That was you? I can't believe I didn't recognize you. But then again, I was drunk. I was always drunk." His shoulders slumped as he looked back up at John.

"There's no reason you should recognize me. I was just fourteen. Not even a man." How had this man survived? "Those men beat you badly."

"They did. Maybe, you could say, they beat some sense into me. My life changed that night. You stopped those men, and the sheriff took over and had me taken to the doctor's place. Someone sent for Chuck. When I woke up, he laid out an ultimatum. I was to leave and never return. There were divorce papers from Melissa and a hefty sum of money, which was mine if I would simply sign and leave."

What? Could that be true? "I still don't understand. . . ."

"There's more I need to tell you. You see, I gambled away everything. I was a drunk and a terrible husband. Oh, I loved Melissa and my girls something fierce, but the alcohol always called to me. And I let it. Over time, I was unfaithful to my beautiful wife and got another woman pregnant. But you see, Esther had a boy. I'd always wanted a boy. And for some reason, that made me feel more like a man. So I continued on in my behavior. Chuck found out. The fight I got into that night was a great excuse for him to get rid of me for good. Those men were his friends."

"You had a wonderful wife and three beautiful daughters—"

"I know. And I threw it all away. But I'm not the same man I was. I wanted to come back and make things right."

"I'm not sure how you can do that now. Especially at a time like this." There was no way he was letting this man near the Powells. Yes, God was a God of forgiveness, but putting Havyn and her sisters through the added pain of hearing this man's story?

No.

Chris slid his hands into his pockets. "After I signed the divorce papers and left, I married Esther. But I went into an even worse spiral of drinking and carousing. Esther had our second baby by that point, and was pregnant with another. She put her foot down and told me we were going to move in with her parents. They lived down in Colorado Springs. I refused. But the next time I got drunk—which was the next day—she already had the wagon loaded and had a couple fellas throw me in the back. By the time I woke up, we were almost there. Her parents helped me get dried up. Eventually they even got me in church. Something Melissa had been trying to do for years. Then they let us help with the family business—a mercantile." He hung his head. "Esther died about six months back. I didn't deserve her. Just like I didn't deserve Melissa."

While he wanted to believe that the man had gotten himself right with God, John resisted. What if it was all a lie? "Why did you come to Nome? And where are your children?"

"They're with Esther's sister, Ruth. Her husband came up to Nome to search for gold, and she hasn't heard from him in a long while. She's afraid he's turned into what I used to be. So I came up here to find him and send him home. But God was also asking me to make things right with my family. I never lost track of them. I knew one day I'd have to face them." He leaned forward. "I have to let my girls know that I'm alive."

"I'm not sure that's the best idea right now."

Chris straightened and leveled a gaze at John. "Well, you need to realize that it is. Either let me tell them, or you do it. I'm going to be at my wife's funeral, and you can't stop me."

TWENTY-EIGHT

Sitting on a chair by the fireplace, Havyn set her chin on her hands and peered out the large window. Normally, this was her favorite place to sit and look at the view. But today, her heart was broken into a million pieces. The sky had turned gray, and it would probably rain.

All too fitting for saying good-bye to Mama.

A figure in the distance rode toward the farm. Her heart lifted. John. She needed his strong presence right now. She went out the door.

It was him.

"Hi."

He looked so . . . burdened. "Hi." She went to hug him. "Thank you for all you've done. Pastor Wilson just left."

"I know, I passed him on the road. I'm thankful you were able to get it all figured out." He took her hand and led her inside. "There's something we need to talk about. In private. Where are your sisters?"

"Whitney is lying down. She had a horrible headache, and Madysen is with Granddad. Let's go by the fireplace. There's a chill in the air."

He followed her, and Havyn got the impression that the subject he needed to broach was serious. Hadn't they had enough of that lately? She needed some uplifting.

She settled by the fireplace, and John sat across from her, putting his elbows on his knees. "Havyn, there's something I need to tell you, and it's not going to be easy to hear."

What could this be about? He wasn't going to tell her they shouldn't get married . . . was he? She could barely nod.

"I'm not sure where I should even start. But your dad had a second family."

Whew! That wasn't so bad. "I had a feeling he did." At John's puzzled look, she went on. "One night he was drunk and he talked about how a woman named Esther was pregnant with his baby. I had no idea who Esther was, but she obviously wasn't Mama. It's so sad that he abandoned more than us when he died."

He took a deep breath. "That's the thing. Your father . . . well, he didn't die."

She sat there, frozen. "What do you mean? Of course he died. Granddad even showed us where he was buried."

"No, honey, I'm sorry. Your dad is very much alive and . . . he's in Nome."

"*What?*" She stood and balled her fists at her sides. "Dad's *alive*? And here? How do you know this?"

"I met him this morning on my way home. He was walking out here to see you all. Said he knew you. I didn't know who he was. Then I got here and found out your mother had passed, so I went out and told him there was a death in the family and that it would be better if he came back to see all of you at a later date. When he found out it was your mother who died, he started weeping. Not something you see a grown man do very often. He left then, but when I went to see Pastor Wilson, he found me again."

"And you're sure it's him?" She put a hand to her stomach. It was all in knots and tumbling over itself.

"Well, you'll have to be the ones to see for sure, but his story seems to line up with the facts that I knew. I was actually there the night he got beaten. I had heard he died, but apparently that wasn't the case."

Her stomach roiled. Was she going to be sick? "I don't think I can deal with this right now." She put a hand to her forehead.

John stood and put his hands on her shoulders. "I'm so sorry, sweetheart, but you have to. He says he is going to be at your mother's funeral, and that we can't stop him."

Closing her eyes, she took some calming breaths. Only one thing to do. "We've got to talk to Granddad about this. Without Whit and Maddy. But I'm afraid it's going to crush him. How could he have been mistaken?"

His next words were almost her undoing.

"I don't think he was, Havyn. I think he planned the whole thing."

"Granddad?" A hand on his arm made him open his eyes.

Sweet Havyn stood over him, a troubled expression on her face. "We need to speak to you about something quite important. Are you up for that? Do you need something to drink?"

He blinked several times and shook his head. He'd been hoping that the nightmare of losing his daughter had been just that—a nightmare. But that didn't seem to be the case. Havyn was dressed in black.

John pulled the door to Chuck's room closed, then moved forward. "I'm sorry for the timing of this, Chuck, but you'll understand we don't have a choice."

Oh no. What had happened now? How could he deal with anything else disastrous? He lifted his hand and signaled for his pencil and paper.

Havyn sat in the chair beside his bed. "Granddad, are you sure you can do this?"

He tilted his chin forward.

She went to the armoire and pulled out the box that held his writing paper and pencil. She pulled out a clean sheet, closed the lid, and placed the paper on top. She put a pencil in his hand, then sat again, her hands clasped in front of her.

"Granddad, there's a man coming to the funeral tomorrow who says he's Christopher Powell. He came by this morning, but John turned him away not knowing who he was. When John went into town to see Pastor Wilson, the man approached him again."

So.

The secret he'd kept hidden for so long was about to see the light of day. His stomach seemed to take a dive toward his toes. This couldn't be . . . could it?

"Granddad, are you all right?" Havyn turned to John. "He's awfully pale. What if he can't deal with this?"

"Naaaaahhhhmm . . ." Chuck shook his head *no* and lifted his left hand a few inches. Taking the pencil, he wrote on the paper:

Talk to John . . . private. Now.

Havyn frowned, but she nodded. "All right." She stood and walked toward the door. "I'll keep Whitney and Madysen occupied."

He gave a slight nod. The most he could manage. After

she'd closed the door, he looked to John and then wrote. It seemed to take forever. Each letter took a lot out of him, but finally he accomplished his thought.

You need be my voice.

John's brow furrowed. "I will do whatever you need me to do."

You know?

"Chris told me a lot. I haven't told your other granddaughters. Only Havyn. And only that a man claiming to be her father is here. And that he has a second family."

Chuck watched John's face. From the younger man's hesitant expression, it was a good bet his foreman knew he'd played a part in making Christopher Powell disappear. John had been only a boy back then, and Chuck had never planned on him being involved.

"He said his second wife died not long ago."

Chuck wrote: *Look in box.*

No matter how much it hurt, no matter how hard it was, it was time to tell the truth. And his granddaughters just might hate him for it.

John picked up the writing box and raised his eyebrows.

Chuck nodded.

John picked through the box and found the folded letter he'd started. "Is this it?"

Another nod.

Read it.

Chuck closed his eyes as the young man read his horrible confession. Oh, why was this happening now, when he was too weak to defend himself or to convince the girls that he had been in the right? Perhaps this was God's way of humbling him.

Completely.

Chuck wrote again as John folded the pages.
I need you to read this to them. Now.

The bedroom fell silent while John looked at the papers in his hands. Havyn sent a prayer heavenward. She sat with her sisters and waited. A glance at Granddad didn't ease her tension. Whatever it was he had to share with them, it was going to be difficult.

What she'd already learned was probably only the beginning of the truth. Was she ready for this? Did she have any choice?

"First, thank you all for being patient with me as I try to speak on your grandfather's behalf. This isn't going to be an easy conversation, and the day has already been one of the hardest you've ever faced."

Whitney spoke up. "It's all right, John. We appreciate you being Granddad's voice. But we Powells . . . well, we're strong. Just be honest with us. We can handle it."

If only her sister meant it. As far as Havyn knew, she was the only one aware of Dad's other family.

It was going to be a long night.

John looked at her and her sisters. "Second, it's important that I tell you something else that happened today. Around three o'clock this morning, I was headed home from Reynolds's shipping warehouse when I came upon a fight in the street. A man held a gun on Dr. Kingston and accused him of killing his daughter by giving her fake medicine. That man shot the doctor, who died in the street."

Havyn gasped along with her sisters. How horrible! While she didn't like the man and had her suspicions about what he'd done to contribute to Mama's death, she hadn't wanted him dead.

John gave them a moment to recover. "I'm not sure who will take on Kingston's patients while they wait for another doctor, but Judas assured me that he would send his own personal physician out to check on Chuck and help him with his recovery." John looked at Granddad for a long moment and then looked back at the papers in his hand. "Now to the hard part . . ."

John cleared his throat, unfolded the papers in his hand, and began reading.

"My dear girls,

"After my bout of apoplexy, God got ahold of me and I knew I had to confess. So here it is. Melly, I'm sorry. Please forgive me. Girls, you too.

"Christopher was not a good man. I know you all loved him, but he started stealing from me the day after he married you, Melly. Then he had the gall to come to me and ask for help with his debts. This went on for all the years you were married. He'd use the same excuse that I wouldn't dare let you starve. It worked.

"By now you know that Christopher was a drunken gambler, but I don't know if you realized he was a womanizer as well. There's so many things I should have done to help him, but I didn't. Instead, I figured out a way to get rid of him."

Madysen gasped. Havyn put a hand on her sister's knee and nodded at John to continue.

"You see, I found out that he had gotten another woman pregnant. And when the baby was born, it was a boy. I spent all your married years paying for his

*debts, Melly, and for all his bills since he couldn't seem
to be responsible. I didn't want my daughter to have
to live like that, but I know it was your choice. And I
kept my mouth shut.*

*"But one night, I finally had enough. I found out
Christopher had been beaten up. In yet another bar
fight. I already had everything in place, divorce papers
and a way out for him. I went to Doc's place. Told him
if he signed the divorce papers, left, and never tried to
see our family again, I would pay off all his debts and
give him money to start over. I told him he needed to
move away. He figured out that I wasn't going to tell
you, Melly, that you were divorced. He knew I would
say he was dead. It only seemed to bother him for a
moment. He took a drink and signed. I had the doc
spread the word that he'd died."*

Whitney bolted to her feet. "Dad's not dead?"

Havyn fixed her elder sister with a calming look. "Sit
down, Whit. Let John finish reading." She clung to Madysen's hand. Had Mama known? It must have broken her
heart if she did. . . .

John took a deep breath and went on.

*"For all that I wanted him gone from your lives, I
couldn't believe a man could walk away from his beautiful wife and daughters. But at that point, he was too
deep in debt and too drunk to realize what he had.
I knew he loved you girls. Just not enough to clean
himself up. I'm sorry for the part I played in all this. I
don't want you to think I'm a monster. I did it all out
of love. But it's time for the truth to be told."*

John folded the papers. "Chuck started this note to your mother, but when the apoplexy hit a second time, he couldn't finish it."

Havyn looked at her grandfather. He looked so frail and broken.

"There's more." John straightened. "Christopher Powell is alive and he's in Nome. He found me today. His second wife has died, and you have half siblings. And . . . he's determined to come to the funeral."

Looking from Whitney to Madysen, Havyn waited for an outburst. But none came. The whole sordid tale had been told. Her heart ached within her chest.

When John put the pages in his pocket, he looked up again. "Your grandfather is deeply sorry. He loves you all more than life itself and thought he was doing the right thing by protecting you and taking care of you. The last thing he wants is for you to be angry at him. He's asking for your forgiveness. This has been a heavy weight on him for a long time."

Madysen was crying. Whitney was silent. Which wasn't a good thing.

Havyn reached over and took her older sister's hand and squeezed.

She loved her grandfather, but how could he have done this? And how would they get past it? "Granddad, I don't know what to say. Other than I can't imagine the place that you found yourself in. Now that I'm an adult, it's easier to understand your reasoning, but I still hate that you took our father from us. As horrible as he may have been. We loved him." She wiped a tear from her eye. "But I forgive you."

Whitney squeezed Havyn's hand back. Hard. She spoke through gritted teeth. "Granddad, I love you. And what you did was horrible, but I understand why you did it. It was easier to think of my father dead than to live with who he had become. I can forgive you too, but I don't think I'll forgive him. And I don't care if we have siblings. With the loss of Mama so fresh, I can't even contemplate my feelings on that. And I can't promise I will even speak to that man tomorrow."

Maddy had been weeping, and now she swiped at her cheeks with a hankie. "I can't deal with this news right now." She stood and ran out of the room.

Havyn exchanged a glance with Whitney. Her older sister's features were hard, but Havyn could see the pain behind her eyes. How long would it take them to heal from this? Would their lives ever be the same?

Whitney let out a long breath. "I need to go be with Maddy. Tomorrow is going to be a very difficult day." She stood, straightened her shoulders, and left the room.

Havyn looked at Granddad. Tears streamed down his face. She went over and hugged him and then wiped away his tears. "I'm so sorry about all this. I know you are grieving as well." Looking up at John, she wanted to jump into his arms and weep.

The man who'd told her he loved her looked at her with sorrow in his eyes. "Are you all right? Can I do anything?"

She shook her head and walked away. What she needed the most was a good, long cry.

Twenty-Nine

The next day dawned beautiful and cheery, which hardly seemed fair. A day like today—with the funeral of a woman far too young and beloved of her family to be gone—should be gray, dull, and gloomy.

John wasn't looking forward to dealing with the potential conflicts today. What would he do when Christopher showed up? He wanted to be there for emotional support for Havyn, but he also wanted to protect all the Powell women. What was the man up to? And why was he so determined to come to the funeral?

As John walked to Chuck's room, a dozen scenarios ran through his mind. The fact of the matter was, he had no place to judge anyone. So he would focus on getting Chuck dressed and cleaned up. Just do the best he could to help the man feel comfortable and presentable for his daughter's funeral. It would be the first time anyone from town—other than the doctor—had seen Chuck since the apoplexy.

Judas had brought a wheeled chair over last night so Chuck could attend the funeral. How the man had found one baffled John, but he'd be forever grateful. They owed Reynolds a debt larger than money.

The decision to have the service at the farm had been Chuck's. There was a nice little section that he wanted to be the family resting place. In a note, he'd told them all his request. Then wrote to John that he fully expected his time was coming soon.

John encouraged him to keep getting better because his granddaughters needed him. But the physical toll on Chuck's body had been great. And his grief only made things worse.

It took about an hour to assist Chuck since he was only able to move his left side a little bit. The man had been diligently doing exercises, but it was slow progress. John just kept talking to him through the whole thing. How difficult it would be to have to swallow pride and allow someone to help like this.

John shaved his boss's face and combed his hair. "You know, Chuck, life isn't over until God says so. You're still here, so the good Lord must still have some work for you to do. And if that means working even harder at your convalescence and your exercises, then I'll help you."

A slight groan came from Chuck's lips.

"Well, I agree, it's not going to be easy . . . but not only does your family need you, I need you as well."

Chuck's eyes glistened. All morning John watched his friend fight tears. Even so, Chuck had been able to hold it together. John didn't think he'd be that strong under similar circumstances.

He situated Chuck in the chair and tucked a blanket around his legs. "How do you feel? Is it comfortable enough? Do you need a pillow?"

Chuck lifted his left hand a bit and motioned for the pencil.

John set the box with paper in Chuck's lap and placed the pencil in his hand. The past day Chuck had gotten more proficient at writing and had a bit more stability in his hand.

I'm fine. Thank you. Today payday?

Oh, good heavens! "It is. I forgot about it. Thanks for the reminder."

"I didn't." Whitney's voice made him turn around. "I talked to the workers this morning. They all said it could wait because of the funeral, but I told them that a worker is due his wage. So I said we would take care of it later today." The redness around her eyes showed her grief, but her mouth was set in a determined line.

"Thank you for doing that."

Chuck was writing again.

John looked down.

Need talk finances.

At least the man was coherent and communicating now. Whether the tragedy had forced him, or by sheer will, John was grateful. Maybe he could finally find out where the other ledger was. And where Chuck kept the family's money. "Will do, sir. It will help us a great deal if you can share how you did things, but let's just see how you do at the service first."

Chuck nodded.

Moving behind the chair, John started to push Chuck out of his bedroom and into the parlor, where they would gather until the pastor arrived. When they made it to the large room—the place where memories abounded of music and laughter and family—Madysen and Havyn rushed to their grandfather's side. They both knelt in front of him.

Havyn buried her face in her grandfather's lap. Her shoulders shook with silent sobs. When she lifted her face, tears glistened on her cheeks. "It's so wonderful to see you up and in this chair."

Chuck seemed uncomfortable—he must ache to communicate with his family—so John jumped into the conversation. "I'm sure he wishes the circumstances were different, but your grandfather is a strong man."

Havyn wiped at her cheeks. "Today's going to be a hard day, but I know we can get through it together. I love you."

"Yes, Granddad. Me too. I love you. " Madysen's smile was genuine.

John stepped back to give them a few moments alone. The day would probably be the hardest that any of them had ever faced.

Lord, please be with us all.

———

The number of people who came to her mother's funeral touched Havyn. Deeper than she'd thought possible.

Funeral.

How could they be burying Mama? Just a few months ago they surprised her and celebrated her birthday. Havyn could still see the look of pure joy on Mama's face. If only they could go back to that night . . .

She just *couldn't* be gone.

But the small pine coffin offered proof. The lack of Mama's sweet voice welcoming friends, offering coffee or something to eat, and seeing to everyone's comfort made Havyn's heart ache even more.

Tears flowed from her eyes and her breath caught in the back of her throat. Who would she talk to when she was confused about something? Who would be there for advice when she got married and had children? Mama had taught her so much. . . . Who would be that mentor to her now?

Life without Mama was unfathomable. And yet . . . it was reality.

Picking lint off her black dress, Havyn didn't even want to look around, because the temptation to search the growing crowd for her father was great. Her sisters were probably doing the same. Would he still come?

She turned her head and saw John coming toward her with a blanket in his arms. Probably for Granddad. The air was chilly even with the sun shining. The sight of him calmed her burdened heart.

Stalwart John. Ever faithful. He'd been good to all of them, never once putting himself first. Taking care of the farm. Taking care of Granddad. Taking care of . . . her.

And he loved her.

Havyn had never been in love before, but Mama once said that when she finally fell in love it would change everything.

Mama was right. *Oh, Mama . . . I miss you so much.* A sob shook her and she allowed the tears to flow.

"Friends, I thank you for coming today to help us say a momentary good-bye to Melissa Powell," Pastor Wilson said, beginning the service. "Momentary, because we know this earth is not our final resting place if we belong to Jesus Christ."

There were a few murmured *amens.*

John wheeled Granddad even closer and stood at Havyn's side. He took hold of her hand and gave it a squeeze. She could feel his strength, and it comforted her like nothing else could.

"A while back Melissa and I were talking after church." The pastor looked around the crowd. "She mentioned then that if she should pass on while I was still preaching here in Nome, that she wanted me to conduct the service as a celebration. She wanted her family and all of her friends to know that death was not the end." He looked at Havyn and then at her sisters.

"She asked me to remind everyone that Jesus overcame death on the cross, dying on our behalf, taking our sins. Through that one action we were set free from the laws of sin and death.

"Melissa put her trust in Jesus, and it was her heart's desire that others do the same. She wanted folks to know the joy of trusting in the Lord. When I spoke to her daughters, they felt the same way. Dwelling on our loss here on earth serves no good purpose, but dwelling on the eternity we have in Jesus will deliver us from the depths of sorrow and bring us into joy. The joy of knowing that this life—and death—isn't the end. Jesus tells us in the book of John that He is the way, the truth, and the life. Jesus is the only way to the Father and eternal life. Melissa knew that truth, and she wanted to make sure you knew it as well."

Havyn smiled. Leave it to her mother to make sure the Gospel message was preached at her funeral.

She looked up and tried to refocus on the pastor's words, but then she saw him. Standing there, just beyond Mr. Norris.

Papa.

Dressed in a dark suit, he held his hat in his hands. He looked . . . different. Thinner. Shorter. His face weathered. Aged. Something else was different too . . . but she couldn't place it.

The last time she'd seen him, he'd been so broken—

Oh! That was it. He no longer looked broken.

She stiffened and John leaned close. "Are you all right?"

Nodding, Havyn lifted her chin. Strong. She had to be strong. Granddad needed her and so did her sisters.

How would their father's return affect them?

Now they all had to face the deception and lies, and not just from their father . . . but from Granddad.

The pastor asked everyone to join him in prayer, and while Havyn bowed her head, she didn't pray. She couldn't. She couldn't stop thinking about the man across the crowd. Would he want to be a part of their lives? Or was he just here for money?

She cringed at her own thoughts.

"Havyn?"

She looked up at John's voice. The prayer was over and people walked around, speaking in soft tones.

"Are you all right? Do you need to go back to the house?" John's face showed his concern.

Oh, how she loved this man. Havyn glanced across the way to where her father had been. He was no longer there. A part of her wanted to seek him out, but another part wanted to hide away. "I have the feeling that everything is going to be different now. With our father back in our lives . . . with him here and Mama gone . . ." She shook her head.

"Try not to worry. Things *will* be different"—John squeezed her hand—"but God will see you through."

An older man she recognized from the Roadhouse stepped up beside her. "Miss Havyn, we're sure sorry to lose your ma."

Havyn lost track of time as person after person came to offer their condolences to her and her sisters and to Grand-dad. He sat so still, a trail of tears down his cheeks.

So many people loved and respected their mother. It was beautiful—but also gut wrenching and exhausting.

Judas Reynolds was the last in the long line. "Miss Powell, your mother was the most incredible woman I'd ever met. I'm deeply sorry for your loss."

"Thank you, Mr. Reynolds. I can't thank you enough for all you've done."

"Think nothing of it. That's what friends do." He looked down at the ground. "I'm very sorry about Dr. Kingston and what he did."

Havyn had tried to push the thought of that man out of her mind, especially since he'd been killed. "Let's not talk about it, please. God and I have been working on forgiving the man. And I pray that he found peace with God before he died."

"Yes. I do too." He tipped his hat to her. "If there's anything at all that you need, just let me know."

"We are in your debt, Mr. Reynolds. Thank you."

He took her hand and kissed it, then walked away.

Pastor Wilson came up to her. "If it's all right, I'm going to ask the rest of the people to leave so that you can have some time together as a family."

"That's very understanding of you, Pastor, thank you." Havyn lifted her hankie to her eyes, but it was soaked from all the tears she'd cried already.

He nodded and went to the small gathering of people still talking around the mound of dirt in the ground.

Havyn couldn't take her eyes off the grave. Mama was gone. It shook her to the core.

Several minutes later, Whitney approached with Madysen in tow. "There's something we need to talk about."

"I'm so weary, must it be now?"

"Yes." A tear trailed down Whitney's cheek. "Let's go inside the house."

"All right." Might as well get it over with, whatever it was. Whenever Whit got a bee in her bonnet, it was best to just let her have her say.

They entered the house, where John sat beside Granddad in the parlor. They both looked . . . weary. Weren't they all. *Oh, Lord, I just want this day to be over.*

Havyn lowered herself on the settee and Madysen sat beside her. Whitney stood in front of all of them. "John, I'm sorry to drag this out again, and I'm sorry that I've been untrusting of you." She pulled a paper out of her pocket. "We've discussed this contract before. After I found it, I was angry and I'm sorry for that. But I didn't know you then." She looked at their granddad. "I still don't understand why you did all this, Granddad, but I'm sorry I didn't trust you either."

What was going on? "Whit, why are we talking about this today of all days? We just buried our mother." Havyn's head hurt from all the crying. Why would her sister bring them any more grief?

"I'm sorry. But we have to talk about it, because there's a man outside that claims to be our father. The father we thought was dead. And I'm concerned, because the memories I have of this man are not good ones." She paced in front of the piano. "I might have turned him into a bigger monster in my mind than he actually was, but I'm still concerned that he's going to try to steal from Granddad. And from us."

Whitney turned to John. "So . . . are you willing to fulfill this contract and marry Havyn? I know it's terrible timing, but I asked the pastor to stay. He's in the barn waiting right now."

Havyn felt her eyebrows rise almost up to her hairline. *Shock* was too tame a word for her reaction.

John's jaw dropped and then closed. "Whitney . . ."

Madysen walked up to Whitney and wrapped her arms around her. It stilled their older sister's movements. "Whit, I love you, but I think you're making a mountain out of a molehill."

Whitney shook off Madysen's embrace and looked at them all, eyes wild. "Don't you *get* it? What if his whole purpose in coming today is for all of this?" She spread her arms. "Why else would he be so determined to be here for the funeral other than to assert some kind of rights?"

Granddad moaned.

John stood. "I don't think the law would be on his side, Whitney, if that is what he's up to. But the fact of the matter is, we don't know why he's here or what brought him. Other than what he told me."

"Which could be a lie!" Whitney's cheeks were bright red. "I really think you and Havyn need to get married right now. I'm serious." She slapped the contract down on the small table in front of her and crossed her arms over her chest.

A little of the shock had worn off and Havyn shook her head. "I'm really glad that you consider John worthy now"—her words held a hint of sarcasm even though she wasn't aiming for that—"but even though John knows that I love him, I don't think it's fair to throw this at him. Especially on the day we buried Mama. When I get married, I want it to be a joyful day. Not a day full of tears."

"But we don't have any time to waste! I don't want that man—"

"Ahem."

They all turned to the doorway.

Their father stood there, his face full of sadness. He looked down to the hat in his hands. "I can see this is a bad time. Is it all right if I come back tomorrow morning?"

John walked over to the man. They shook hands. "That would be fine. Around ten?"

Dad nodded and walked away without another word.

What if Whitney was right?

THIRTY

Whitney's heart raced in her chest. "See?" She walked over to John and tugged on his sleeve. "I'll go get the pastor. We need to get this taken care of right now."

John shook his head. "Whitney, please, calm down." He took her by the arms. "As much as I love Havyn, there's a lot we still need to discuss. And plenty we need to talk to your grandfather about. I don't think it's necessary to rush into anything." He released her and ran a hand through his dark hair. "I didn't see any evidence in him that he came here to try to steal anything from you."

"What if that's just what he *wants* you to believe?" At that moment, tears burst forth. All the anger she'd held toward her father rose to the surface. He'd hurt them. Left them. Abandoned them. And she couldn't forgive what he did. She *couldn't*.

Madysen was at her side, sliding an arm around her waist. "Let's go talk in my room for a few minutes." She offered a hankie.

Her younger sister brought her to Granddad's chair.

Whitney leaned down to hug him. Why didn't she feel anything? It was as though all her feelings were just . . . numb.

Granddad moaned and she looked down at the paper he'd written on: *Please forgive me.*

While she didn't blame her grandfather—she was actually thankful that he'd taken action to get Christopher Powell out of their lives—she couldn't respond.

How could she when she had no idea how to truly forgive?

———

John walked the length of the sheep pen, hands deep in his pockets. He'd already checked on the dogs and the chickens. Even though the farm workers had gathered that morning and worked out a schedule for everything to get done without him or the family.

He stretched his legs and went down to the lower pasture. After Christopher's departure, they'd all taken a break. Havyn went to check on Madysen and Whitney while John settled Chuck back into his bed. Chuck had asked for Havyn. After John asked her to go see her grandfather, he went for a walk to clear his head.

He'd asked everyone to rest for a couple hours. Chuck wrote to Havyn that he had been working on a letter to them all, and needed to finish it. Maybe they'd soon be able to put to rest the matter of the financial state of the farm.

If he could get the workers paid again today and get the ledgers caught up, he'd be able to breathe a sigh of relief. For all of them. So they could move forward. Then they could all work with Chuck each day to get his exercises done, so he could build strength and get back to the farm that he loved.

It seemed the only way to get everyone back to normal. But there was still Christopher Powell to deal with. . . .

Whitney's fear had clearly gone a bit overboard today, but what if she was correct in part? What if Chris had some ulterior motive for being here?

He pushed the thoughts aside. It had been a hard day. But they'd made it. So far. They just had to get through one day at a time after this.

As he walked back toward the house, Whitney's demand that he and Havyn marry today barreled back to him. He couldn't restrain a smile. As much as he wanted to marry Havyn, marrying her out of fear on the day of her mother's funeral wasn't right. But oh, how he wanted to marry her.

He wanted to shout from the rooftop that he loved her, but he'd wait for her to get past her grief. He could wait. She was worth it.

When he made it back to the house, he found the sisters all gathered around their grandfather's bed.

"John, I was about to come find you." Havyn's smile greeted him. "Granddad wrote a note for us."

Whitney stood. "Granddad asked me to read a letter from him."

Their grandfather pushed her several sheets of paper. Whitney cleared her throat and began to read.

"Whitney, Havyn, and Madysen, my dearest grand-daughters. By now, you probably know the story. Doc Gordon hounded me for months, saying my symptoms showed there was a bigger problem coming if I didn't make changes. I ignored him because I needed to keep things running. You all depended on me. So when John

showed up, I hired him. I knew him. Knew his grandpa.
The whole reason John came was to fulfill his grandpa's
last request."

John held up a hand and grinned at Chuck. "Did you ever
open the box?"

Chuck held up one finger.

"I take it that means to wait."

A slight nod.

"I'm sorry. Please continue reading, Whit."

Whitney actually grinned at his use of her sisters' nick-
name for her. Then she read on.

"Yes, I asked John to sign the contract, but there's
more to that story as well. And he was good enough
to help me out. When I met his grandpa in the mine in
Cripple Creek, we often shared stories of our families
to pass the time as we chipped away at the mountain
searching for gold. When I left for Nome, I told him
that we should try to get our families together one
day. Giuseppe joked that maybe his grandson would
even marry one of my granddaughters. It was nothing
more than that. Just talk between two friends. But we
wrote letters back and forth over the years. I told him
about all of you, and he kept me up to date on him
and John."

Whitney peered over the papers at their grandfather as she
turned the page and then looked back to the letter.

"John spent every last cent he had to fulfill his grand-
father's request. When he got to town, he had no money,

no place to stay, no way to feed himself. He went searching for a job and Doc Gordon sent him out here. Ironic, isn't it? The very man that he'd come to see in Nome. Then I hired him. Knew I could trust him. He wasn't a stranger. And I confess I was desperate. It was hasty, I know. But John's a good man. I've given my blessing for him to marry Havyn."

Whitney looked at Havyn, gave her sister a wink, and then went on.

"You don't ever have to worry about money. I've got plenty of gold hidden away. As for your father, and my part in lying to you and your mother, I'm sorry. I did what I did to protect my own. I know it wasn't right, but I forged your mother's signature and my friend the judge declared them divorced. She never wanted it—your mother believed marriage was for life. I just couldn't see God being so cruel as to expect her to bear a lifetime of your father's deceptions and affairs. I only wish I'd been able to ask her forgiveness as well. I hope you will forgive me. I have no way of knowing how much time I have left on this earth, but I know I couldn't bear it without my girls."

Madysen leaned over and hugged Chuck. "Oh, Granddad, we couldn't bear it without you! I don't understand why all of this has happened, but I love you and I always will." She wrapped her arms around him and sobbed.

Whitney walked around the bed to where John stood and then bent down. She reached under the bed and came out with a box and ledger. "Granddad said the box was for you all along, John. Not for him. And here's the ledger. It's all we need to pay the workers. He gave me the key to the money drawer too." She held up the key and handed it to him, a small smile on her lips.

"Thank you." It might take time for them to become friends, but at least Whitney seemed to trust him now.

Havyn came over and took his arm. "So this is what you brought all the way from Colorado?"

He looked at it and nodded.

"Why don't you open it? Granddad said it was for you."

John laid the box on the end of the bed and opened it. On top sat a letter addressed to Chuck. It was already open, so Chuck must have read it all those weeks ago when John first gave the box to him. John lifted it out and laid it on Chuck's lap.

The next letter in the box sat atop an oilskin packet. It read *John.*

Just the sight of Nonno's handwriting made him smile. How he missed him.

He unfolded the paper and read.

My dear John,

I know this letter comes as a shock, and so I wanted you to have the company of my dearest friend when you read it. You probably know by now that Chuck and I have formed a partnership of sorts. A conspiracy to plan your future, you might believe, but, I assure you, it was designed with only your very best interests in mind.

Chuck will see to it that you understand, but let me say that I have long believed God would see our two families joined together. I hope that you feel the same way, and I believe with all my heart that because this is something God has ordained, you will. I have left you all of my worldly goods. My desire is not only for your own benefit, however. I want you to use this money to help take care of Chuck's family should he pass on. We both pledged to take care of each other's families, and while I realize you are a man full grown, fully privileged with making your own choices, I hope you will honor my final desires and take on my pledge to Chuck. It is the last thing I will ever ask of you, Patatino.

Nonno

The letter almost made him want to laugh out loud. Who would have ever thought that two old men would be match-makers? And very good ones, as it turned out.

"Would you read it to us?" Havyn's sweet voice broke through his thoughts.

"Sure." He read the letter to them and looked up to see the left side of Chuck's lips lift in a smile. "You two . . ." John shook his head.

Looking back down at the box, John unwrapped the oil-skin package. Whatever it was, Nonno hadn't wanted it to get wet.

Two large stacks of gold certificates lay within. Thousands of dollars. John laughed. "I carried thousands of dollars on my back as if it was nothing more than a sentimental trinket!"

"Sounds like Giuseppe Roselli was quite a man." Madysen smiled up at him. "Just like his grandson." She patted him on the shoulder. "I'm looking forward to you being my

347

brother-in-law. I always wanted a brother. Sisters can be so annoying."

This time John didn't hold back. He laughed out loud.

An hour later, all the workers were paid. Whitney had graciously gone with John out to the barn with the ledger and a bag of money from her grandfather's safe. While she hadn't said anything to him, they worked together well.

He turned to her now. "Thank you for all your help. I couldn't have done it without you."

Her eyes misted as she handed him the bag and ledger. "I'm sorry I've been so hard on you, John. You didn't deserve that."

Whitney might have a hard exterior, but he'd seen the warm and loving sister that was underneath the layers. It must have been hard on her, being the oldest in the circumstances they'd lived through. "No, it's good for you to be protective of your family. Don't ever change that, Whitney Powell."

She considered him for a moment, and he had the impression she was restraining a smile. "I think Madysen's right. It will be nice to have a brother." She wiped her hands on her apron and walked away.

"How did you manage that?" Havyn came up behind him.

He turned. "Manage what?"

"I heard Whit apologize to you. I'm impressed." Her light laugh washed over him.

He smiled and pulled her close. "I'm glad that everything is out in the open. From now on, let's agree not to have any secrets between us. *Especially* where matters of the heart are concerned."

She nodded. "Then let me be the first to say that I love you and I can't wait to marry you."

John gazed for a long moment into her eyes. "And I love you, Havyn Powell. Now and for the rest of my life."

For what seemed a long time neither one said anything. Finally, he stepped back. "I should probably let you get to your chickens. That was where you were headed, right?"

She lifted her face to kiss him. "They can wait."

———

The next morning, Havyn opened the door to their father. "Please come in."

The first few moments in the parlor were quiet. John sat next to Granddad. Madysen and Whitney were with Havyn on the settee.

Dad looked at all of them. "By now, you probably know the whole story. I didn't come to rehash everything. I just wanted to see you. To apologize to Melissa." His voice cracked.

"And you never once thought about how much it would hurt us to believe you were dead all those years?"

Good ol' Whitney, always went to the heart of things.

"It couldn't have hurt you as much as having me alive had." Their father looked down at his feet. "I was no good. I was a drunk and a slacker. Your grandfather tried over and over to help me with jobs, and I constantly sabotaged myself. Look, I don't expect you to understand, but in time I'm hoping you'll forgive me."

"Ha!" Whitney stood and stepped away as if she'd been stung. "You're a fool to come here expecting that."

"Whitney, don't be that way." Madysen went to her sister. "I know you probably remember more of the bad things because you were older, but God said we should forgive."

"Then He expects too much. How am I supposed to forgive someone who hurt us like he did? He was our *father* and he walked away. Made another family and left the first one behind to believe he was dead." She looked back at their father with a scowl.

It cut Havyn like a knife. All these years, she'd had time to digest it all. Her sisters . . . they were just now having to deal with what their father had done. And as adults, it was harder and more real. Looking from Whitney to Madysen, she prayed that they would all be able to get past this. Someday.

"I'm sorrier than words will ever convey." Dad lifted his eyebrows and stood tall and straight. "But it was for the best. I knew your mother needed more—knew you girls needed a better father. After I signed the divorce papers, I knew your grandfather would think it best to let you think I was dead. I saw it as a way to give you a better life. He told me if I did it his way, he'd take care of all of you for the rest of your lives, but if I stayed . . . he would walk away. I weighed it all out and knew you would be better with him than with me. And if we hadn't done it, I'd be dead anyway. God used all of that to clean me up. That's why I'm here. To show you that I'm different. To ask for your forgiveness."

Whitney glared at him. "Don't count on it."

Havyn wanted to weep. For the last half hour words had flown between Whitney and their father. Madysen tried to mediate, but made little progress. A glimpse at Granddad showed all this was making him miserable too.

She jumped to her feet. "I'm sorry. I can't hear any more of this! Dad, I'm glad you're alive, but it's going to take us all a lot of time to work through it. So why don't you come back next week? In the meantime, we need to grieve our mother, and we will work on forgiveness." She gave a pointed look to Whitney. "Won't we?"

Whitney didn't answer.

What else was there to say? "It's been a really tough week. I need to think. I need time alone." With a glance to John that she hoped he understood, she turned and walked out of the room. As she left the parlor, voices erupted again.

Let them deal with it. She had a different plan.

Outside, she walked to the chicken yard and took deep, long breaths.

God, I know You have a plan. This isn't the one I would have chosen, but I keep reminding myself that You are God. I don't know how we will make it through all of this, but I'm tired of carrying around this huge weight. The secrets that I carried, that I felt guilty for, the worry about the future, everything about the farm, Granddad, and Mama. Lord, help me to let go. Help me to lay all this at Your feet and rest in You. I want to follow Your will. Not my own.

The chickens followed Havyn around the yard as she paced. Buttercup and Sally jabbered at her in their chicken talk.

"I know, you're right."

Several other chickens chimed in.

"That's true." She threw out some scratch for them and smiled at their antics. Pretty soon a song came to mind. Lifting her voice up to the heavens, Havyn sang:

> "When peace like a river, attendeth my way,
> When sorrows like sea billows roll
> Whatever my lot, thou hast taught me to say
> It is well, it is well, with my soul."

EPILOGUE

Two Weeks Later

E ven though it was only August, there was a taste of snow in the air as Havyn stepped into the Roadhouse. The many layers of satin and lace in her wedding gown reminded her of Mama. She'd stashed away boxes of fabric for their weddings over the years, praying for the husbands that God would bring her daughters. If only she could look down from heaven to see . . .

Lord, thank You for this man and for how You brought him into my life. Please tell Mama how much I miss her. . . .

Tears threatened. But they were tears of joy. This was her wedding day! Her heart overflowed with love for John. She couldn't wait to see him.

Oohs and *aahs* reached her ears. Men filled the room, all with their hats in their hands. Friends. Fellow churchgoers. And plenty of those who came to listen to her and her sisters sing every night.

Madysen nodded from the stage and began a beautiful

melody on her cello. Havyn walked down the makeshift aisle. Dad was still in town, but she'd asked him to respect this special family time and not come to the wedding. Too many years and heartaches still separated them. And it wouldn't be good for Whitney right now.

Things hadn't been great between her and Dad, but she and Madysen had prayed a lot about how to build a relationship with the man they barely knew. It would take Whit a lot more time. If ever.

Forgiveness and healing were beautiful—things that Havyn begged God to give her. But they would take time.

She looked ahead but couldn't see John amid the crowd of standing men. Her heart thundered in her chest.

There.

Tall and straight. In a dark suit, he looked more handsome than ever.

As soon as their eyes connected, she wanted to run the rest of the way. Even two weeks had seemed too long to wait for this day, but God had done a mighty work in them both during that time. Had done a mighty work in her whole family.

And she would always be grateful.

The last few steps brought her up next to her grandfather. He sat taller and straighter in the wheeled chair than he had before. It was good to see him gaining strength every day.

She leaned down and kissed his cheek and then whispered in his ear, "I love you, Granddad. Thank you for being a matchmaker. It worked."

His lopsided smile was the best gift he could've given her.

The pastor asked a question and Granddad answered, but Havyn had looked up again at John—and she couldn't take her eyes from him.

And as he came to her and took her hand, she never wanted him to let go.

"You look beautiful." His voice was husky and soft.

Whitney went behind Havyn and fixed her dress and fluffed her veil, then stood next to her. They'd worked on the dress together for the past two weeks. And by the look on John's face, it was worth it.

"We are gathered together today . . ." Pastor began.

It all passed in a blur as she and John exchanged their wedding vows. She wanted to savor the moments so she could remember them forever, but she got caught up in the man before her.

John.

She was marrying him. Right now. A dream come true.

He smiled down at her.

Then he pulled her close, their hearts beating against one another.

Time stood still as he put his forehead on hers. "I love you, Mrs. Roselli. Always and forever."

And then he sought her lips with his own.

The Roadhouse erupted in whoops, hollers, and cheers.

But the only voice she wanted to hear was John's. And the only place she wanted to be was here . . .

In her husband's arms.

THE END

A Note from the Authors

Tracie and I are so grateful that you chose to join us for THE TREASURES OF NOME series. We love Alaska and love sharing our knowledge and research of this great state with you. We hope you join us for more of the Powell sisters and the rest of their stories as the series continues.

For two years, I've been waiting for the right story to add in my own personal research of pertussis. And when I say *research*, I mean the most intense research I've ever done. With lasting effects.

I found out I had contracted whooping cough—the hundred-day cough, otherwise known as pertussis—during our trip for our son's wedding. When the simple cough that had been there for three weeks changed and I couldn't breathe, the doctors discovered pertussis and I had to be treated so I wouldn't spread it. Then I was quarantined for seven days. It took four months for that horrible cough to run its course.

The CDC had several phone conversations with me. The poor people who were around me had to get used to the horrific spasms that would overtake me. And my dear, sweet, amazing husband didn't get a whole lot of sleep.

Even the folks at Bethany House had to endure this with me. And they were so gracious. Dave Long and Dave Horton were troupers as we did our best to get through meetings with my hacking.

That terrible disease is only a memory now, but this spring we discovered it scarred my lungs, gave me asthma, and damaged my soft palate so that I have acute obstructive sleep apnea. I have a whole new respect for this horrible disease, modern medicine and inoculations, and how so many people suffered and died from it years ago.

But through it all, God is good and He is faithful. I've learned a lot. And I was able to use it in this story.

As we all travel through the days we have on this earth, it's important to remember how precious life is. Every moment counts. I pray you hug someone today and tell them that you love them. Don't wait to let people know that you care. And please, don't hesitate to share the Good News with the lost and dying world around you. That should be our priority. Each and every day. Because someone right next to you today might not be here tomorrow.

Thank you for reading!

To God be the glory!

Kimberley

Acknowledgments

First and foremost, we'd like to thank the Lord God for giving us the stories to tell.

Second, to our amazing husbands. They are our supermen. Without their support and prayers, we wouldn't be able to do this.

Third, to all the team at Bethany House. What an honor and a privilege to work with you again. You are the best!

Fourth, to our incredible editor Karen Ball. You made this book shine. I thank you for all your hard work. For helping us to dig deep and keeping us on our toes. You are a gift.

And last, to our readers. We could *not* do this without you. We read every comment, post, email, and message you send our way. Thank you for blessing us.

Tracie Peterson is the award-winning author of more than one hundred novels, both historical and contemporary. Her avid research resonates in her many bestselling series. Tracie and her family make their home in Montana. Visit www .traciepeterson.com to learn more.

Kimberley Woodhouse is an award-winning, bestselling author of fiction and nonfiction. A popular speaker and teacher, she has shared the theme of "Joy Through Trials" with hundreds of thousands of people across the country. Kim is a pastor's wife and is passionate about music and Bible study. She lives and writes in the Bitterroot Valley in Montana. Visit www.kimberleywoodhouse.com for more information.

Sign Up for the Authors' Newsletters!

Keep up to date with Tracie and Kimberley's news on book releases and events by signing up for their email lists at traciepeterson.com and kimberleywoodhouse.com.

More from Tracie Peterson and Kimberley Woodhouse

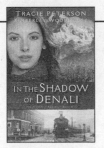

This series blends excitement, history, breathtaking scenery, and romance while introducing three adventurous women who find refuge at the Curry Hotel, near the foot of Mount McKinley. Will they each have the courage to rely on their faith as they search for hope, healing, and forgiveness?

THE HEART OF ALASKA: *In the Shadow of Denali, Out of the Ashes, Under the Midnight Sun*